A STORY OF SCORPIONS

Gabriel Everett

A STORY OF SCORPIONS

COMPASS PRESS
AN IMPRINT OF WHEELER PUBLISHING, INC.

Published in Large Print by arrangement with Crown Publishers in the United States and Canada.
Compass Press Large Print Book Series.

Set in 16 pt Plantin.

Library of Congress Cataloging-in-Publication Data

Everett, Gabriel.
   A story of scorpions / Gabriel Everett.
      p. (large print) cm.(Wheeler large print book series)
   ISBN 1-56895-500-6 (hardcover)
   1. Large type books. 2. Murderers—Fiction. 3. Forgiveness—Fiction.
4. Revenge—Fiction
I. Title. II. Series
[PS3555.V328S76 1997]
813'.54—dc21   97-37561
                                                CIP

For John,

Visser der Menschen

Oh, full of scorpions is my mind, dear wife!
Macbeth, Act III, scene ii

Behold, I have given you authority
to tread upon serpents and scorpions...
Luke 10:19

A STORY OF SCORPIONS

Part One

Part One

1

I have not been to see a psychiatrist since the interview that preceded my ordination. I have, of course, had several "spiritual directors," but they don't count. They have not counted for a while.

Then, my interview had been to determine my fitness for professional ministry, to see if I was the type prone to diddling altar girls or boys, or having nervous breakdowns at church expense. One did not have to be a genius to guess the answers to many of the questions, or to separate those questions intended to elicit information from those intended to gauge honesty. "Do you fantasize often about sex?" the psychiatrist had asked. "Do you masturbate?" "Have you ever had sex with an animal?" "Do you ever have the sensation that bugs are crawling up your arms or legs?" "Have you ever wished someone you love were dead?"

I had maintained good eye contact and answered each question as truthfully but briefly as possible, confident in the knowledge that four years of college and two of seminary had confirmed in me beyond any shadow of a doubt: that I was in few ways unusual, and in no way abnormal. I was right. I was recommended for ordination without a snag.

This time would perhaps be more difficult.

For one thing, the psychiatrist was a woman, and I have been ill at ease around women since my wife was taken from me. For another, I was applying not for admission to the ministry but for entrance into a maximum security prison. I was interested to see which institution would prove more exclusive.

I would guess Dr. Michelowsky was in her late thirties, my age or a bit younger, a dark-haired woman with pale skin, blood-red lips, and aggressive eyeglasses. In heels she was as tall as I, but she walked awkwardly in them— maybe she was just stiff from sitting—and she smiled awkwardly, as if it made her sad to smile. She also wore a rather short skirt and a silky blouse unbuttoned to what we male seminarians used to call "amulet depth." I wondered if she wore that skirt when she interviewed prisoners.

For my part, I was wearing a black shirt and a clerical collar, but with sport slacks and a maroon cardigan to give me a softer appearance. I tactfully did not attempt to match the firmness of her handshake. When we sat, I gave her crossed legs a complimentary glance ("Do you ever look at an attractive woman's legs?" "Occasionally, yes.") but then glued my eyes to hers ("Have you ever been charged with or disciplined or dismissed because of sexual misconduct?" "Never, Doctor."). At her suggestion, we met at her main office in downtown Paterson instead of in the smaller quarters she occupied three days a week at

4

the prison. I think they were afraid to let me get even that close to Alex Leonard.

She surprised me a little with her lack of preliminaries. She probably wished to disarm me. And in this case, unlike that psychiatric interview more than a decade ago, I had come armed.

"Reverend Pierce," she began, "or is it Father Pierce—what do you prefer to have me call you?"

"Alson is fine, or people call me Al. Just not 'Father.'"

"All right. Alson—you and I are both professionals, we both have educations, we're both in helping fields, so I want to be as direct as possible with you."

"Please do be."

"You have made a very unusual request," she went on without a pause. "And the correctional authorities have engaged me to determine whether or not they can and should honor it. Of course there are others involved, including Mr. Leonard's attorney. But that's the task here—not to make judgments about you or your beliefs, and certainly not to add to the suffering you've experienced. Of course I know about your tragedy, your ordeal."

"Everyone does." When I hear the word *ordeal*, I imagine some instrument of torture, except I can never see it clearly. I only know it turns, like the world.

"I don't wish to be insensitive. Believe me, I've thought hard about what you've been through, in anticipation of our meeting, but the nature of your request makes it impossible not to touch on your experience in some ways."

"I realize that. I appreciate your tact. But please proceed. Feel free, I mean. I'll be fine."

On the wall above her desk was a large reproduction of what I supposed was a French Impressionist painting: a mother combing the hair of her child. Madonnas all look like crucifixes to me now. I hate to look at either. Outside the window a great crane rose from the skyline like the neck of a dinosaur, its wrecking ball dangling like a swollen tongue.

"I'd like to start with the letter you wrote to Alex Leonard. It's dated July twenty-third and it was received by the correctional facility on the following day."

"Has the letter been delivered to Mr. Leonard?"

"I'm not sure. I believe the prison administration may be holding it for the time being."

"I see."

"Your letter, or what I take to be your letter, reads:

Dear Mr. Leonard,
I am the husband of the woman and the father of the boy you murdered. Obviously the word "dear" is a formality only.

You have dealt me the worst blow that any man can deal another. And you dealt it with incredible malice and cruelty.

Oddly, it is my lot in life not only to have loved your two victims, but also to have been baptized into a religion that commands me to love my enemies. I take the commandment seriously.

Therefore I am writing to you and to the authorities where you are incarcerated to request permission to see you, and, as much as is possible, to be of service to you. It is not my intention to reproach you for what you have done, to convert you to my religion, or in any way to harass you or to interfere with your life. Nor do I have any intention of pretending that you are anything other than what you are: my *enemy*, whom I am commanded to *love*.

My only goal is to obey my Lord Jesus Christ, in hopes of one day joining those persons you have so abruptly sent to him.

I wait for your reply.

Sincerely,
(The Rev.) Alson Pierce

PS. "Love" for my enemy can include reading to him, assisting with his correspondence, interceding with prison authorities on his behalf, delivering messages, obtaining diversions or entertainments (e.g., cassette tapes), and performing any other tasks he desires and the law allows.

"Is this your letter,?" she asked.
"Every word."
"And I'm to take it at face value?"

"Absolutely."

She looked at me intently.

"I have no hidden agendas. I'm not planning to smuggle dynamite into his cell to blow him to kingdom come."

"Have you ever fantasized about blowing him to kingdom come?"

"My dear lady," I replied with the authority that is the privilege of all survivors of atrocities, an authority I am only beginning to appreciate, "blowing Alex Leonard to kingdom come is a good deal less sophisticated than the fantasies I've entertained over the past nine months. If you or the prison authorities desire, I'll be glad to make some sketches. If you have a program set up, I'll do them on your computer. In a pinch, I might even be able to impersonate some of the sounds I imagine him making in the course of my revenge."

The trick here was to seem credible, but not unstable. The volume was a notch too high on the last remark, I thought.

"Pardon me—you'll recall that I've had some experience in hearing cries of pain and terror. But as you said at the outset, Dr. Michelowsky, our purpose here is not to peruse my nightmares or my fantasies—though I'm prepared to share both if necessary. The purpose is to decide my fitness and your employers' willingness to let me see Alex Leonard."

"Assuming Mr. Leonard wants to see you."

"Assuming Mr. Leonard wants to see me. I'll only add, with all respect, that if the purpose of this meeting is in any way to measure my determination to see Mr. Leonard, let me assure you I intend to renew my efforts to do so for as long as I live or Mr. Leonard lives. I will not give up."

"Mr.—Reverend—Pierce, why do you want to do this?"

Calmly now, I told myself, calmly. "I believe I make my reason clear in my letter."

"But I want to hear you tell me. Please."

I sighed wearily. "I am a Christian. That means I am a follower of Jesus Christ. I am also a Christian minister. I preach the words of Jesus Christ. Jesus said, 'Love your enemies, do good to those who hate you, bless those who curse you, pray for those who abuse you.' I'd be quite content if he'd said otherwise. To tell you the truth, there's a part of me that would be quite content not to believe in Christ at all. But I am what I am, I'm a Christian and a Christian minister, and as a Christian minister I think I have a special obligation to practice what I preach. I've lost"—here my voice broke spontaneously—"everything that is dear to me. Integrity may be the only thing I have left."

"I see. But is this the only way to show your integrity?"

Her manner was softer now, less aggressive. She uncrossed her legs and leaned forward over her slightly parted knees.

"Can't you follow Christ by working in a homeless shelter or becoming a missionary? Why this? I'm not religious, but certainly, when I think of Jesus, I can't imagine him expecting anyone to do what you're asking your-self to do. It's too cruel."

"It seems that way, doesn't it? And yet he allowed a cruel thing to happen to my family. He allowed a man like Alex Leonard to draw breath on what is commonly called 'God's earth.' Perhaps God is cruel. Perhaps love is cruel."

"And you intend to love Alex Leonard, no? Will your love be cruel?"

She stunned me with that.

"I spoke from the bitterness of my experience. If you want to play games with my words, I assure you, you'll win." This time the break in my voice was artificial—or so I told myself.

"I don't mean to be doing that. I'm just try-ing to suggest to you some aspects of this that maybe you haven't considered. For exam-ple, suppose everything goes through the way you want. Have you given much thought to what it will be like to sit in the same room with this...individual? What are you going to do when you first hear his voice again? What if he talks about the crime? The crimes. What if he tries to taunt you with them? Have you thought of all these things?"

"I have. I've thought of them a lot. I can't say I know for sure how I'll react. Listen, I can't say I'm not going to get in there and run away screaming. How can anyone predict how he'll act in a situation like that? I can't predict how I'll act any more than I could have predicted how I'd act the first time I saw him in my house. I know two things. I've thought about this. I know he's harmless to me now. There's nothing more he can do to hurt me. And the other thing I know is that he can't do or say anything that isn't already inside my head."

I was perspiring now, in spite of the air conditioner. They say that sweat cost Nixon an election. I hoped I looked dryer than I felt. "There are the key words, Reverend. 'Inside my head.' None of us knows all that's inside our heads, do we?"

"No, we don't."

Neither of us spoke for a while. Even with the windows closed I could hear a siren, a man shouting "motherfucker." Were the mother and the daughter in the painting family to the artist, or merely models, I wondered.

"I just don't see how you can love someone like that," she said finally.

"You can't, probably, in the sense of having affection. But love in the New Testament is an active word. I *can* perform acts of service."

"Even that ..."

"Listen, for me there are only three possible responses to what I've been through, and only two authentic ones. I can follow my gut instincts and attempt to hurt this man in some way. I can devote my energy to devising elaborate plots for his destruction. Or, instead of following my gut instincts, I can follow Christ and attempt to love him."

"What's the third? The two you gave me are the supposedly authentic ones. What's the inauthentic one?"

11

"'Getting on with life,' as they say. Contrived amnesia. Apply for another parish, maybe a different job altogether. Sell driftwood or run a hotel. Get out of Jersey. Erase myself and all memory of my wife and son. In other words, finish the job for Alex Leonard. Just humiliate and lie us all off the face of the earth and call it 'a new beginning.' Boy, what a line to use in a bar, though. 'Excuse me, miss, I don't mean to be too forward, but ever since my wife and son were slaughtered by a deranged sex-killer, I can't seem to resist buying drinks for beautiful women.' No thank you."

"I don't think you're being fair," she said. I could tell I had offended her—and realized I had wanted to. "Is this the way you counsel people in your church? Is this how you would respond to someone attempting recovery—"

"No, it isn't." I cut her off. "But are all your counsels effective for yourself? Is every cure effective for the doctor?"

"No, but the word you used was 'authentic.'"

"Words again. Bad word, my mistake. It doesn't work for me, that's all. Let me share a somewhat bitter observation. It's an interesting society, isn't it, where someone like Alex Leonard is more free to walk into my home to destroy my family than I am to walk into his prison cell to offer him my love. Maybe that's why there are Alex Leonards in the first place. I'm sorry."

"Don't be sorry, if that's how you feel. Look, I take a good part of the responsibility for this, but we've gotten a bit off our track here. As you can well imagine, the textbooks and my experience don't offer too many suggestions for a case like this. To say the least, Reverend Pierce, you are an unusual man—and I respect you, though we have some radical differences."

I was nodding, attempting to smile, trying to hold my rage in check. I had meant to seem sincere but wounded—credible, in other words—but I sensed I'd let too much of my anger show. I appeared unstable, I am sure. I so wished I could start the interview over. The impressionistic mother sat serenely in her timeless pose, combing the hair of her unassailable daughter.

"If you'll bear with me, I want to turn to a more conventional format."

"That's fine. Like you said, the conventions are hard to locate with this sort of thing."

I managed a weak chuckle, but she ignored it.

"I'm going to ask you a few more questions in a very random sequence, and I want you to respond as immediately and succinctly as possible. Don't worry about giving too much thought to your answers."

"All right."

"How long have you been a minister?"

"Almost fourteen years. It'll be fourteen this October."

"Did you have any substantial job before that?"

"I worked for two years as a high school social studies teacher, before seminary."

"How long has it been since the crimes in which your wife and son were victims?"

"About nine months."

"Do you have any flashbacks of the experience, times when you believe you are reliving it?"

"No. I have nightmares, and I think of it. But I never think it's present instead of past."

"Do you remember your dreams?"

"Yes."

"How often would you say you have nightmares?"

"Several times a week." Often several times a night.

"Are they all related to the crimes in some way?"

"No."

"Can you describe one of the others? Briefly?"

"In one I am suspended by a string over a live volcano."

"Who holds the string? Anyone?"

"I'm not sure. That's part of what makes it a nightmare."

"Do you have any pleasant dreams?"

"Yes. I dream of my wedding."

"With your deceased wife?"

"Yes."

"Is there anything unusual about the dream?"

"Yes. Our son is the ring bearer. I look down at where he's standing, and he winks at me."

"And your son was not born until after your marriage, wasn't the result of a previous marriage or relationship?"

"No."

And so it went. Most of the questions and

their weaving together were familiar from the ordination test. The only jolt in the remainder of the interview came when she asked if I ever felt aroused by the rape of my wife. Did I ever imagine myself the victim or the rapist, or more of a witness than I had been? She was careful to preface the question with an apology.

I looked at her, and for just a moment I imagined myself gripping her throat and shaking her till her earrings jangled like chandeliers in an earthquake.

"Never," I said firmly, but I hoped without menace. "At times I have tried to imagine what my wife went through, but that is not the same thing as you're talking about."

She would not even murmur an assent to that. I wanted to spit at her. Of course, if I had answered yes, she would have told me that such thoughts were "not unusual" and thus "perfectly natural." I would give a great deal to sit in on one of her interviews with Leonard.

"I can't predict how your request will be handled," she said at the close of our session.

"Can you tell me what you'll recommend?" I asked.

"No, I really can't. To be honest, I'm not yet sure what I'll recommend. I need to think about this."

"Fair enough. I'll pray for you."

"That's...nice of you." She stood up and took my hand. "Reverend Pierce, have you given any thought to what you'll do if your request is unconditionally denied, which it may very well be? It's none of my business, but if we say no, what do you do then? The question is well intentioned."

"I'm sure it is." We still clasped hands, though I could tell hers was ready to be released. "If my request is denied"—and here I squeezed her hand more tightly—"my next step is to resubmit my letter to Mr. Leonard through the pages of every major newspaper that will take my money to print it. Perhaps a wider range of dialogue will result in some broader perspectives on the issue."

I finally let go of her hand, but not of her eyes.

"In this, as I'm afraid in so much else, Dr. Michelowsky, the issue will not be decided by psychology *or* by religion, but by politics. Let's pray that my fears are unfounded. Thank you for your time."

I walked swiftly from her office to the elevator, repeating the scripture to myself: *Behold, I send you forth as sheep in the midst of wolves. Be ye therefore wise as serpents,* I said aloud, and then, after the doors had closed and I began my descent to the lowest level, I whispered, *and harmless as doves.*

2

I have not read a newspaper since the day before I was on the front page of one. I have not watched the news on television, or kept my radio on during the news. No news is good news.

I do not read the newspapers, because I get too distressed over what is in them. That was hardly a problem before. I used to read about other crimes, other victims, and shake my head or even groan, but I never questioned the essential rightness of the world. I asked what it was coming to, rhetorically, like everyone else, but I do not recall ever missing a dinner, a movie, or a night of lovemaking because someone had been murdered, tortured, or raped. I never walked to the pulpit and said, "I have no words for you this morning because of something that happened to a neighbor last night, something that tears all words from my mouth and threatens to tear the very wings off the Dove of Heaven." I slowed down to look at the auto wrecks, but I never abandoned the highway. I always had somewhere to go.

I guess I still have. This afternoon I was asked to meet with my spiritual director, or counselor if you will, whose place in my life is guaranteed by the conditions of my paid leave of absence. This sabbatical was granted to me by my church shortly after the murders—as much, I suspect, from the fear that I was contagiously unlucky as from any sense of compassion or obligation. My director told me there was something in today's newspaper that we needed to discuss. He knows I don't read the papers, that I have yet to read the accounts of my wife's and son's deaths, but he was probably afraid that someone would mention a detail to me, and he wanted me prepared, I suppose. My sexton walked his message to my house. I have no phone, so I had to call him back from the public one up the street.

I wonder if he is tired of me. I cannot blame him if he is. He sounded annoyed with me on the phone. He was curt.

Now there is an ancient worry I had almost forgotten: the fear that someone doesn't like me, the fear I have given offense. How I used to live in thrall to that! It was a bigger presence in my life than God himself, that anxiety to be on good terms with everybody. How strange that I could have lost that fear, along with just about everything else, and still be alive.

Andrew Nelson, like the psychiatrist the other day, opened our meeting and cut to the chase. No one wants to take time on preliminaries with me. I guess I am a man with whom small talk is impossible.

He started right in after the "quiet time." He doesn't open sessions with a prayer anymore. He can't decide whether he's a Quaker or a Zen master. No word to the wise is sufficient. The last I heard, he was hellbent on "exploring deconstruction," which as nearly as I can tell means taking apart everything from the Godhead on down, not counting one's salary and benefit package.

"I take it you're still not reading the papers, Al."

"I'm not."

"So I'll read this for you."

"If it has anything to do with the crime, I won't have it read. You'll have to summarize."

I had adopted my survivor's limp, the mannerism that says, *Don't push me, I'm still very vulnerable.* I hate it.

"There's no need to summarize. You've just about written the article yourself."

He allowed me a moment to register the shock before going on. Like Leonard. The sadist's pause.

"This was on page three of the *Great Falls County News*, morning edition. 'Prison Refuses Pastor's Request to Love His Enemy.'"

He looked up at me to make sure I'd heard him, and then went on:

"'The Sermon on the Mount is not in the governing code of the New Jersey Department of Corrections. At least that's the message it's sending to the Rev. Alson Pierce of Lenapee Borough.

"'Following the murder of Pierce's wife and son in their home last November, Pierce wrote to their convicted killer, Alex Leonard, asking for an opportunity to meet him and "love his enemy." Leonard is serving a life sentence in Hamilton State Prison for the stabbing deaths of Cynthia Pierce, age thirty-six, and James Pierce, age four. Mrs. Pierce was also raped before her death.

"'"It is not my intention to reproach you for what you have done," Pierce wrote in his letter, "to convert you...or in any way to...interfere with your life."

"'Pierce offered his services to Leonard, including "diversions or entertainments," as a way of serving Christ. Pierce hopes his efforts on Leonard's behalf will enable him to join his deceased family in heaven.

"'According to prison administrator Frank Amazo, Pierce's request was rejected out of concern for the minister's emotional health and because Leonard has no wish to see him.

""'We have to respect the inmate's wishes in a matter like this," Amazo said. "We also feel, on the advice of our professional staff, that such a visit is not in the victim's best interest."

"'Amazo added, "We certainly respect Rev. Pierce's sincerity. He's obviously trying to practice what he preaches."

"'Rev. Pierce could not be reached for comment on the decision. He is currently on leave from the Smyrna Federated Church in Lenapee, where he has served as pastor for the past six years.

"'Pierce had been hospitalized because of a savage beating received during the murders of his wife and son.'"

Incredible. The powers and principalities. They had beaten me to the punch. I had threatened them with a public request, and they had bested me with a public rejection. Force is met with force. The nature of retaliation is escalation. This is why we are told to turn the other cheek. Andrew was talking to me. I was now holding the clipping in my hand.

"Are you with me, Al?"

"I wasn't, but I am now."

"Alson, what are you up to?"

"It seems the newspaper pretty much explains that."

"No, it doesn't. I want you to explain it."

"There's nothing to explain."

"I'm sorry to disagree. I'm beginning to wonder if you need more qualified help than I'm able to provide."

"Beginning to worry that I'm becoming a biblical literalist, maybe? Have no fear. I have no intention of testifying to the Virgin Birth in a letter to the editor."

"Don't be funny."

"I'm not being funny. You're being funny. This whole stinking business we're in strikes me as hilariously funny, Andy."

I knew he wouldn't like the nickname or the display of temper. I stood up for emphasis.

"We waltz around in black robes and take vacations to the Maine coast on money earned from proclaiming the relevance of the Gospel, especially the moral and social relevance, go light on the hocus-pocus and the 'opiate of the people stuff,' of course—we make Gandhi and Dr. King into the new Saints Peter and Paul—and then somebody tries to put some of it into practice, and we act like he needs a straitjacket. If that's not hilariously, uproariously, sidesplittingly funny, tell me what is."

"Sit down, Al, you're flailing."

"Don't tell me to sit down, Andy!" I shouted. "I've been told to sit down one too many times. Told to sit down with a goddamn gun pointing at my kid's head and tied like an animal to a chair!"

21

I shook my finger at him, then sat down. Andrew was silent for a minute.

"And what were you intending to do, pray tell, when you walked into Alex Leonard's cell and he said, 'May I offer you a chair, Reverend Pierce?' Tear out his eyes? Or is that your secret hope? Are you trying to go out like Gandhi or Clint Eastwood?"

"Go to hell, Andrew."

"*I* am not a biblical literalist, so I'll take that as no more than a generic curse. Oh, Al, let's not do this with each other."

"Who threw down the gauntlet? It wasn't me. Who called me in and read me the newspaper?"

"Was it news to you? Was this the first time you heard of their answer?"

"Yes. I haven't checked my mail yet today. There could be a letter there."

"You should get a phone, for God's sake. You could hook it up to a machine at least."

"I'll get a phone when I'm good and ready. Not having a phone is about the only pleasure I have these days, but it's a pleasure, let me tell you."

"I'm sure it is. Al, are you able to see why I'm a little upset here? I mean, I don't expect you to kiss my ring, but I've stood by you through this whole nightmare. I used my credentials to up my job description from your spiritual director to your counselor, not that I was ever much of either, frankly—to you, I mean. I used that new status to argue for you to stay out of court, I went with you to court

22

when you had to identify the madman, I helped videotape the better part of your testimony—and there was a job I wouldn't give to my worst enemy. It was horrible. For you most of all, I know, but for me too. I've put my nuts in the wringer to spare you exposure, I've bullied the regional directors on your behalf, I've kept your governing board from pulling a coup while you're out of the pulpit, I've met with you and listened to you and wept with you, and then you go pull this stunt without a word to me. I read it in the paper, for God's sake. I mean, never mind if it's the right thing. Maybe you've got the Holy Spirit and all I've got is hemorrhoids, but I read it *in the paper*, and it reflects on me, too, because I'm supposed to be your counselor and guide. What do I tell people? I endorsed this? Or Pierce is totally out of control?"

"You can drop me if I'm an embarrassment."

"Is that what you want? And that's the other thing, Al, and it hurts, I'm suddenly like the enemy here. If you plan to do any soul-searching on this, I hope you'll remember me. I mean, who am I? I'm your friend. I was Cindy's friend. I am also grieving."

It was probably no exaggeration for him to say so. I always thought he was sweet on Cynthia. Whenever he met her, he seemed to take on the attitude of her soulmate, the one who truly understood her because they both understood me. I was more or less their child—in his eyes. Cynthia often spoke of

23

him as a blowhard. Still, she glowed in his attention. She blushed, even. What does any of this matter now?

"Blessed are those who mourn," I said.

"Give me a break. Jesus! You know what this is, Al, as well as I do. This is the delusional paranoia of somebody about to develop a prophet complex. You're going to do a mighty deed, and the rest of us soul-blind Pharisees had best just stand back and marvel. Everybody's an enemy now."

"I have only one enemy, Andrew, and he's not you. And I intend to love him. If it kills me."

"Oh, Christ, Al."

"Oh, Christ indeed, Andrew."

We engaged one another's eyes for a silent moment. I noticed the number of gray hairs in his goatee. He is a good man. He has served as my spiritual director since the time of my second church job, as his assistant over in Holland Grove, and even though I stopped following much of his advice some years ago, I never stopped in my grudging admiration for his guileless decency. Even his sins—his infatuation with my wife, for example—were transparent, "natural," harmless. Andrew, if ever you find what I have written here, know that I mean what I say when I call you a good man.

"I'm not sure we should wait till tomorrow."

"Don't worry. I'm not going to do anything drastic. Apparently I'm not even going to visit a prison. I can wait. I need to wait."

"Okay, but go home and try to sleep. You got medicine?"

"Yes."

"Still doing the journal every night?"

"Yes. More than ever, lately. That's been a helpful suggestion, Andrew."

"I'm still interested in having you share some of it, you know."

"Sure. Let's just wait a while on that."

"Your call completely, Al." He stretched out his arm across the desk to me. "Look, why don't you sleep at our place tonight."

"No. Go home to your family, Andrew. I'll see you later. Leave an appointment with Bob. I can make anything. I have no engagements. I just had my hair cut."

There was a letter in my post office box, which I checked on the way home. It came from Alex Leonard's attorney. Mr. Leonard had "no desire" to see me, it said. And Mr. Leonard's attorney did not advise him to. There's this joke about a dispute over the boundary between heaven and hell. I heard it in the barbershop. St. Peter threatens to sue the devil in order to establish the property line, but the devil just laughs in his face.

"Where are *you* going to find a lawyer?" he says.

3 ✦

Let the words of my mouth and the meditations of my heart be acceptable in your sight, O Lord, our strength and our redeemer.

The text for my message this evening to you, O Church of the Invisible Congregation, is taken from the tenth chapter of Paul's First Letter to the Corinthians, beginning and ending with the thirteenth verse.

Paul writes: "No testing has overtaken you that is not common to everyone. God is faithful, and he will not let you be tested beyond your strength, but with the testing he will also provide the way out so that you may be able to endure it."

Now every word of this wonderful verse is important, but what concerns me most this evening are the words "he will not let you be tested beyond your strength." Immediately, if we are paying close attention, we are struck by how these lines are addressed to us as individuals. Like so much of the Gospel message, they are spoken to the whole Church, yet also speak to us as singular persons. The Good Shepherd calls each of us by name, and you can take this or any other verse and find your name written on it.

For if God will not let us be tested beyond our strength—and notice the words "let us be tested," God does not test us, actively, but *allows* us to be tested, passively as it were—but if God will not let us be tested beyond our strength, that means that as my strength differs from another man's or woman's strength, so my testing will differ also.

Don't we often interpret our testing as a measure of our sins? "What have I done to deserve this?" we say. "What have I done?" And our question sounds so humble, so penitent, but at its root is the grasping, overweening pride of life. We suppose that what befalls us is somehow measured out according to what we deserve; it is our responsibility, and therefore within the domain of our will, and our power, and our so-called willpower.

But no, says the Apostle, we are tested according to our strength. And who among us is the author and creator of his own strength? We can no more *be* strong than we can *be* happy, though people are continually advising us to do both. No, we are weak and strong as God has decided, and insofar as we are weak or strong, God allows us to be tested.

Isn't there a certain liberation in looking at the matter this way? And isn't there also a certain terror? A certain blind, helpless terror? For if this is how things stand, the strong are, of all men and women, the most miserable.

But do not suppose that I am going to spend the remainder of my sermon on exegesis. Rather, I am going to tell you a story. I know that announcement will delight many of you. So many times, one of you has come up to me after a sermon and said, "Oh, Reverend Pierce, I like it so much when you tell stories. I find that's what I remember from your sermons. The other things are important, I know, but the stories stick in my head."

And so this evening we shall have a story. And I can assure you, this story will stick in your heads. This story will stick in your heads like the spike that the biblical Jael drove into the head of the sleeping Sisera.

For this is the story of a thing that happened to me and to a woman and to a little boy who were my wife and my son, a thing for which I cannot even find a suitable word.

Now I see some of you glancing at your pewmates. I see the distress on your faces. I see some of you preparing to flee with your children. That is one of our most basic instincts, isn't it, to protect our children?

But what did you suppose? That I would parcel out this tale in pieces, a little here, a little there, like clues in a mystery novel? No, I intend to tell you everything I know, here and now, without embellishment or equivocation, without exaggeration, but also without mercy. So go if you have to go.

A man is sitting at his dining room table with his wife and son. It is November, roughly two weeks before Thanksgiving. The dinner is tuna noodle casserole, which is a favorite of the little boy, also carrots, and if everybody cleans their plates, a dish of vanilla ice cream. The boy is four years old. The boy is named James. The boy is usually called Jimmy. The boy weighed seven pounds, fourteen ounces when he was born. Even though it is November, he is sitting at the table in his underwear, white briefs and a T-shirt. He once saw his grandpa Cornelius eat breakfast this way, and it made a great impression. His parents indulge the fancy now and then, and turn up the thermostat so he will not be cold.

The wife is named Cynthia. The wife is very pretty. The wife does not look like a minister's wife. I'm not sure what that means, but I was not the first person to say it. She is wearing a blue work shirt rolled up at the sleeves, and slightly darker blue jeans. She is also wearing silver earrings that look like sand dollars. The man remembers thinking how beautiful she is when the family says grace. The man also remembers, because of its irony, thinking how lucky they are that the phone has not disturbed them at the start of dinner. The phone in a parsonage is always ringing. I wonder if the phone rings over there now, or if you have disconnected it. No one has lived at the parsonage since that evening. You have a lamp set with a timer that goes on at dusk and off at eleven o'clock. You hope to discourage anyone from breaking in.

I do not even know now how the man got in that day. I guess I am going to speak of myself in the first person after all, so as not to confuse myself with him. He is the man and I am I. We heard no noise until the man appeared in the doorway from the hall. I don't know if he walked in through an unlocked door or climbed in through a window. I don't know if he was there, waiting, all along, listening as we made supper, as we played and kissed and flushed toilets, or whether he entered the house right before we saw him. I have sometimes imagined that he simply appeared there, out of thin air, like an angel from hell.

His hair was scruffy and greasy, the same shade of blond as my wife's, and he was clean-shaven. He wore what they call "a muscle shirt," and he was very muscular. He had tattoos on both arms, which I later noticed were of a scorpion and a naked woman. I did not notice what the tattoos were at first, because he was holding a handgun. He said nothing. My wife drew in her breath audibly. The man smiled. For a single desperate moment I hoped he was someone's tasteless idea of a practical joke.

They say that most people automatically freeze when they see a gun. And we were all three of us frozen for a moment. But quite soon I rose to the occasion. I became gallant. And my gallantry, invisible brothers and sisters, had nothing to do with courage, or even love, or quick thinking. Least of all with quick thinking. No, my short-lived gallantry was the automatic response of a man who had always discussed a moment of crisis like the one he was in with an automatic clicheaa. Let me try to explain what I mean.

I have, as you know, preached several times from this pulpit on the subject of gun control, and many other times on the subject of violence. I have from time to time offended those of you who participate in sports that use guns, or belong to organizations that uphold, as they say, your *right* to own guns. As a few of you will never forget, or let me forget, I even wrote an editorial for our national church newspaper, *The Fisher*, in which I sketched out a theology for universal disarmament.

And so, because of my stand on that issue, I was always having to answer the question, "What would you do if your family was threatened by a rapist or murderer?" Because, as you know, that is how we often probe the convictions of our ideological opponents. We rhetorically take their loved ones hostage. "How would you feel if someone came to murder your family?" we ask the man who does not believe that a follower of Jesus Christ ought to maintain an arsenal of assault rifles in his living-room closet. "How would you feel if your thirteen-year-old daughter was impregnated by a rapist?" we ask the woman who believes that a human fetus just might have more value than a troublesome appendix.

And, of course, within our rhetoric there is a secret wish, is there not?—a slight but wicked wish that our opponent will indeed suffer what we describe in our hypothetical example, and so come to know in his broken heart the stupidity of his convictions. At the very least, we wish to afflict him with the imagining of the horribly unimaginable. For I also have taunted my adversaries by saying, "And what if your child were to find the gun and accidentally kill himself, or purposely kill himself in a moment of emotional distress?" We have all used this device, haven't we, all made hostages of our neighbor's wife and child, and thus we are all in danger of the wrath of God.

But I am preaching, and I promised a story. I had only meant to explain how I could act gallantly in such a threatening situation, and said that I had acted automatically. You see, whenever someone had posed the terrible question, what would I do if my family were threatened by an armed assailant, I had given the stock reply of pacifists and peacemakers everywhere. I would give my life, I had said. I just would not *take* one. I had never discussed, nor had anyone ever challenged me to discuss, how giving up my life would protect anyone or anything except my own self-righteousness.

So when Alex Leonard stood before us in our dining room, showing his gun but not yet pointing it at any of us, I immediately knew that I must give my life. I had practiced that response so often that I knew it by heart. I rose from my chair, I turned and took up the iron poker from the cold hearth at my back (even then, you see, I was not a complete pacifist), and advanced toward him, shouting, "Get out of our home!"

And perhaps, just perhaps, if he had killed me, he might have panicked and run. In another situation it might have worked like that. In this situation it did not. In this situation a gun would not have helped either, unless I'd been in the habit of laying it next to my knife and fork on the table.

The man simply pointed the gun at Jimmy's head and said, "I wouldn't yell at me if I were you. And I'd put that down before somebody gets hurt with it." He waved the gun back and forth, like a serpent's head, from Jimmy to Cynthia. And glancing at Cynthia I had the horrible sensation not only of having been utterly disarmed, but of seeing her forced to agree with him.

"Do what he says, for God's sake," she gasped. And as Jimmy pressed his face into her breast, I dropped the poker, which hit the rug with the dull thud of a severed head.

One of the man's hands had apparently been held behind his back, for when I next looked at him he was holding a coil of rope. A wave of nausea passed over me. What else did he have with him? What else had his preparations included? I managed to hold down my dinner. All the little proprieties we cling to until the very end. It has occurred to me that vomiting might have disgusted him enough to deter him, or at least delay his intentions. As you all know, we were moments from rescue. Just moments. Or I could have vomited and he might have shot us all on the spot. In either case, I wish I had vomited.

The man pulled one of the chairs out from the table, using the hand that held the rope. Then, once again raising the gun so it was aimed at my wife and son—he had momentarily lowered his arm, I guess—he said, "I want you to sit down right here, Reverend. At the head of the table. Right now, Reverend." He shot a glance in the direction he was aiming his gun.

How did he know I was a clergyman? I wasn't wearing a clerical collar, and we had no sign outside the house identifying it as a parsonage. My eyes rose questioningly to his pitiless face for one moment before I turned to sit. Cindy was still holding Jimmy's face to her chest. Tears were running down her cheeks. Did I know this man from somewhere? Like someone in a burning building tearing through the pages of a phone book, I leafed through impressions of my congregation from Sunday to Sunday. The rope wound around me like a terrible dry snake, first at my feet, then up my legs to my chest. Had he come to the office one day? Sometimes strangers, transients, do come. Some of you have even told me that it makes you nervous having them around. Had I refused him something? For what might I apologize? *Did I know this man?*

He cut the unused rope from me with a knife. He refolded it and pocketed it. He moved from behind my chair to where my wife and son were clutching one another. It was then that I saw the scorpion on his right arm as it passed me.

"Now, Mother, we need to have the boy come over by his daddy." He went to lay his hand on Jimmy, and she rose with him in her arms and inhaled sharply, grimacing to scream. At the same time I shouted, "No!"

Leonard grabbed the boy roughly away from

his mother and pressed the gun against his ear.

"Noises make me very nervous, all right? You understand that, honey? You understand that? Nod your head, honey, so I know you understand."

Cynthia nodded and then pressed her face between her hands. She looked ten years older. And what was her last impression of me, I wonder, tied up and sweating with fear? Did she know her fate even then?

Jimmy was completely motionless, his face completely white, as the man turned and placed him on my lap. He put his arms around my neck, but stiffly, like the corpse of a child instead of a living one. But I could feel his short breaths; his face was pressed to my face.

When I moved mine aside, to see but also to catch my breath, my face was shadowed by Leonard, who bent close to us. He was a hot, suffocating presence. His breath reeked of alcohol.

"Mommy and I have some things to talk about," he said in a calm voice, but with his chest heaving. "We'll be in the next room, and you have to sit right here on your daddy's lap."

Leonard straightened, stepped back, looking at where Cindy stood petrified, but pointing his gun at us. Before he turned away, I saw the other tattoo, the naked woman. Surely this is a dream, I thought, but with absolutely no faith that it was.

"Now, it's very important that the little

boy stay right there. If the little boy disturbs Mommy and me, that won't be very nice, will it? And if the little boy tries to run away, he could get hurt very bad because there's a monster in the hallway. He's my friend and he does whatever I want. Are you listening, Reverend? Pay close attention, Reverend."

Was there another? Would he appear soon? Were there more than two? Would they also go into the other room with Cynthia? Now I feared I would black out. I could scarcely manage the breath to speak. We had the thermostat turned up so high.

"Someone's coming," I said, and for just a moment he seemed to freeze.

"Shut up," he hissed, listening. Then he shook the gun he was still aiming at me and Jimmy.

"You trying to bullshit me, man?" he snarled. "You bullshitting me?"

"No, no, I don't mean someone's there right now, but someone will come." This meek exclamation, with its implicit wish, was as close as I probably came to a prayer throughout the whole ordeal. That's true, I never thought to pray. Would it have changed anything if I had? But I am a minister, and in my darkest hour I never thought to pray. It occurs to me just now: Could it be that God himself paces the halls of heaven, muttering what I mutter pacing here below: *Where was he?*

"I have an appointment," I lied. "My building committee, the guys who take care of the church building, are supposed to be here any minute."

The mention of such ordinary business in that dreadful context almost made me laugh. Since then, all the pursuits of the sons and daughters of men have often struck me in the same way. Life, liberty, and the pursuit of happiness—to me they sound like Larry, Curly, and Moe.

"Well the guys are just going to have to come back, aren't they, because nobody's home. Nobody's home. The reverend and the missus just turned in early. Do not disturb. Isn't that right, beautiful? The reverend doesn't buy you very nice clothes. He's got you dressed up like a fucking man. But you're not a man, are you?"

He draped his arm around Cynthia's shoulder. The gun barrel dangled over her breast. In his other hand he carried the remainder of the rope. She turned her head to look at us, and I could tell she was trying with all her might to smile. "I'll be right back, Jimmy," she said, but it was as if she were speaking solely to me. It was the last I saw of her—and even that moment was violated by the insistent impression of the similarity between the color of her hair and his. Had we all survived, I would have asked her to dye it.

The two moved languidly into our bedroom; but as soon as they were there, he kicked the door closed with violent force. The dining room had become a waiting room, and the feeling, strangely—or perhaps not strangely enough—was something like I'd known after delivering my wife into the hands of a male doctor. You will think this contrived, but for the first time I noticed a couple of magazines lying on the unused side of the table.

There is so much to wonder about an event like this. The facts of it cut like one of those high-speed European trains through a vast landscape of possibilities. Why did Leonard not tie the boy as well? That is what I wonder almost more than anything else. If he didn't want the boy out of my lap, why didn't he tie him there? A question not unlike asking why God put the Tree of the Knowledge of Good and Evil in the Garden of Eden if he didn't want Adam and Eve to eat its fruit.

Jimmy began to whimper almost at once. His partial nakedness, the coldness of his bare arms around my neck, was terrible. Oh, the helplessness of those minutes, hours, however long it was! A soul without a body is no more helpless. A man had unhusbanded me and unfathered me, and how was it that I was still alive? What had I failed to do? He had taken my wife from me, though she was only a room away. He had taken my ability to hold my own son in my arms, though he was on my lap. Do you doubt for even a minute, you blind, foolish sheep, that heaven and hell are close by, that the damned and the saved are damned and saved by inches?

"I want Mom," he cried.

"Mom is all right. Mom is coming right back."

38

I said it again, louder, as he said "I want Mom" louder.

"I'm all right, Jimmy," I heard Cynthia call. "Mommy's coming."

The last words came out of her like a twisted gasp. Then she could hear us. I shushed Jimmy, and for a moment heard muffled, indecipherable words from Leonard, dull sounds of movement, then silence. Then Jimmy crying again. What was he doing to her?

Suddenly Leonard burst out of the room, moving toward us with his head turning from side to side like that of a carnivorous dinosaur. Jimmy hugged me more tightly. "Cindy," I called. "Cindy, are you okay?"

I think she uttered some wordless sound before Leonard barked at me to shut up.

"You got a camcorder?" he said.

I heard him perfectly, but wondered if I had. "What?"

"A camcorder, asshole. A camcorder! What you make videos with. You got one?"

"No, no, we don't."

And here, brothers and sisters, you may see how quick we are to hope and how just as quick we are to despair, for I immediately assumed that somehow a camcorder might be the ransom for my poor wife and that for lack of one I could not save her. We had talked seriously about getting one. Of course, ransom was not the man's intent at all. I cried out stupidly, "I could give you money to buy one."

"You're nuts, you know that?" he sniggered after a brief pause. "You sure you ain't got a camcorder? You got a CD player"—he pulled it off the shelf and onto the floor—"you got a VCR in the bedroom, you got a fucking answering machine on your phone, you got a fucking computer upstairs with everything on it, and you mean to tell me"—he bent his face toward us—"you ain't got a fucking camcorder? Are you sure?"

"I'm sure," I said. He grabbed a fistful of my hair.

"Because if when I'm done I find one, you and this kid here are in deep shit."

He was away from us and into the bedroom before I could say a word. My mind panicked for a moment with the thought that perhaps we had rented a video camera and forgotten to return it. Leonard swore "Jesus Christ!" and slammed the bedroom door. Jimmy trembled and wailed.

I said, as soothingly as I could manage, "Jimmy, it's okay. Shh. Shh." I had not ceased to work my hands and arms back and forth in the ropes. "Listen to me, Jimmy, listen, okay. You can't cry or Mommy will worry. Come on, Jimmy. Let's sing, Jimmy." And I started to sing a song that Jimmy had learned and sang constantly, "Jesus loves me." I sang hoarsely. "Jesus loves me. Come on, Jimmy. Jesus loves me, this I know, for the Bible tells me so."

But he would not sing with me. And I thought, no matter how things turn out, whether we live or die, he will never be able to sing that song again.

As if she had read my thoughts, Cindy cried

out from the next room. I could feel Jimmy freeze on my lap. She cried again. And then I did what is the only act or word of that day that I do not revise over and over again in my head, wondering if another act or word would have been better. With this I am content. If all my body and soul are destroyed in hell, let this still echo through eternity—I cried out, "I love you, Cindy. I love you with all my heart."

"We love you, Mommy," I cried for the boy and me, and then he himself cried it.

Oh, but even about this there is reason to wonder, isn't there? For with those words I might very well have killed her.

The rest goes very fast.

"I love you, too," she cried back in a voice I can only call wretched.

"Shut your mouth!" I heard Leonard say distinctly.

Cindy cried out in pain.

Jimmy bolted from my lap and ran to the bedroom, shouting, "Mommy!" He was like a little machine gone haywire, like a movie of himself and the projector running amok—pounding the door, turning the knob, as I cried in vain to call him back.

I heard shouting, screaming, scuffling. I never heard a shot. I began to scream myself. I bellowed and roared, as much to drown out their cries, I think, as to call for help. It seemed we cried out like that forever. With a jerk of my body I tipped over the chair and crashed to the floor, where I continued to make a wordless

41

uproar for as long as I was able. Then, hoarse and exhausted, I drew breath to scream one more time, and heard silence.

What a horrid silence!

To this day I do not know the details of what occasioned that silence, though some of you may. I was warned that the newspapers were unsparing in their reports.

The cry that came from me next was the loudest of all. I felt as if I were literally going to disgorge my heart and lungs. And then I felt his feet kicking my head and body, shouting at me to shut up. I cried out for as long as I was conscious. I remember hoping he would kill me.

But he did not kill me.

You know, of course, that the police arrived, and that their arrival probably saved my life. A neighbor who had seen Leonard enter our house called them. Or, rather, that neighbor called another neighbor, and she called them, apparently after some discussion. The two neighbors have never identified themselves. They remain invisible, like you, my brothers and sisters. I, I only, am escaped alone to tell thee.

So there is your story. Doesn't a sermon seem to go so much faster when it contains a story? Everyone seems to think so. But we must not forget our message. Do any of you recall the text with which we began? Think for a moment, and then I shall close by reading it.

"No testing has overtaken you that is not common to everyone. God is faithful, and he will not let you be tested beyond your strength, but with the testing will also provide the way out so that you may be able to endure it."

God has not yet revealed—at least not to you—what will be the "way out" that makes this man's endurance possible. Presumably death was the way out for his hapless wife and son.

But one thing should be clear to you all. Applying the text to the story, there is only one possible conclusion. This man who stands before you, this man who was powerless to save his family, a man you pity and fear and avoid as if he were a contagion of bad luck, this dry cake of animated dust who goes by the name of Alson Pierce, is in fact the strongest man in the world. Behold!

Why do you flinch? It is not loaded. It is not pointed at any of you. It is not the same weapon that menaced my family, though you can draw some vacuous moral association between the two, if that satisfies you in some way.

Do not miss what I am revealing to you. I am showing you the culmination of my career. Oh, yes I am. What is preaching, but the attempt to make a text as simple as a stone, as clear as a crystal, as portable and applicable—as a gun? "He will not let you be tested beyond your strength, but with the testing will also provide the way out so that you may be able to endure it."

This is my way out, brothers and sisters. Only if I can find the way in.

4

I dreamed of our wedding again. I stood at the altar with my best male friend beside me, a man who now lives in Alaska. He was craning his neck to see through the great wooden doors at the back. The stained-glass windows on either side of the church were all engorged with sunlight, golden yellows, Canterbury blues, blood reds, and the deepest forest greens; crowns, swords, suns, mantles, wounds and halos, vine leaves and grapes, all resplendent. There was no stained glass in the little college chapel where Cynthia and I were actually married. These windows and their stone casements were quarried from the memories of various holidays we took together. The congregation likewise contained people who had died before we were married, and friends we would not make for years to come.

The music was from a CD we had at the parsonage, *Organ Masterpieces of Johann Sebastian Bach*, one of those magnificent Pentecost preludes invoking the Holy Ghost. (At our wedding, a friend had played a folk guitar.) As the notes rose, Joe tapped my shoulder and Cynthia appeared on her father's arm, in a dress much grander but no prettier than the one she had actually worn. She moved like the live golden figurehead of a schooner with its sails cut free. She filled the aisle with triumphantly undulating whiteness. Even from a distance I could see the tanned skin of her face, breast, and arms, the living flesh against the pale white. Her blue eyes pierced my whole being with their love.

I could smell her perfume as she took her place beside me, halting ever so gently, like a sailing vessel brought skillfully to dock. It was not the perfume she wore at our wedding, or any other commercial fragrance, but all the smells of her skin turning through my memory like colored lights thrown onto a Christmas tree by a rotating filter: her skin in the sun, her skin wet in the rain, her skin musky in the warmth of a night's sleep, the smell of her sex.

When the minister said "Dearly Beloved"— which were not the opening words of our wedding service, either—I looked to my right and saw instead of my best man (who I knew was behind me) our son Jimmy, holding both of our rings on a velvet cushion. He was standing up as straight as a little spruce, and his hair was combed. He smiled up at me, and then his glance moved slightly forward to gaze upon his mother. He winked. I felt a swooning pleasure in his eyelashes moving, in his fist scratching at his perfect ear. I knew he would not be born for another decade, yet he was there with us, according to the timeless, flexible logic of dreams.

When the minister led us through our vows, I said "I will" so earnestly, as if I had said so before with questionable success and intended to do better this time. For her part, Cynthia said "I will" with complete confidence—she seemed to be saying, "I don't mind your asking, but do you really need to ask?" Her eyes were never long off Jimmy; she was interested in his impressions of all this. She was hoping he understood everything.

It was only when we kissed that the sweetness of the dream acquired its taste of worry. I felt we were kissing each other good-bye. But when Cynthia's eyes opened, I saw no sorrow in them. "We should go," she said, intimating with her voice and eyes that better kisses were soon to come.

"Let's wait a while longer," I said, suddenly anxious. "Let's wait till the rain passes." By then I knew it was raining, the knowledge instantly confirmed by an ominous pattering on the church roof. We turned and faced the people, who were now fumbling with umbrellas and tying on plastic rain hats. The light was gone from the stained-glass windows.

"We won't melt," Cynthia said. "Come on, Jimmy."

She took his hand and, with an impish glance over her shoulder, said, "Last one out's a rotten egg."

The congregation laughed as Cynthia and Jimmy ran down the aisle. I followed close behind. The church doors swung open to reveal a dark night laced with bullets of rain and riven by lightning that lit nothing.

"Wait!" I cried.

But we were all three sucked into a terrific wind that lifted Jimmy like a kite above us and tore his mother's gown and blew its shreds away into the darkness. I yelled "No!" with all my might, and woke trembling and sweating in my bed.

I knew instantly that I was awake, and yet the darkness of the room seemed one with the darkness of the dream. The blue numerals of the digital clock radio told me it was only 10:23.

I felt I must leave the house. I rose and dressed quickly. The air outside was muggy; a bug-infested haze surrounded the streetlamps. In the distance I could hear the car tires snapping over the seams of Brandon Avenue, but in the immediate neighborhood most of the houses were quiet and dark. These people had to get up for work in the morning.

Walking at night past the statuary of a largely Italian neighborhood can give one the impression of walking through a graveyard. Mary after Mary. Here and there a Joseph. The Holy Family. I, in turn, began to feel like a ghost.

Crossing Brandon Avenue did nothing to make me feel more substantial. Willy's Service was closed by then, of course, and so were the bakery and the dry cleaner up the street. There was not even the suggestion of a breeze. In seminary we learned that the Hebrew word for *wind* is the same as the word for *spirit*, and both connote life. For just a moment I wondered if I was not in fact a ghost, and this the land of the dead. Had I died in my dining room on that awful day? Had I died in a storm at my wedding only moments before, and was all the rest a dream?

I knew that none of this was so. I knew I was real, and I knew I was very much *there* on the street, and I could trace all of the events that had brought me there. I was not lying when I told the prison psychiatrist that I did not have flashbacks, and that my grip on reality was firm. It is just that since the ordeal I am not sure reality is firm. I find myself pausing for a moment to wonder about things I know are so, or can never be so. The habit began when I first saw Alex Leonard. I could not believe my eyes when I saw him, or my ears when he spoke. I could not believe anything that followed was happening when it happened. Many days I still cannot believe it.

The moon above was pale and shrouded in the same haze as the streetlights. I walked through another neighborhood of modest houses, then across the Van Ness Bridge toward the more or less suburban homes where many of my former parishioners live. The river made the dry, guttural sound of a dying old man. It smelled like a dying old man. Downstream a hundred feet or so, an overturned shopping cart lay gleaming in the shallow flow like a cage in hell.

It was foolish to head that way, of course; I knew from having gone there before, other nights after other dreams. Yet I felt drawn there with the same irresistible homing force that pulls those silly, monogamous penguins through frozen oceans filled with predatory seals back to their old rookeries.

The light was still on in the parsonage. The timer would not shut off for another five or ten minutes. On other nights, especially in the beginning, I had told myself that I was just checking on the house, performing a small, self-appointed duty in exchange for my paid leave of absence. The humble, widowed caretaker.

I no longer came with an excuse. I had come several times lately to watch the light click off, and then to return home. It had the feeling of an act of reverence, like waiting for the candles to be extinguished before leaving the pews.

Tonight, with the dream still in my head, and the ghostly sensation of the humid darkness, and the knowledge that I had taken my best shot to see Alex Leonard and had failed and therefore lost any purpose whatsoever for existing, I was seized by and readily yielded to the suggestion that I had at last been led by Providence to the great loophole in my fate.

Inside that house, my wife and son were alive and well. The newspapers had printed the stories of their deaths in order to protect them. They had come home to live after the trial of Alex Leonard. They knew I was alive, and had heard I was traumatized, and they, too, suffered from God knows what nightmares, wounds, even mutilations. Everyone had told them it was best to wait a while for a reunion. Children are resilient, and Jimmy was making good progress, and this in turn worked for healing in his mother. She asked for word of me every day, and someone brought it—probably Andrew. The sting of jealousy somehow made the possibility more real.

Now, having gone to the extreme of asking to see Alex Leonard, I had been spared by the strange and incredible mercy of God. I had been led home to take up my life with a gratitude already eternal in its profundity. No matter what terrible memories lay inside that house, no matter what hideous scars marked the minds and bodies of the woman and boy who lived there, I was ready to love them. I need wait—they need wait—no longer. I was home. I was standing at the window. I glimpsed the bare frame of our bed through the slit between the drawn drapes.

Then the light switched off, as at the end of a bedtime story told by a heartless automaton.

I wandered for much of the night, and returned an hour or so before dawn. It is strange to recall the last time in my life when I was an all-night walker, in those heady days of working out my "call" to the ministry. It was autumn when the crisis seized me, taking the form of an irresistible restlessness. I was in good physical shape; in fact, I coached both wrestling and cross-country running at the high school where I also taught history, and in those cool, nearly frosty nights I walked for miles and miles at a pace close to a run. Sometimes I did run. I would fancy myself running from God, but playfully, in the manner of a lover, looking behind to see if God would catch up with me.

Cindy and I lived in Warwick then, up near the New York State border. There was a big chemical plant tucked in the crook of the arm of Route 19, just below where it joins up with the New York Thruway. I'd walk or jog old Route 104 under the dense foliage of ash, maple, and elm, and past the sedate colonial houses out to the highway ramp, then mount it like a spiraling stairway up to the cement lanes where the tractor-trailers went wailing by at all hours, and glance over at the chemical plant, which in those days was going at all hours too, and just stand out there like a dazed hitchhiker gazing up at the few stars bright enough to defy the artificial light of that vast Milky Way of diners, gas pumps, and clip joints stretching from Warwick to the New York City skyline, which I could see glinting like another galaxy in the distance. I would walk to this place because it was always awake, as God is always awake, and because I thrilled to imagine myself hitching a ride north to Canada or south into the bowels of the city, to know that these were choices God had placed at my disposal under those few daring stars.

Where had they led, my choices, my religious

zeal? To waste. On those rocky romantic coasts in Maine, Cindy and I, and later Jimmy, would find fragment after spiny green fragment of broken sea urchins. The seagulls fly them up into the air and drop them on the stones to split their shells and eat their still living bodies. That is the image I see when I think of my life, broken sea urchins, broken heart, lost faith retreating like the tide.

Of course, if I am honest, I will admit that my estrangement from God began before I met Alex Leonard. As a minister, I became married to God, and what as a minister I had seen happen to so many marriages—what had not happened in Cindy's and mine—happened in my religious life. God and I quite simply drifted apart. We talked every day, yet it soon became impossible to remember when we had last had a conversation. I sent the obligatory bouquets of worship on special occasions, but I never would have thought to stop and pick some flowers on the way home from work. When Alex Leonard appeared in my house, even when I sang "Jesus Loves Me" to comfort my petrified child, God was the farthest thing from my mind.

Apparently, by that time, so was I from his.

I slept soundly for several hours, but do not remember any more dreams. I woke in the middle of the morning. I showered, ate a piece of toast with a glass of juice, and sat down in my living room with the emptiest feeling I had known since the moment when I knew for sure that my wife and son were dead. I simply, utterly, did not know what to do next. I had run out of everything but time. *"Eli, eli, lama sabachthani,"* I muttered to myself, attempting to be wry and even blasphemous, but knowing I had prayed instead. I do not know for sure how long I sat there before the doorbell rang, or how many times it rang before I noticed it.

I opened my door to find a young man in rumpled khaki sitting like a parcel on my front step. He got up as soon as I appeared.

"Jesus, you scared me. I thought nobody was home. Hello." He extended his hand. "Are you Reverend Alson Pierce?" "Why?"

"I'm Harold Stevens from the New York *Daily News.* I wanted to ask you some questions about your letter to Alex Leonard, if you don't mind. I would have called, but you don't have a phone."

"There's nothing to say. The papers have already said everything." They send somebody to talk to you about your heart and soul who's dressed like a tropical explorer who sleeps every night in his goddamn clothes. I felt a sudden rush of anger—as if my family had been destroyed by nothing more than an excess of informality.

"Are you sincere, Reverend Pierce?" he asked, with his pen poised over his notepad. "Is your letter to be taken at face value?"

I looked hard at him, one of those blunt young

persons who are so assertive that they wind up being innocuous. "Yes," I said, "it's to be taken at face value." There was something else I could have added, clever and sarcastic, but I did not know what it was. "I need to go back inside."

"But how do you love a man who's murdered your family?" he said. "I know that's a hard question, but it must be one you've asked."

"God help me," I sighed.

"What?"

If I had uttered so much as that during the Calvary of my wife and son..."God help me," I said, louder, lost in another time. "Why don't we talk about that, about God."

My eyes focused on a blue Mercedes that had stopped decisively at the curb near my front walk. An immaculately dressed man slammed his door and walked with a crisp step toward us.

"Are you Alson Pierce?" he said.

This time I just said, "I am."

"I see you haven't lost any time," he said to the reporter.

"Have you reconsidered what we discussed?"

"No," he answered, shaking his head, "and I won't." Then he turned to me.

"I'm Joseph Lincoln, attorney for Mr. Alex Leonard."

The blood froze in my veins, as if he were the angel appointed to take me to the depths of hell.

"I have here a communication from Mr. Leonard, which I am delivering personally to you at Mr. Leonard's insistence and over my strong protest. This is completely off the record as far as I'm concerned. And I'm putting you on notice that I will scrutinize, with the closest professional attention, any overture made by you or anyone else to my client. I'm also telling you what I have told Mr. Leonard in regard to you, that this is the last time you will see me outside of a court of law. Good-bye."

He handed me the envelope and strode away. The reporter hurriedly followed the lawyer to his car, saying, "Would you wait a minute, please?"

I did not watch to see if he waited. I was through my door with the letter, and locked it behind me. In a few minutes there came a knocking, which I did not answer.

5　✦

Dear Rev. Alson Pierce,

If you want to love your enemy I'll tell you how to do it. You can get your fans to lay off my girlfriend! She never did A THING to hurt you or your family. They can do what they want to me but leave her alone!

I tied you up before I did your family but at least I did it on my own. Now you got society to tie me up in here and there's nothing I can do about it, you didn't have to lift a finger. The cops are on your side to because she calls them, even my lawyer calls them and they don't do a dam thing to protect her. If I ever get out of this place, I'd say something but I can't.

You wrote to me 1st or I wouldn't of wrote to you. You don't need to see me you can just call your fans OFF. I'll believe you meant what you said when she says she's alright. My lawyer doesn't even want me writing this, he says the whole thing is bogus as far as he's concerned but I'm giving you a chance which is something I NEVER GOT, and maybe you say I don't deserve one but she does in every way which as a minister I shouldn't have to tell you.

These are my terms and their final!!!

A. Leonard

I found that I needed to concentrate to keep the letter in my hands. My fingers seemed about to die. When I finished reading, I laid the letter down and closed my eyes. My heart was pounding like the fists of a man who's been entombed alive. My mind was a mixture of rage and mad glee.

To settle myself, I turned on the radio and sat in my rocker. I rocked gently but rapidly, slowing down as my breathing did. Thank God for classical music; it either has no words or its words are usually in another language. This was piano, Chopin from the sound of it. I tried to imagine the sea, rolling to shore wave after wave, crashing on the rocks. The gulls wheeling overhead, piercing the air with their elongated orgasmic cries. Not a person in sight, not even a boat. An empty, rocky shore. Dark pine and balsam in the distance.

I don't know how long I sat like that before I took up the letter again. It was midafternoon when I looked at the clock. Surely some of my weakness came from lack of sleep the night before, and from having had hardly any food since waking. I hadn't eaten since my piece of toast at breakfast. It was not just the letter that made me feel weak.

It was so strange to see Leonard's words in what I took to be his handwriting, a blocky printed script. I could imagine his voice too, but I did not want to hear it. He felt tied up, he said. He was tied up in his own awkward sentences. He was helpless to help someone he loved, a thought at which I felt neither pity nor satisfaction. I was no longer even outraged much at the impertinence of his comparison. I was just a little fascinated by his lack of power.

Mostly I was trying to figure out what my next step ought to be. The letter implied a deal of some kind: *I'm giving you a chance... These are my terms...* What I needed to do next was find out who his girlfriend was, and where she lived. And who were my "fans"? What were they doing to her, I wondered. If I could somehow convince Leonard that I had called them off, as he put it, then he might agree to see me.

The most obvious course seemed to be to contact the lawyer. He'd said he wouldn't see me again outside of a court, but that wouldn't be his choice if I showed up unannounced at his office. Or would my chances be better with a tactful call?

57

I decided to wait until evening to leave the house, in case that reporter was still lurking about. I'd need to walk to a public phone to look up the lawyer's address and phone number. At least I should keep a phone book around here, I thought. The lawyer's name was Lincoln. Fortunately for me, he had a memorable name.

For supper I fixed an enormous plate of spaghetti with butter and grated cheese. I wolfed it down. I can't remember the last time I showed such an appetite; I have lost close to thirty pounds over the past months. I even drank a glass of wine with an ice cube. After supper, I walked to the phone booth next to Willy's Service Station and looked up the number. I came home, listened to the radio, and went to bed.

I slept soundly, and with no nightmare I can remember, though once in the night I did wake with a start. Superstitious, I guess, is the word for what I did next. I got up and took Leonard's letter off the table, pressing it between the pages of an old Bible. Then I opened my front door and dropped the Bible into a small gray box on the front step outside, which I assume was once used for milk deliveries. Looking up at the clear night sky, I thought how, so much less than a light-year away, all the milkmen had disappeared and I had hardly noticed, or cared. My mother just started buying milk at the store.

Joseph Lincoln's office was all the way over in Oakshire, so I would have to take my car. Since the murders, I have tried to avoid driving as much as possible. When your life is empty, you're not interested in making the earth smaller or in gaining more time. You want a trip to the grocery store to occupy the better part of a morning. You hope to be tired enough from carrying home your groceries to sleep a little in the afternoon. I wasn't even sure my car would start, but it did.

I entered Oakshire, a prosperous town of gabled stone manors, Jews and Episcopalians, linked to the city by a shiny commuter train. Even the station looked rich and Anglican. Lincoln's office was upstairs, over a dress shop. The shop was closed because it was not even eighty-thirty.

So was Lincoln's office. "Nine to five" hadn't been on my mind. But the mistake was fortuitous, I thought. He would mount the stairs and find me at the top of them, standing serenely in my black shirt and white clerical collar. If others were with him, he might feel a need to show me some courtesy. At least he would not be able to have his secretary tell me that he wasn't in.

As I waited, I was struck by how trusting Leonard was in telling me of his girlfriend's plight. Did he have no fear that I would use her for my revenge, an eye for an eye, a rape for a rape, a murder for a murder? In fact, I think he had no fear of me at all. He knew I couldn't harm the woman. Aren't men like Leonard so successful at what they do because they can count on our scruples, our habits, our fears and reflexes? They know us as well as a lion knows a zebra or a wildebeest or any other kind of herd animal. They watch patiently for the moves they know we always make, having no worry for the moves they know we'll never make.

But I had made an unusual move, hadn't I, offering love to my enemy? What did the lion make of it?

I did not have to wait until nine o'clock. In a few minutes the door opened at the bottom of the stairway, and Lincoln entered, briefcase in hand, behind his young secretary. I could hardly see his head behind her frizzed-out hair, and he didn't yet see me. She was telling him something about her mother that he found very funny.

He noticed me about two thirds of his way up the stairs, but I don't think he recognized me until he reached the top. Even then I wasn't sure whether his obvious annoyance was at me personally, or just at being accosted by a stranger this early in the day. Nevertheless, when he did speak to me, he managed a smile and a cordial tone of voice.

"Can we help you with something?" Then, to his secretary, "You can go on in, Jennifer. I'll be in in just a moment."

"I'd like to talk with you for just a few minutes," I said.

"I'm not sure we have anything we can talk about, Reverend." He continued to smile. "I thought, though I may be mistaken, that I had made that reasonably clear yesterday. Did I fail to do so?" "No, you made it clear, but I'm not sure you're completely clear about my predicament."

I had to choose between rushing forward or waiting for him to invite me inside. I chose the former, wisely.

"Mr. Leonard has made a request," I went on, "which I wish to honor but which I cannot honor without more information."

"Mr. Leonard has made a very foolish request, and I was probably very foolish in delivering it to you. But then, I'm not sure you're clear about *my* predicament—with Mr. Leonard, that is. So why don't we just leave it there? I don't think you need to feel any obligation to assist Mr. Leonard in this matter."

"I want to, though. I think I can help you if you will tell me either who his...girlfriend is, or who the people are who are harassing her."

I found myself wondering at something that had escaped me until then: What was someone like Leonard doing with an Oakshire lawyer? I could picture this guy in his bathrobe, petting a spaniel in the J. Crew autumn catalog.

"Mr. Leonard is my client, not yours. Anything I know about Mr. Leonard is privileged information. Surely, as a clergyman, you can understand that. Now, I have a busy day ahead of me." I tried a more aggressive tack. "Why would you deliver a letter that you would have no intention of helping me understand? Is this some extra little treat to make me suffer? A little practical joke with the help of legal counsel?"

I hit the nerve.

"Reverend Pierce," he said, his voice rising to courtroom pitch, "may I remind you that it was *you* who initiated contact with Mr. Leonard, and not the other way around. I resent your insinuation. I very reluctantly agreed to deliver his letter, but not in hopes of finding him a bodyguard or a father confessor. I did so in the probably naive hope that Mr. Leonard would desist from certain self-destructive behaviors that he gave no indication of stopping until we'd acquiesced to some of his demands. He seems to feel that you are going to be more effective than a police force in protecting his fianceé from some hoodlums. My only interest in this matter is to prevent Mr. Leonard from compromising his chances for an appeal, which he certainly deserves. What your interests are in this are highly questionable. Now do you mind if I go to work?"

He gestured toward his office door. His smile had become a smirk.

"You can't even tell me who is harassing the woman, his fianceé?"

"If I could tell you that, would he have felt a need to write you a letter? If the police were doing their job, would we even be standing here having this pointless conversation? I have no idea who's harassing her. Why don't you try the good, God-fearing people of your church? I'd lay pretty good odds that you'll find your culprits there, or somewhere thereabouts. Isn't that where vigilantism usually begins, someplace between a Bible and a pigsty?"

He wanted to leave me, of course, but he could not resist the attorney's impulse to win every fight with a knockout. Angering him was in fact the best way to hold him, I thought.

"Why are you so hostile toward my religion?" I demanded. "And why are you so hostile toward me? May I remind *you*, Attorney Lincoln, that I am your client's victim, not his oppressor."

"Everybody's a victim," he said with more calmness. "You're a victim, he's a victim."

"He's a victim, huh?"

"Yes, he's a victim. That is not so absurd as you'd like to make it sound. He's a victim, among other things, of a society that supposedly separates church and state but vetoes every law that the church finds offensive, and railroads every poor son of a bitch who lifts a finger against a church. I'm sorry, but if you'd been an agnostic orthodontist, I'd have been a more successful lawyer, at least as far as Alex Leonard is concerned, I'll tell you that. That's gospel if there ever was a gospel. He might as well have raped and murdered Jesus himself. Listen, I feel sorry for you. I wish I could undo all that's happened to you. If you want to use your tragedy as the basis for some religious crusade, if that's how you find your way out of grief, that's up to you, but you're not going to use me to do it, and you're not going to use my client. I can't make it any simpler than that."

"I don't want to use him," I said. His hand was now on the door. "I want to love him."

"He doesn't need your love. He's had all the Christian love he can stand."

"I don't think so."

"You don't, do you? Well, here's something for you to chew on. Alex Leonard was raised to be a good Christian. Oh, yes. Alex Leonard's father was a Baptist minister. Alex Leonard had sweet Jesus shoved down his throat before he could swallow mashed peas. You don't know the half of what's happened to him, all in the name of God. I'm sorry, but if we stand here for one more minute, I'm going to say some things I'll regret. I have to go."

He had the door closed in my face before I had fully registered what I'd heard. But my mind was racing on ahead of him. One thing that was clear to me on the ride home was how foolishly hasty I'd been in shaking off that reporter the day before. I stopped at a phone as soon as I saw one, and called his paper.

I could not remember his name, or if he'd even told me his name. I described him as well as I could to the woman who answered the phone. I identified myself by my name and the crime and the article that had already been written about my failed attempt to see Leonard. I refused to leave a message, but said I would wait by the phone for another thirty minutes. If I heard nothing, I'd return to the phone whose number I'd given her between six and six-fifteen that evening. And if I'd heard nothing by then, I'd assume that the paper was no longer interested in my story and I would go to another.

The phone rang within five minutes.

"I want to see you at my house on Sunday morning, no later than nine o'clock," I said to the young man.

"Does it have to be then?" he said.

"Yes it does," I said. "I'm taking you with me to church."

When I had hung up on him, I called the telephone company and ordered a phone.

6

Harold Stevens, New York Daily News reporter, and I sat in my car a block from my church, like two detectives on a stakeout. It was drizzling, and many of the people walking from their cars to the church carried umbrellas. Because we did not have our wipers going, I recognized no one through the rain-blurred windshield. I had almost forgotten how cozy and protective a car feels in the rain.

I had taken charge of Stevens as soon as he showed up at my door, in sport coat and tie, no less. I told him that before the morning was out, he would have material for a story, but that he must not talk to me until I told him to. I needed quiet in which to think, I told him. I told him we would enter the church a few minutes after the service began, and sit at the rear.

He must not take out his writing tablet until I gave him the nod. Finally I told him I would leave the church before he did, and he must not follow me. He could remain until after the service in order to gather more material for his story, or he could walk out after me and go in some other direction.

The young man did not offer a single protest. Perhaps the unfamiliar combination of wearing a tie and getting up early on a Sunday morning had shocked him into docility. He stood in my tiny living room, towering a foot or more above me, with his rain-dampened hair and his tie patterned after a dynamited flower box, nodding at my every word. Jesus might have chosen him for a disciple, I said to myself. He would have misunderstood every single parable, and run for his life from the Garden of Gethsemane, eventually to be martyred for the Word, skinned alive in some remote Roman province.

To make his vow of silence easier for him to keep, I turned my car key to "accessory" and played the radio softly as we sat. The rain and the music filled up the silence. A crash of thunder sounded, but on the radio—the start of a song about a storm. I listened until the singer began describing a hitchhiker who would murder the family of anyone who gave him a ride. I switched off the radio. Stevens did not seem to have noticed my reason for doing so. Had I hallucinated the lyrics?

When most of the worshipers had arrived, I checked my watch, and we entered the church at about three minutes after ten. With extraordinary luck, we found a seat at the end of a rear pew. The congregation was on its feet, singing the opening hymn, "Faith of Our Fathers." The thought of Leonard's father flared in my mind like a struck match, but I let it go out. I took up two hymnals from the back of the pew in front of us, and handed one to Stevens. The poor fellow actually made an attempt to sing. And then a sound that nearly frightened me, so long had it been since I'd heard it: my own voice singing.

How odd to be back in my church, to see the place where I once stood, now occupied by an earnest younger man, and the pew where Cindy and Jimmy used to sit, up front to be near me—now conspicuously vacant in the crowded church. I had that ghostly feeling again. This church, with its ancient words and its already dated "modern" architecture, and its bereaved former minister—nothing in it seemed to belong to the moment. I glanced sideways at my companion, who was himself looking sideways out the window. Perhaps he belonged to the moment.

I touched his arm when the minister had finished the announcements that preceded his sermon and asked if anyone had any announcements to add. I raised my hand, and Stevens rushed to take his notepad from a pocket in his sport coat. He seemed almost to have forgotten why he was here.

"Yes?" the minister said, as I rose to my feet

and heads turned to see me. "Reverend Pierce, of course," he added, nervously, I thought, when I was on my feet. I could feel the congregation inhale all at once.

I walked slowly and deliberately to the front of the church. I bowed my head to the minister, who stood in the pulpit above me. Then I turned to face the people.

Had they ever looked at me so intently? A few seemed positively horrified. Others nodded and smiled as if to say, "Go ahead, Alson, we're listening. We're glad to see you." There were a few new faces, and later I would recall some old faces that were missing. I locked eyes for a moment with my old faithful sexton, Bob, with that ready butler's expression of his, as if all I had to do was give the sign and he'd carry the cleric behind me bodily out of the church. There was Alice, the closet lesbian, and Mark and Hope, an infertile couple who flinched at every scripture announcing a miraculous birth, and the jovial and maddening Richard Aiken, The Most Contented Man in the World, who truly believes that God is in every respect like himself, a retired fella who's done some fine work in his day and is decent to everybody he meets and has no mystery about him whatsoever except how he can be so dang-blasted happy every minute. I could see Stevens, taller than his pewmates, and distinguished by his head nodding up and down from his writing tablet like that of a nervous bird.

Yes, and there was Ellen Fabian, looking as

worshipful as ever—more worshipful, even—with her abundant auburn hair and her slightly heavy face, like a Pre-Raphaelite muse who'd eaten too many slices of jam toast. The fall from grace had occurred for her when her husband had callously rejected her for another woman, and she looked for hope of human regeneration in Christianity and magic crystals and "sensitive men" like me. Cynthia always said it was only a matter of time before I found her waiting naked in the pastor's office some Saturday night. Cynthia never seemed concerned. It was typical of her to trust me more than I sometimes trusted myself.

"I don't want to take much of your time," I said, "but I do have an important announcement. All of you know that my family and I have suffered a terrible tragedy. And all of you know the person who was responsible for our sufferings. It has come to my attention that this person's fianceé, a woman I do not know, is being harassed and threatened. This person's lawyer has even suggested to me that those involved might be well-intentioned but very misguided members of this church. I have no way of knowing whether that's true. But I wish to go on record as saying that I strongly disapprove of such actions. Anyone who loves me or loved my family should remember the teachings of Jesus Christ, that we love our enemies and do good to those who hurt us. And I say this as the living person who has been hurt most in this affair. I also say this as your former and perhaps future pastor. Should I ever learn that anyone in this church has acted in this vengeful and cowardly way, I shall draw no other conclusion than that my preaching and my other labors in the name of God have all been in vain."

I fixed their eyes for a moment, then began to walk toward the back of the church. Stevens's head was bowed now; his shoulders trembled with his scribbling. Before I was halfway down the aisle, the minister spoke my name, pausing until I turned to face him.

"I hope you know," he said, "how much all of our prayers are with you. You are an inspiration and an example for all of us of what it means to be a disciple of Jesus Christ."

I glanced above his head to the painting in which Jesus carried a lost lamb on his shoulders. I said nothing as I turned again and climbed back over the fence of the sheepfold.

There were footsteps on the wet sidewalk behind me, and I turned furiously, ready to expel my tension by tongue-lashing Stevens till he backed away. But it was not Stevens who was behind me. Instead I faced Ellen Fabian, with tears in her bright green eyes.

"What's wrong, Ellen?" I said, sounding surprisingly pastoral. Drops of rain caught in her hair as the tears rolled down her cheeks.

"You shouldn't walk out on us like that," she said.

"I'd finished what I came to say, and—" I meant to add that my continued presence, after my announcement, would have been a distraction, and a discourtesy to the preacher, but she didn't allow me to finish.

"I felt like you were accusing us. I felt like you were accusing me."

"Well I certainly did not mean to do that," I said, but immediately wondered if Ellen felt so accused because she was, in fact, so guilty. I think she is capable of stalking an enemy. Hadn't she told me some of her revenge fantasies involving her husband and his lover, vividly rehearsed in her head years after the man left?

"I just wish you weren't so stern with us. We haven't seen you. We just read about you. You forget, we're not as evolved as you."

She continued to weep, and we were both getting wet in the rain. I felt an impulse to take her shoulders in my hands, but resisted it. Had I done so, I might have shaken her.

"Listen, Ellen, there is no easy way to do some of the things I have to do."

She interrupted me again.

"I mean, anybody could be doing it. The woman's face was in the paper almost as much as yours or that creep's. All the stuff about her 'moving testimony,' which was a crock of the most sickening bullshit. Anybody could be doing it. Why ask us?"

"Because you're what I have left of a family," I said. She threw her arms around me so suddenly and with such force that she almost knocked me over. She must have felt me stiffen, because she drew back almost at once.

"I'm sorry," she sniffled. "You're so thin," she said miserably, as if I were melting before her eyes in the rain. She had hugged me several times in the past.

"Ellen, I didn't know this woman had appeared in the newspapers. I don't read the papers. I guess I should, but I can't bring myself to...go over all the details just yet. I've saved every one from back then till now. I have this big pile in my living-room closet." With the next sentence I began talking to myself out loud. "I guess I need to find somebody to go through the papers for me. It just never occurred to me that the name of Leonard's fianceé might be in the papers. Why didn't the lawyer just say so?" Then I said directly to Ellen, "Do you know her name, the woman, the fianceé?"

"No," she said, shaking her head with an expression so innocent it seemed feigned. "But I'll help you go through the papers if you want."

"I'm sure you're busy. Anyway, we're both getting wet." Getting sticky, is what I thought.

"I have lots of free time. When would you want me?"

"When could you do it?" I was hoping she'd name several times, all of which I could excuse as impossible. Did I hope that?

"I can do it right now," she said.

"Now?"

"Why not?"

"Now is not really good," I said.

Just then, Stevens stepped out of the church.

72

He began gesturing at me. Two people walked out in front of him. It seemed much too soon for the service to be over, but if it was, I would very soon be apprehended by my flock.

"Okay, now, then," I said, and pointed to my car.

"This is where you live now?" she asked as we entered my front door. I just then remembered that my Bible was still in the milk box outside. I hoped the box was waterproof.

"This is where I live. But I'd prefer to keep my address a secret."

Up till that moment only a few people in my church were supposed to know where I lived. And yet both a reporter and a lawyer had found me, on the same day, seemingly without any trouble. There was a positive side to this: perhaps I could find Leonard's fianceé with the same ease.

Ellen told me that my secret was safe with her. She took off the large silky scarf she had wrapped around her bare shoulders and began to look around as if she intended to move in. There was not much to see. With the exception of a photograph of Cynthia and Jimmy in my bedroom, I have no pictures, plants, or other decorations. My rented house is a square, squat, two-bedroom bungalow-type dwelling, with no redeeming aesthetic features except a few shrubs and a small dogwood tree outside. And there is also a cement birdbath in back.

"I can make us some tea," I said, pointing to the kitchen. "We're both pretty wet. I'll show you the newspapers."

Ellen was standing in the middle of the living room, untangling her damp hair.

"If you had a robe or a blanket for me, I could put my dress in your dryer while I worked. Would that be all right?" she said.

"It would, but I don't have a dryer. I do my clothes at the laundromat."

"Do you have a hair dryer?"

"No. Short hair. Listen, I should take you home where you can dry off. You can help me another day."

"I'm fine, I'm fine. I just thought if you had some kind of dryer, that's all. You make our tea and I'll go through the papers."

I opened up the living-room closet, which I admit seemed less threatening with another person nearby. The papers were stacked in three piles, two of them almost as tall as I. There was nothing else, not even hangers. I keep my coats on a tree near the door.

I told Ellen that the papers from the time of the crime would be at the bottom of a large pile on the left. I lifted off the top of that pile, in two armloads, and laid it on the floor outside the closet. I told her I would like to keep the papers in order according to their dates, and that I was only interested in the name and, if given, the town of residence of Leonard's girlfriend. I'd also be interested in a picture, if she found one. But I wished to hear nothing else.

When I brought in our tea, I told Ellen that I'd feel more comfortable waiting in my room while she went through the newspapers. I did not want to be around them. She sat on the floor with her bare legs crossed in front of her Indian-style, taking snarls from her hair as she turned the pages. I looked at her hair to avoid seeing the papers, and then discovered myself looking out the window to avoid looking at her hair.

I went to my room and closed the door. I didn't feel right changing my clothes when she was unable to, so I sat at my desk with my tea and waited to dry. A moment earlier, in the living room with her, I had registered the faint stirrings of a long-dormant lust, like green shoots on a forest floor after a great, timber-blackening fire. My manhood was not altogether dead, then. Still, I felt nothing in my body, only a tremor in my head, and then something approaching nausea in my stomach. I closed my eyes and sipped my tea.

Ellen knocked on the door, and I told her to come in. Sitting while she stood before me, I saw her nipples hardened behind her still-wet dress and brassiere. I looked at once into her eyes.

"I've found it," she said.

"Wait." I fumbled for a pen and paper. I exhaled noisily. "Okay."

"Her name is Monica Zeller. According to this, she resided with Alex Leonard in Thornwood. There's a picture here if you want to see it."

I took the paper from her hand. The face looked no older than a teenager's, with plain features and long dark hair. There was an expression of long-suffering devotion in the eyes. Above the picture was a caption: "THERE'S GOOD IN HIM THAT NOBODY SEES," says killer-rapist's girlfriend.

"Can you cut this out for me?" I said, handing the paper back to her. "I think I have a scissors in the drawer. Leave the rest and save the paper with the others. I just want the picture. I appreciate this."

I turned away from her to my desk, but she remained standing by the side of my chair. Then she knelt, placing her hand on my thigh. With her other hand she laid the newspaper and scissors on the desk. The picture of Leonard's girlfriend was more tangible to me than the hand on my thigh. Ellen seemed to know it; she reached and turned the paper over before speaking, now with both hands on my leg.

"I'm nowhere near as spiritual a person as you, and I consider myself a pretty spiritual person ..."

"Stop," I said, but she gripped my leg and continued.

"Please don't shut me off, Alson. Please listen to me. I think I understand what you're trying to do, and if you want, I'll help you to do it." I turned to her involuntarily and scrutinized her face, then looked away. "But I can't help how much it pains me to see you trying to protect this man's lover, when you don't even have a woman of your own. Because of him! I know you're a wounded healer, but the wounded healer needs to take care of some of his wounds first, doesn't he? Just so he can heal other people."

Her hands were kneading my legs now. When I looked at her face, with its eyes moist again, she laid her brow on my thigh.

"I'd do anything for you," she said.

I placed a hand gently on her hair without letting it sink to her scalp. She might not have realized I was touching her. I don't know if it was the strain of the day, or the closeness of this woman, or the discovery of Leonard's woman, or my consciousness of the photograph of my slain family sitting on the end table of my bed behind me, but I felt Cynthia with me more palpably than at any time since her death. She was present not as a part of my conscience, wagging her finger at the possibilities, but as a finger laid gently to the lips of my will. I could remember the way she would repeat my full name with soft determination whenever she wished to calm me, to call me to my senses. "Alson, Alson," she would say. Accept nature, she seemed to say now. You won't be using her any more than she wants to be used. There's no exploitation here, believe me. And I know it won't be the same as me. We know what we had, Alson. But this is one of God's life rafts, darling. Jump. Jump and save yourself while you can.

"I have a woman," I said. "She's just not here now." I put my hand back on the desk.

Ellen rose and took the newspaper and the scissors. I heard the sound of her cutting in the next room, and then the sound of my front door opening, and latching shut again.

I took the picture of Leonard's girlfriend with me to the pay phone that evening. I wanted to look at it when I heard her voice. Somehow I thought it would give me an advantage, an extra convincingness. Ellen had clipped out the headline along with the picture, perhaps the subtle fury of a woman scorned. If she did so for that reason, she would soon reproach herself for it. "THERE'S GOOD IN HIM THAT NO ONE ELSE SEES," SAYS KILLER-RAPIST'S GIRLFRIEND. If the whole world canonized me, Ellen Fabian would still be capable of making such a statement about me—that is, such a claim for herself. The vanity of women, I have decided, does not consist of courting admiration from another's eyes, but in believing that love provides a unique insight to their own. Only God can see all they can see, and perhaps, they fancy, even God occasionally falls short of their all-knowing and thus all-forgiving gaze.

There was no listing in the phone book for Monica Zeller. I looked and looked, considering that the papers might have misspelled her name. There were no Zellers of any kind. A downpour strafed the phone booth as I searched my pockets for some change to call information, and re-skimmed each column of names beginning with Z. I wonder: Does God himself ever look vainly through the Book of Life, sure of finding a name that has vanished from its pages forever?

7

The story of my announcement to the church appeared in the New York *Daily News* the next morning. I don't know on what page the first article had appeared, the one that Andrew had read to me in his office, but this one was on page three. "LOVE MINISTER" ATTEMPTS TO PROTECT GIRLFRIEND OF WIFE'S KILLER, said the headline. I steeled myself and read a newspaper article for the first time. There was nothing new to upset me. How easily they had omitted mention of Jimmy in the headline, for the sake of symmetry, I suppose. He was mentioned in the article, though, after the phrase "brutal murders." Stevens had managed to copy my remarks almost verbatim. He'd also gotten a few quotes from the congregation. One person had called me "a saint." Another had said, "This may be the Christian thing to do, but it doesn't seem natural"—striking testimony to the way a person can profess a religion all his life and still not get the main point.

I bought four copies of the paper and brought them home. I cut the article out of two, and sent one copy each to Leonard's lawyer and to Leonard in care of his prison. I would take a third to Andrew later in the morning. The fourth would accompany me to Thornwood that afternoon, when I would begin to look for Monica Zeller. Andrew did not say very much to me during our session. His attitude was one of resignation—masking bewilderment, I believe. The only explanations he could find for me or my actions were theological, and that was bound to make an assimilated clergyman like Andrew feel uncomfortable. I described my condition as that of a soul "born again," and I even used the words in the hope of making him wince. But I never broke his stare. I told him that my appetite had improved, that I was driving again, that I'd ordered a phone, had even had a single woman over for tea!

"And you've been to church, too, I hear."

"Yes, and I brought the story with me, to read it to you myself. Instead of what happened last time. I thought that would be a collegial reciprocation. I'm reading the newspaper again." I shook the paper in front of me like a matador's cape.

"You ascribe all of this to your Alex Leonard mission?"

"To what else would I ascribe it? Andrew, life has dealt me a vicious blow. I have made a conscious choice to strike back—with the weapons of the Gospel. It's the *only* choice for me. It's that or be knocked down forever."

"Do you realize what a stir you've caused?"

"Well, two articles in the paper is hardly a stir."

"It's more than that. I don't have to read your article there. I've been getting phone calls since you showed up in church yesterday. Since the paper came out this morning, there've been phones ringing all over the place. It's like the FBI around here. Reporters—you're a news item now."

"You mean 'again.'"

"Whatever. And not all the calls are what I'd describe as nice." He paused. "What you're doing offends a lot of people."

"Isn't the Gospel always an offense?"

"Probably," he sighed. "I hope you realize that I—that nobody—is going to be able to protect your privacy much longer if you keep this up. I mean, after the crime you were insistent on privacy, although you were just as insistent on not leaving the area, which is where I think we should've drawn the line. It was like hiding someone who'd squealed on the Mafia or something. Now you're out in the sunshine, Al."

"I know. I'll always be grateful for all you've done—and continue to do. I'm not after publicity, believe me."

"Well, it's going to be after you. It is after you. And there's another consideration. This may be premature, but I think you should be aware of it. I've heard at least one person on your governing board say, 'If he's well enough to take care of Leonard's problems, he's well enough to take care of ours.' If you keep it up, it won't be long before others are saying the same thing."

"Perhaps by that time I *will* be well enough," I said. It was true, I felt an incredible vitality. Perhaps *momentum* would be a better word.

Everyone in Thornwood knew that Monica Zeller had lived there with Leonard at the time of the crime, but no one knew where she was living now. It turned out I was asking all the wrong people; I realized that when a woman behind the counter of a delicatessen told me that Monica Zeller had been a student at the town high school when Leonard had been arrested. In spite of her young appearance in the photograph, I was surprised.

"What do you think," she said, glancing at my white collar as if it were the badge of an imbecile, "they have to wait till they're twenty-one to become tramps? Christ, they start dropping babies when they're twelve years old. They say she had one, you know, but she give it up for adoption before she came here. Supposedly it was a little colored baby, and Leonard made her get rid of it. Colored, white, it don't make no difference, a girl like that's got no business in school. And the school has to take these pregnant girls, you're not allowed to keep them out, you know. Christ, they'd probably have to let Leonard in if he asked. Give him a couple of shop classes in the morning and then let him out early so he can go rape and murder people in the afternoon. Hey!" she said, her eyes opening wide as she pointed at my collar.

I thanked her and left before she could speak again. It was foolish to have worn clericals. They were soon to be a dead giveaway for anyone who reads the papers and heard me ask about Monica Zeller. I remembered what Andrew had said about "not nice" phone calls. From now on I would travel in street clothes, carrying a spare clerical shirt and collar for when they might be an advantage.

The people I needed to talk to, then, were not adults but teenagers. I drove through the neighborhood, and then along the brook-bisected park that runs the length of Thornwood, until I saw a group of teenagers gathered near the duck pond. They were listening to music from a black box, shoving one another, flipping up skateboards and a little bean bag with their feet.

I approached in a leisurely way. My inquiries would probably be easier if none of them had read the papers, and I was betting that none of them had.

"Hello," I said when I was near.

A space opened in the circle. The tallest boy raised his chin and squinted through the smoke of his cigarette—an acknowledgment. We practically shouted the first few sentences of our exchange before someone thought to turn down the music a few notches.

"I'm looking for a girl that I've been told used

to go to Thornwood High School. I have a message I'm supposed to deliver to her."

"Who is it?" asked a boy with half his head shaved.

"Monica Zeller."

"Oh, fuck," said yet another boy, but a girl jerked his arm and said, "Craig!" then looked at me and turned around, giggling and sputtering. The boy who'd said "fuck" gave her several sharp blows between the shoulder blades, as if she were choking on a piece of meat.

"She doesn't live around here anymore," said another girl.

"Probably in jail," said the boy with half his hair.

"Or dying from AIDS," said Craig.

The tall kid with the cigarette now felt it was proper for him to speak.

"She lived with Alex Leonard, the pervert who killed the minister's wife and kid right in their own house. You're not him, are you?"

"Gracious, no," I said, strangely giddy from the lie, "but I know him slightly. A terrible thing. What happened to Monica? Doesn't anybody know where she went?"

"I heard she was taking her GED over at summer school in Runcie," said the girl who'd giggled. "They don't got to take her back here because she turned eighteen last year. So she went to Runcie, where her grandmother lives. Her best friend told me that."

"Who's her best friend?" Craig asked.

"Kelly."

"Vandervliet? That wasn't her *best friend!*"

said the tall boy. From his tone of voice one would infer that the girl's statement was more unforgivable than the murders he had mentioned thirty seconds before. "Kelly just felt *sorry* for her."

"Well, she was one of the few people that did, and did something to show it!"

"Yeah, but that don't make her her best friend."

"I hear she's living with a nigger now," Craig interrupted.

"Jesus, watch your mouth, Craig," said the girl beside him, to which Craig replied with an affectedly stupid "What?" and another girl asked, "Kelly?"

"No, retard. Monica! I heard she was living with"—Craig tapped his skull to make it work, like a lightbulb—"a multicultural guy."

The tall boy snickered. "You're something else, Craigy. A multicultural guy. Jesus. Hey, look, there goes a bunch of multicultural guys in an Oldsmobile."

"I don't believe it," said a girl beside him who'd said nothing until now. Her sudden interjection quieted the others.

"I heard it, too," she went on, "but it's bogus. She had a baby with a black guy, but that was before Leonard. She wouldn't be living with anybody else. She loved that guy. She adored Leonard."

"Loved to get raped," said Craig, clasping his throat with both hands and sticking out his tongue. "The rough stuff."

"He wasn't like that," said the girl, who seemed to command a certain authority, perhaps because she was so attractive. She could have changed from her mismatched laundry into an evening gown and looked the same. "Not to her. He was good to her."

"Define 'good,'" said Craig, with mock seriousness.

"Define 'multicultural,' Professor Pud," said the tall boy, snickering again.

"He protected her," said the girl, looking straight at me. "He never let anybody hurt her. Ever."

With that, I thanked them and turned to go. I had reached my limit.

After some deliberation, I decided to wear my clericals when I went to Runcie High School to inquire after Monica Zeller. I had considered stopping home to change, but in the end, I felt I had more to gain in authority than I might lose through suspicion. A clerical collar is not unlike a gun in that respect: people see one and freeze. You can usually make them do what you say.

My best chance lay with another teenager, ideally one who looked as if she couldn't spell *confidentiality*, but all I saw were a few secretaries in the office and two custodians waxing the floors. I walked the halls for a while to see if any classes were in session, but none were. I didn't really expect them to be—the halls were dark except for the exit lights and the muted sunshine coming through the windows of the locked classrooms. The dimness, the humid air, and the rows of steel lockers combined to create a particularly oppressive atmosphere, like that of a crypt or a morgue. No wonder kids hate these places, and deface them when they can. It would not take much imagination to believe that the souls of the damned are imprisoned in steel tombs in a place just like this.

Finally, I glanced at my watch and stepped into the office.

"Can we help you, Father?" the secretary asked at once. By the expression on her face, I could tell that I looked lucky to her.

"I certainly hope so, but God bless you either way. I spoke this morning with the grandmother of a Monica Zeller, who told me that I might find her here and could talk to her in regard to an employment opportunity. I understand the girl has had a hard time. The grandmother said that Monica's class was over at two o'clock. Can you tell me where it meets?"

"Oh, no, Father, the classes here are all at ten A.M. We're on summer session, you see. They're all done by noon."

"Oh dear. I thought sure Mrs. McCarthy said two. She's my secretary." I began to make a search through my pockets—the befuddled cleric. "But Mrs. McCarthy has trouble hearing. In fact, that's why we're looking for some help for her. It's a delicate situation. She's worked for us so long."

"I understand."

"And I don't think I've got the grand-mother's name and number. I'll have to drive all the way back to the church."

"You can call from here."

"Oh, you're so kind. But Mrs. McCarthy only works until noon. And I'd only make her feel bad if she thought she had botched the message. I guess the whole world has shut down on me this afternoon. You wouldn't know the grandmother's name, would you?"

"We might."

She rose from her chair immediately. All I needed now was a curious principal to come walking out of his office into the room.

"We keep emergency cards on the students that usually have that information. Here we go. Monica Zeller. Hmm. Hers is the only name on this. Does she live with her grandmother?"

"That was my impression, yes. Well, where does Monica live? Maybe the street will ring a bell." I boldly stepped behind the counter and stood beside her, my arm touching hers. "Appleton Street. Apartment six, at number 110. That sounds familiar. Just let me jot that down."

"I could call her from here, if you'd like. It would be a shame for you to go all the way over there if she isn't even home."

"Oh, no," I said, and paused a few damaging seconds. "You see, this is a rather delicate matter. Monica doesn't exactly expect me. And her grandmother fears she might make herself scarce if she did. We're hoping that...face to face, I could persuade the girl to give our job a try. You know, kids that age all want to work at a Burger King and sell Whoppers to the billions, but we think the parish office would be a better environment. Don't you?"

"Oh, absolutely."

"So this is sort of a conspiracy." I nudged her arm ever so slightly. "And now you're a co-conspirator. It's best, I think, that you keep my visit with you on the q.t., if that's all right."

"Certainly."

"And I won't mention anything, either. We never saw each other," I whispered, and she laughed.

In the car, I considered how easy it was to dissemble, and how careful I should be about doing so. A trail of lies might hurt my work in the future.

I also came back to that scripture about the children of darkness being wiser than the children of light. How gullible we Christians are, how easy it is to break into our confidences—our houses. It is a wonder there are any of us left. We have survived, I suppose, only because a good number of us practice the religion loosely, some a good deal more loosely than others.

I inhaled a deep breath with every other step up to Monica Zeller's apartment, and exhaled it mounting the next. My legs were weak.

This is the test, I thought. It will test my self-discipline. It may also test my sincerity in Alex Leonard's eyes. If I can greet her in a compassionate manner, and help rescue her from her harassers, he might agree to see me.

I felt for Leonard's letter and today's news article in my pocket as I knocked on the door. I hoped that the grandmother answered instead of Monica. For just a second I wondered whether I had invented the grandmother back at the school, or actually heard of her back at the park.

The door opened to reveal a slim, short girl in tight denim shorts and a blue T-shirt. Her dark hair was carelessly folded up and fastened to the back of her head like a piece of plumage. Above a small, fishlike mouth and a pug nose, her eyes wore that squinting, world-weary expression one finds on girls who were still dressing Barbies when they started having sex. I had seen those eyes on dozens of faces when I taught school. She took me in from head to toe and then stepped back, looking as if she might slam the door.

"My name is Alson Pierce," I began hastily, "and I am here at the request of Alex Leonard, who wrote to me about some harassment you were having."

"Alex Leonard didn't tell you to come here," she said. Her voice was so like a cartoon character's, nasal and high as she spit out the words, that for a moment I thought she was making it up to mock me. "Alex told you to call off your fans. I got the letter he wrote to you."

"And I've done as he requested," I hurried to say. "I have a newspaper article here to prove it."

"I don't need to read no article. The reporter who wrote it was just here. He said he's been to your house and your church, so don't pretend you don't know him."

"I don't pretend at all." I was momentarily disoriented—why should I pretend I didn't know him?—but I pressed forward. "Do you know who these people are, the ones who are bothering you?"

"No, I don't, because they ain't got the balls to show their face. If Lennie was here, they wouldn't come near this place. But you probably know them."

"I wish I did."

"Why, so you could pay 'em? They're doing this for you. They're doing this because everybody feels so sorry for you. Here, I'll show you the kind of postcards religious people send to their neighbors."

She flew from the door, leaving it open before me. I had a glimpse of her squalid little kitchen—and a poster-sized photograph of Alex Leonard on the wall opposite where I stood. He had the same smile he wore the last time I had seen him, as if he were savoring the taste of a very small seed just behind his sealed lips, a seed that broke against his teeth and oozed with the blood of my pounding heart.

She materialized in front of me again, and thrust a picture postcard into my face. I think

I must have gasped audibly as I took the card in my hands. On it was the photograph of a naked woman's torso with an old cavalry saber thrust almost to the hilt into her bleeding vagina. She was blond.

"What is this?" I asked, breathless.

"This is what I find taped on my fucking door when I wake up in the morning. Oh, and it says 'Charge!' on the back. Real funny, ain't it? But you probably feel your fans got a right to do this."

I was fighting my way up from the bottom of a pit. I raised my eyes to hers and fought to steady them there. If I looked above her head I saw Leonard; if I dropped my gaze I would see the atrocity in my damp hands.

"What makes you think that people from my church are doing this?" I managed to say.

"I didn't say people from your church, did I? You need to see a counselor or something, don't you? I said your *fans*, your good holy fans."

She snatched back the postcard and took an aggressive step forward. I believed she was going to hit me. I stepped down from the landing, steadying myself on the rail. We were now almost the same height. She could have pushed me down the stairs if she'd wanted to. My hand was numb on the banister.

"Why fans? Why do you think these people have anything to do with me?" I said. "I just want to find out who they are and make them stop."

"Because the holy rollers always had it in

for Lennie, and now, because of you and your sweet little family, it's going to be even worse. They've been on his case ever since he ran away from home. His daddy was some big-shit preacher, but Lennie wasn't going to take his shit. They could beat him and molest him"—she choked back tears, as if this were all happening to her—"and hurt him worse than anybody I know's ever been hurt, but they couldn't take his head." She beat her own head with tiny, impotent fists. "They want to take over the whole fucking country, but they couldn't take over Lennie. Goddamn born-agains. They want the whole world in their hands, them and the niggers. It was a born-again who first fucked Lennie in the ass, and a nigger who got me pregnant, but Lennie said 'Fuck you' to all of them. And that's what I'm saying to you, and to the creeps who sent me this." She flung the postcard defiantly over the railing and screamed, "Fuck you!"

I began to back my way down the stairs.

"I'm going to try to put a stop to these people," I said. "I'm going to get to the bottom of this."

"Fuck you!" she screamed again. "Fuck you! Fuck you! Fuck all of you!"

She went into her house and slammed the door behind her. I could still hear her screaming inside. Then she flung the door open again and pushed past me. She thundered down the wooden steps and ran to the curb, where she threw herself into a shabby red car and lurched out of sight. I turned to see several of her neighbors dumbly watching me from the windows of their houses, like passive witnesses to a violent crime.

8

I rode endlessly through the neighborhoods until it was dark. I rode through the loops and around the cul-de-sacs of housing developments, I rode slowly down the parked up, party-bright business streets and over the bumpy lanes of surreal industrial parks, I drove back and forth over murderous stretches of New Jersey highway, where the changes in pavement lower the pitch of your tires' moaning, then raise it, then lower it, making a tormented music that stretches out before you seemingly forever, and I rode through the vast, numbered lots of shopping malls whose towering lights obliterate the Milky Way. I did not want to leave my car. I did not want to kill time on foot.

I drove and drove until finally I came to rest at the curb of the street where Monica Zeller lived. Her car was parked in front of her house once again. The sun was down, and the street was empty of people. I decided I would wait and see for myself what happened. I would wait all night. If necessary, I would wait for the rest of my existence. What else had I to do?

I was parked behind a ridiculous little

candy-colored pickup truck with enormous tires, enormous antennae, and a thick chrome roll bar. Before killing my headlights, I managed to read two of the half-dozen bumperstickers on the tailgate: SAVE A TREE, EAT A BEAVER. HOW'S MY DRIVING? DIAL 1 800-EAT-SHIT. I decided to eat a sandwich. I had packed a peanut-butter-and-jelly for myself that morning. I took it out from the bag and unwrapped it slowly. What I had said to Andrew about my improved appetite was not entirely true. I was still eating mainly to stay alive, often as an afterthought, that evening almost for spite. There is a certain spitefulness, isn't there, at the root of survival as well as suicide.

Before I'd even chewed my second bite, a sharklike black car cruised to a stop beside number 110, then went up the street, turned, and came slowly back. I slouched in my seat, though I was pretty sure that in the darkened place where I had intentionally parked, the driver could not see me. Peering over the dashboard, I saw two young men get out of the idling car. One of them ran upstairs with what appeared to be a small parcel, while the other stood on the sidewalk nervously glancing up and down the street. I thought to get out and accost them, but curiosity and fear kept me in my place.

The boy was soon down the stairs again, at which point he and his companion both hurried back to their car. I slid back up in my seat in readiness to follow them. When they came back to the car, only the driver got in. The other bent down over the passenger side, and reappeared with a stick or bar of some kind. I slouched back down in my seat. He ran to Monica's junky compact, parked several yards away, and struck the windshield two shattering blows. In an instant he was back in the car, which burned rubber and screamed away.

I started my car in something of a panic. I was parked facing in the opposite direction, and by the time I had turned around, they would surely be blocks away from me. I did not dare a U-turn either, for fear they would see it in their rearview mirror and suspect that I intended to follow.

But New Jersey is a crap game of traffic signals, where it is probable that lives and loves and prey are lost and won by random throws of red, amber, and green lights. Quite poetic, isn't it? That's how I felt when I recognized that they had sped to a red light that remained red long enough for me to turn around and follow. Poetic and lucky. Of course, they probably would have run the light but for a car stopped in front of them.

They did not seem to notice me behind. They did a few drag-race accelerations along clear stretches of road, but I attributed this more to their usual habit of driving than to any apprehension of me, and they were always halted by traffic or red lights. They made no sharp, evasive turns up side streets. What would I do when I found where they were going, I wondered.

I found appetite enough to finish half of my sandwich on the way. I confess to feeling invigorated by the chase. We begin stalking, and the predator within feeds fuel to the pursuit. Was this impulse supercharged in a man like Leonard? It is simultaneously horrifying and reassuring to think that I can feel any emotion he might feel—horrifying because I don't want to be anything like him, but reassuring because it is even more horrible to think of him as an incomparable alien presence breathing on the earth, who once breathed into the faces of my wife and son.

The streets grew more familiar, not less so, as we drove on. The possibility that Zeller's tormentors were members of my church seemed more likely, but I would have recognized the boys if not their car, and neither was familiar. "Who gives a damn anyway?" I started at the sound of my voice.

I found myself possessed by a mounting rage, often the most difficult of emotions to trace to its source. Perhaps I wanted to put an end to the agony and frustration of the past days, to bet everything on one desperate move. I was driving very close to them all of a sudden. Had they been sporting a bumper sticker telling me to eat shit, I could have read it now. I was disappointed there was no such thing to read.

I could see the driver's silhouette turning to his rearview mirror. That's right, punk, I'm in back of you. I switched on my high beams.

We were the second and third cars behind a semi truck, with steady traffic coming in the other direction; there was no place for them to go. The driver raised his middle finger in the mirror. I punched my horn.

Like the stirring of my desire in the presence of Ellen Fabian, the stirring of my anger surprised and even thrilled me. Toward Leonard himself I did not feel anger so much as coldblooded resolution, but I was angry now, at the outrageous impertinence of it all—the vengeance falling on Leonard's girlfriend instead of on Leonard, the avengers two anonymous punks instead of me. How dare they! How dare that smug little tramp in the park talk about the chivalry of Alex Leonard, so protective of his dear Monica. What protection was he giving her now? A whole lot, as it was turning out. That I was actually *doing* this, chasing a couple of dog-faced kids down the road in order to ingratiate myself with the man who had butchered my wife and son—I wasn't angry, I was raving and raving with every good reason.

The boys veered into the vacant parking lot of a small manufacturing plant and threw open the doors of their car. Before either could emerge, I took the driver's door off its hinges with a great crash of metal and slammed on my brakes.

I tore the white collar from around my neck. I grabbed what was left of my sandwich and smeared my face with the brown and red gore between the bread.

By the time I was out of my car, the passenger

98

was on his feet on the other side of theirs, brandishing a metal pipe. The other boy was still seated on the doorless driver's side. His feet were on the pavement, but he was bent over his knees, clutching the back of his head with both his hands and groaning the word "fuck." He had probably been about to step from the car when I'd broken off the door, and hit his head on the roof with the impact.

The kid with the pipe was obviously terrified. "What are you, fucking crazy?" he was shouting, doubtless convinced that I was. He held the pipe cocked behind his head and moved cautiously around the front of the car toward me.

"Yes, I'm fucking crazy," I yelled back, kicking the driver's knee and yanking the delirious boy to his feet by one of his limp arms. In a moment of fury that still astounds me, I spun him around, locking his arms and head in a full nelson, and brought his forehead down hard against the roof of the car. He responded with an ejaculation of vomit. I think both of them were a little drunk.

"Stand where you are, or I'll put out his eyes." Those were my exact words, though it's unlikely I could have made good on the threat. Suddenly I was panting and weak.

The other boy obeyed, now almost crying in the frustration of powerlessness—an emotion I know all too well.

"What the fuck is wrong with you?" he cried. "What the fuck is your problem? What did we do? I'm going for a cop, you crazy fuck."

"I am a cop," I gasped, still holding the boy, who seemed to have become dead weight in my hands.

"You open your big mouth once, now or ever, and I'll pull you both in for what you've been doing to that girl. We'll book the both of you. I took pictures of everything."

I think the boy was actually relieved to hear the word "cop." He blew through his teeth with disgust.

"That girl! That girl! You know who that girl is, Officer Wacko, whoever the fuck you are? 'That girl' is the number-one cunt of Alex Leonard, who raped a minister's wife and cut her into ribbons along with her kid while her husband just sat there!"

It was those words, I'm sure, that broke my last restraint and brought that poor boy's face down again on the vomit-spattered roof of his car. I know that at the very least I broke his nose.

Was there a devil in me? I must have looked like one, in my disheveled black clothes and macabre face, and sounded like one too, gurgling my words in a froth of spit and blood, letting the boy drop, and advancing furiously toward the second boy, who stepped back, then tripped and fell backward onto the ground.

My words, surely, were those of the devil. "Alex Leonard is mine!"

Part Two

Part Two

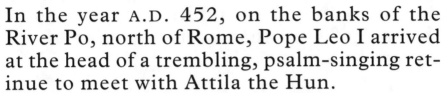

1

In the year A.D. 452, on the banks of the
River Po, north of Rome, Pope Leo I arrived
at the head of a trembling, psalm-singing ret-
inue to meet with Attila the Hun.

"The Scourge of God," as Attila was called,
had devastated all of central Europe. Gibbon
says that in one year he destroyed three hundred cities, a detail that does not fully register until you recall that there are but 365
days in a year. Nothing but Leo and a few miles
of grass stood between Attila and the streets
of Rome.

Leo requested a private audience. It was to
be one of the most momentous and enigmatic meetings in all of history. For after
only a few words together, words that Leo never
revealed, Attila ordered his armies to withdraw.
By the next morning they had vanished.

This morning at eleven o'clock, less than two
weeks after my confrontation with the boys in
the parking lot, and almost ten months since
my wife and son were ripped like abortions out
of this world, I again met Alex Leonard face
to face. I would sooner have met Attila, have
thrown myself at his merciless feet, than have
once again come within the orbit of that man,
though he was chained hand and foot. Yet I
had worked with all my might to come into his

presence—I had not labored to see God as zealously as I labored to look upon his scourge for a second time. I shall be able to look even a third time, for as many times as I desire.

Unlike Leo, however, I shall not be favored with a private audience. Though our parley does not concern an empire, it appears to be the will of God that every member of the empire be a witness.

Immediately after dealing with Zeller's tormentors, I wrote the following letter:

> Dear Ms. Zeller,
> I believe that I have managed to discover the identity of those persons who were harassing you. I also believe that by the time you receive this letter all harassments, from that source at least, will have ended.
> The individuals involved were not, as you supposed, members of my church, but two troubled youths who were using you to vent their personal frustrations. Though I had never seen them until the evening when I caught them in their mischief, I am greatly ashamed for their actions. Given your feelings about Mr. Leonard's arrest and imprisonment, I was sure that you would agree with my decision *not* to turn these boys over to the police, but rather to warn them that the police would be our next step if they did not mend their ways at once.

I understand that some of your property was damaged by these pranks. The enclosed check should more than cover the cost of repairing your car's windshield and any other minor losses. Of course, no amount of money can compensate for the trauma of such abuse, can it?

I am sorry if my unannounced visit the other day also contributed to your distress. Believe me, my only intention was to honor what I felt to be Mr. Leonard's request of me. I promise you that you will not see me again except at your own express request, or that of Mr. Leonard, with your consent.

I sincerely hope that God will bless and comfort you in whatever griefs you have borne in the past, and in whatever griefs that are to come.

Sincerely,
(The Rev.) Alson Pierce

I CC'ed the letter to Leonard and his lawyer, and to Stevens at the *Daily News*, fully aware that none of these was a guaranteed route to Leonard's eyes. But I was pretty sure that since my last letter had reached him, this one would too.

When a letter from the warden of Leonard's prison arrived at my house a week later with an invitation to meet with him and possibly with Leonard himself, I was positive that my own acts of mercy had unlocked the door. I was wrong.

The receptionist led me to the prison

conference room, where I found about half a dozen people standing at their places waiting for me as if I were to say grace, or to be their meal. With one arm around my shoulders, the warden introduced me to the gathering. I have wondered if the increasing demonstrativeness of those around me owes more to my being a victim or to my looking like a victim. I continue to lose weight. A third possibility began to present itself that morning: I am beginning to look like a saint.

"Reverend Pierce, welcome. I'm Frank Amazo, the chief warden of Hamilton Correctional Center. This is my assistant, Rita Hamilton, no relation to the prison, ha, ha, ha, not that I know of anyway, are you, Rita?"

"Ah, no." Rita was a black woman with the girth, deliberateness, and nearly military bearing of someone who's fought her way up from the lower working class.

"This is Dr. Sharon Michelowsky, our psychologist."

"Psychiatrist," she corrected.

"Psychiatrist. She keeps us from going crazy, crazier than we already are. I believe you two have met."

"We have," I said. We shook hands like two people trying to keep the secret that they have slept together.

"And this is Joe Lincoln, attorney for Alex Leonard."

"He knows me, too," said Lincoln.

"Oh," said Amazo.

"I'm not sure I do," said I, pausing for effect. Then I said, "We've met briefly."

"Well, that's good, I guess. And this charming lady is Mrs. Jillian Cohen, a local businesswoman who represents the public on our policy board. Nobody can accuse us of being a sexist organization, can they? I'm the only insider who's a guy."

Jillian greeted me warmly, as the psychiatrist accepted Amazo's patronizing remark with a forced smile that curdled the skin of her lower face and neck.

"And last but not least, the only man without a tie, except for you, Reverend, but your thing here counts as one I guess—I've always meant to ask you guys why you wear that—this is Jerome Roth."

The lack of an identification as well as his placement in the introductions gave Roth the drama I suppose was intended. He was a man slightly older than I, with curly red hair and beard, and round, wire-framed glasses. I guessed from the anachronistic look and from his blue work shirt that he was probably an inmate at the prison. Leonard's cellmate?

"Mr. Roth is a documentary filmmaker."

Roth engaged my eyes as if he'd just been introduced as a plate of tripe, and was about to say, "Now I know everybody hears 'tripe' and says 'yucch,' but did you know that tripe is considered a delicacy in many European countries?" I can afford a little humor now. At the time, I felt the lining of my stomach go as dry and hollow as an empty honeycomb.

"Well, now that that's done, let's sit down and begin. Reverend Pierce, why don't you sit here, at the head of the table, and I'll sit beside you over here. I'm going to be the moderator and the kicker-offer, I guess. So let's begin. In the past month we have received two requests that I can only call extraordinary. At least I have known nothing like them in my thirty-odd years in the correctional system. Well, I guess I've seen something like one of the requests, but when I say 'extraordinary,' I'm talking mainly about the *first* request, which was your request, Reverend. You wrote to us, I guess it was about a month ago, the duration's not really an issue, and you asked to be able to see Alex Leonard to bring the Gospel to him."

"It's more accurate to say I asked for permission to serve Leonard in a loving way. Certainly that's 'bringing the Gospel,' as you put it, but unfortunately that phrase has certain evangelistic overtones"—I cleared my throat—"which do not apply here. I had no intention of preaching at Mr. Leonard or proselytizing in your prison. As I said in my letter, I am merely hoping to follow Christ's commandment to love our enemies."

"I think that's perfectly clear to everyone here," Amazo said immediately.

"That's questionable," said Lincoln, the attorney. "At least I am not clear about what Reverend Pierce meant in his letter or in what he just said."

"That's one reason we're having this meeting, isn't it, for clarification?" said Amazo.

"I hope that's one thing we can accomplish at this meeting," Lincoln shot back.

"We're going to try our very best, counselor. And I think the best way to do that"—he scanned the company for support—"is to allow me to set the framework and the tone, and then allow everyone a chance to ask their questions, and define their points of view frankly and openly. Just let me get started."

"I'm sorry," I offered. "I was the one who interrupted."

"Not at all, Reverend Pierce," he said, standing now as he touched my shoulder. "I should probably stand." But he disliked the height of standing. "That's too formal. Let me sit and let me finish my introduction."

He began again. I thought of Leonard moving through a world of people like us with his knife and rope, like a smug handyman of death. In the time it had taken us to handle our introductions, he had raped my wife. In a few more minutes he would have murdered her and our son. I thought of ancient cities, their elders meeting in councils like this one to dicker over the boundary of a new wall or arbitrate the ownership of a disputed goat, or even to define the nature of the Holy Trinity. From harvest to harvest, Attila would raze three hundred of their like to the smoking ground.

"... your tragedy," he was saying, "your great loss. I don't think there's anyone here who doesn't extend their sincerest condolences to you for what you've suffered."

Even Lincoln nodded at that.

"But your request was like nothing we'd ever had before. I'll admit, we didn't know what to make of it, and we were perhaps too hasty in rejecting it, although I'm sure there's bound to be a difference of opinion on that. I mean, clergymen ask to come into the prison all the time, of course. But not clergymen who are close family of victims of the criminal! I'd say every other year we do get someone who fills out an application to work here, and when we run through everything, we find out they're related to the victim of somebody serving time here. Would you say I'm off, Rita?"

"About what?"

"About the frequency of this kind of thing. Say every other year?"

"I guess so. At least the ones we *catch*. For all we know, there could be somebody on the staff now, just biding his time." She drew out the word "biding" as if it opened the refrain of a hymn.

"Jesus Christ, don't tell me that. Pardon my profanity, Reverend. But Rita's just described one of a warden's two worst nightmares. We have to worry about our people breaking out or somebody else breaking in. I don't know which we're more afraid of. Thank you, Rita, for rearranging my large intestine."

"Always a pleasure."

"Anyway, you will pardon my profanity?"

"God handles pardons, I only work downstairs."

"Ha, ha, ha. You've got a great sense of humor for a man of the cloth. Doesn't he? Anyway, where was I?"

"You were telling him about two extraordinary requests," said Roth, who was eager to present the second, I'm sure.

"Right. Well, as I'm sure you're aware, your request got quite a bit of publicity in the media, which was perhaps not your intention."

I shot a glance at Michelowsky, to whom I'd made my threat to go public—and then realized it was Amazo himself who had doubtless broken the first story to the news. She was looking down thoughtfully at the surface of the table.

"In any case, there've been several stories about this in the news, and about your efforts on behalf of Alex Leonard's lady friend, and then, lo and behold, we get our second request, from Mr. Roth this time, who wants to make a documentary movie about you and Mr. Leonard. Now this is the point where an administrative type like myself says, 'Hold the phone.' Honoring your request would set a precedent fraught with danger. Honoring his request wouldn't exactly be a precedent, they've done films like *Scared Straight* and things like that before, but never here at this place. So I was very skeptical, and to be perfectly honest, I'm a little skeptical still. But to make a long story short, much to my surprise and maybe your surprise, too, the Department of Corrections is interested in the idea, I'm told the governor himself is interested in the idea, which I find interesting because up till now, as far as I could see, he didn't know that such a thing as the Department of Corrections even existed. But he had a good point, that maybe a project like this would help morale, if we could involve some of the inmates, cut down some of the tensions around here, that kind of thing. Anyway, Alex Leonard is interested in the idea, at least as an excuse for handing us a list of demands longer than the Declaration of Independence, and if you're interested in the idea, I guess we ought to pursue it further. Does this surprise you?"

"Yes," I said.

"Mr. Amazo, this is where I'd like to step in, if I may," said Roth.

"Roll 'em."

"Reverend Pierce, your actions in the past weeks, in the light of your terrible tragedy, constitute one of the most phenomenal things I've ever heard. I don't want to patronize you, if for no other reason but that I don't think flattery's going to impress someone like you, but when I...contemplate what you're doing, and then when I think of somebody like Mother Teresa, with all respect to Mother Teresa, she looks easy. I haven't got a saintly bone in my body, but I'd find it a lot easier to go feed lepers in India or whatever than to...show any compassion for a person who'd...made me suffer the way Alex Leonard has made you suffer."

"I haven't been given many opportunities to show this compassion. In that respect, at least, Mother Teresa looks easy to me, too."

"I'm sure. But that can change. And I may be able to help you change it. The story that you have to tell—you don't even have to tell it, your actions tell it for you—is of overwhelming interest to a filmmaker like me. I don't know if you know any of my work, it doesn't matter if you don't, but just so you have some idea of who you're dealing with—"

"*Might* be dealing with," Lincoln interjected. The administrative assistant sighed noisily, as Roth rattled off his credits.

"My work has always been about compassion," Roth continued, "about human caring, alternatives to violence, that kind of subject matter, which isn't big at the box office, but I think it's something on a lot of people's minds. There isn't a person in this country who doesn't wake up and open the morning paper and read about some violent crime and ask, 'What if that was me? What if that was someone I love?' I guess the classic reaction, at least the classic *fantasy reaction*, which is the same thing as saying the classic Hollywood reaction, is to go out and buy a handgun or assault rifle or something. But you seem to be saying to people that there's a way that goes beyond vengeance and fear and paranoia, all the things that the popular entertainment media are feeding us in megadoses. And that goes beyond helplessness and despair. You're saying, 'The religion I'm committed to, the Golden Rule and things like that, is not just some abstract ideal, it's not pie in the sky, it's real, it's alive, it's a viable solution to the madness.'"

113

"I think Reverend Pierce knows what he's saying," said Amazo. "I think he needs to know what you're saying."

"I hope he *knows* what I'm saying. I'm saying he has something to teach people, and I can help that teaching get across. Reverend Pierce, I'll lay it right on the line. I want to make a documentary film about your encounter with Alex Leonard, wherever that encounter goes. And I may be mistaken, but I think my film may be the only means for convincing Mr. Leonard and the other powers that be to even allow a meeting to take place. What I'm asking from you today is a provisional okay to be with you if and when any meetings take place with Leonard. I'm not asking you to sign anything or commit to anything, I'm just asking you to say you're willing to trust me through the first step. These people can contradict me if I'm wrong, but without me there may possibly be no first step. Not because *I* have any power, but because *movies* have power."

"Mr. Roth—"Amazo interrupted.

"Just two or three more short things and I'm done."

"Okay, but please keep them short."

"Reverend Pierce, I can go over all of this again later, but just quickly for now—if, after we've gotten better acquainted, you're willing to commit to this project, I'm willing to offer you my complete cooperation. I'm willing to allow you input on the editing of the film, and there's a financial aspect here as well, which may not be a concern to you right now, but you could stand to receive some substantial moneys, especially if we can sell this to public TV or even one of the commercial networks. But that's down the road, of course."

"Can Mr. Leonard hope to get a share of the profits as well?" I asked.

"No," Amazo said. "Not a penny. He can't make any money off this film, his mother can't make any money, his uncle Oscar back in the old country can't make any money, nobody associated with him in any way, shape, or form. New Jersey Criminal Injuries Compensation Act. Am I correct, counselor?"

"You are, but there are other issues besides money, serious legal issues. I remind you that Mr. Leonard has an appeal slated in several months."

As Lincoln said this, Rita leaned forward with her eyes on mine.

"I think we should make Reverend Pierce aware that Mr. Leonard's only reason for even considering any of this is the hope of seeing his own face on TV. There's no change of heart here, Reverend."

"I thought perhaps my efforts on behalf of Monica Zeller might have been a factor—"

"I think Alex was grateful for what you did," said Dr. Michelowsky.

"Grateful, huh?" said Rita. "Well, you're the doctor, not me, but as far as I can tell, 'grateful' ain't nowhere to be found in Alex Leonard's vocabulary. Old Lennie thinks *we* should all

115

be grateful that the world is so unjust it don't allow him to put *us* all in jail for causing a major inconvenience in his life." She locked eyes with me again. "You should see his list of demands."

"I think we should get back to the issues raised by Mr. Leonard's attorney," Roth said.

"Thank you," said Leonard's attorney.

"We're fully aware that with an appeal coming up, a film like ours can provide incriminating evidence. It can also do just the opposite. What I think—"

"I would like to see the list of demands," said Mrs. Cohen, in a voice that immediately commanded attention. "This lady—I forget your name—"

"Rita."

"Rita said, 'You should see his list of demands.' I want to see it."

"It's just a fantasy that reads like a grocery list," said Amazo.

"Why do you want to see it?" said Roth.

"Because I think it says something about the attitude of the man who submitted it. Look, if my taxes are going to go for this little venture"—she stifled an attempt by Roth to correct her—"let me finish, and they will, because you're going to have to make security arrangements for this, you're going to have to consult lawyers to iron out the wrinkles in this—that's all money."

"Which we can provide," Roth squeezed in.

"I want to hear the demands. Am I not privileged to hear that information?"

"You certainly are privileged to hear it," said

116

Amazo. "But I don't think it will tell you anything you don't already know. Alex Leonard is not a choirboy, right?"

"Actually, he was one," said Michelowsky.

"Well, whatever you say—he says. Maybe he was the Prince of Wales once, too. I don't have the list with me. I can show it to you later if you want. He wants various privileges that he's lost restored to him, to play music whenever he wants, this sort of thing. He wants to be able to sleep an extra hour in the morning, because he says making the movie will tire him out."

Rita snorted contemptuously, and even Lincoln smiled. I could tell Cohen was not amused, though.

"He wants a better selection of reading material."

"Smut, in other words," said Rita.

"Oh, and he wants to be handled only by *white* corrections officers. I don't think we'll give him that one, will we, Rita?"

"I'm sure, sir, that the people of color on our staff would be more than happy to excuse any discrimination in this particular case."

"Well, I won't be. What else? Oh, he wants his girlfriend in the film, he wants money for his girlfriend to buy new clothes so she won't be embarrassed to be in the film. He probably wants a helicopter with his name painted in a big gold star on the side, I don't know. You get the idea, anyway."

Lincoln began to speak. "With all due respect to everybody here, we need to clarify some

117

things. There's a distinction that's starting to blur between what Mr. Leonard wants, however ridiculous that is, and what Mr. Leonard *needs* as a person entitled to certain constitutional rights, the guarantee against self-incrimination being one..."

I did not hear most of what he said. Our wordy negotiations led me to think of the scarce moments of pleading allowed to the murdered and the raped, the few syllables granted to scare or shame or sicken the one with the knife, the strategies now printed in women's magazines almost as often as recipes. Tell him you're pregnant or have a venereal disease. Tell him you're being watched, that your husband, your parents are on their way home. Scream. Vomit. Tell him to come back again tomorrow. Tell him he's handsome. Tell him, yes, you do enjoy it. Tell him what he tells you to tell him. Do whatever he says.

"... but that's not the same thing as editorial privilege," Roth said in a heat. "If you want to delay or speed up the distribution of the film, that's one thing. But editing is another question. That does not have to do with his rights, but with *my* right of free speech as an artist."

"An artist whose subject is my client."

"Can we back up a bit here? Legal rights are not the only kinds of rights," said Dr. Michelowsky. "There are also some basic human rights. I'm the only person here who's spent in-depth time with both Mr. Leonard and Reverend Pierce, and I have some concerns that nobody's addressing. We are talking about a very damaged and so far dangerous individual who I've only recently discovered was traumatized by religious fanaticism as a child. His father was a minister who, as far as I can tell, was the first in a series of men to have molested him. His early experiences with religion may very well have been his motivation for choosing the victims he did. The last thing he needs right now are the so-called services of a clergyman, much less *this* clergyman, and I don't care if it would make a heartwarming movie. I mean, at the risk of being rude, I can't help but notice, Reverend Pierce, that you came to the prison fully equipped today. You're wearing your collar, you've got your Bible, you've got your box with the cross on it, whatever that is."

"It's a Communion set," I said, tapping the box that lay alongside my Bible in front of me.

"A Communion set. You've certainly come pretty well prepared for what you supposed might be a little chat with Mr. Leonard. I mean, do you have any tracts or other literature to go with it?"

"Sharon!" the warden said.

"I want to know."

"I have brought nothing but this Bible and this Communion, which I have very literally laid on the table in front of you. It's refreshing to think that somebody even noticed them. These go with me wherever I go as a minister, and I have come here as a minister."

I scanned the others before turning decisively to her. This was my moment, and I wanted the issue settled once and for all.

"When Alex Leonard entered my home to slaughter my wife and our little boy, he carried a knife and a rope and a gun. He also came well equipped, didn't he? Well, what you see is *my* equipment, and I assure you the last intention I have is to impose my equipment on Alex Leonard in the way that he imposed his equipment on me and my family. I'm sure you're perfectly competent to explain the psychology of murderers and rapists; let me explain my psychology, which comes down to theology, and to a few pathetically simple needs, one of which is to have the visible support of two sacred objects, since I've lost the support...of the two people ..."

I broke off. There was silence. Then Mrs. Cohen spoke.

"Well, finally! I am so glad to hear somebody talk about *your* need. It's just sad that you had to be the one to do it. For the past six months I've been listening to what black murderers and rapists say they need, and then to what white murderers and rapists say they need, and you people telling us what you need to keep the black and white murderers and rapists from murdering and raping each other. And then today I hear what the governor needs, and I hear about this person's artistic needs, and I hear this person tell us about Alex Leonard's needs, I even hear Alex Leonard tell us what he supposedly needs, and needs, and needs, and Dr. Michelowsky tells us even more about Leonard's needs, and nobody even mentions or thinks to ask what this man needs." She pointed at me as she slapped the table with the palm of her hand. "This man is the victim. This man is the person whose family was murdered—not you, or you, or you, or you, or you, or me. Least of all, not the animal locked up in there. Him! I want to know what *he* needs."

"You've put us back on track once again, Mrs. Cohen, as you always do," said Amazo. "We can work out all the legal and artistic and psychological and financial and what-have-you stuff later. Right now the only real question is up to you, Reverend Pierce. Does anything we've discussed interest you? If you say no, we have nothing more to talk about."

Mrs. Cohen had not seemed to hear him.

"I want to hear his demands," she said. "I want *his* list. I'm tired of always hearing the other lists. I want *his* list."

"All we need now—" Amazo began.

"I want his list!"

"Mrs. Cohen, I thank you for your kindness," I said. "My only wish, which I've made clear for some time, is to be able to see Mr. Leonard and, if possible, be of some help to him. It's up to others to decide whether I can do that, and to dictate the conditions. Maybe it'll be a movie, maybe it'll be something else. I'm open. I'm powerless. I'll only say this: If it's to be a movie, then I have some conditions also."

"And what are they?" said Roth, who could barely hold himself in his chair.

"For one thing, I will not be interviewed, on camera or off, about my wife and son. If you want to film me as I meet with Mr. Leonard, that's fine. But I will not rehash the crime or relive my life before the crime for anyone."

"Fair deal. We might be able to talk about some different options—"

"No options. I don't retell the tale. You can do what you wish. You can say whatever you want in the film. I don't talk about it."

"Fine. Fine. Absolutely. Now what's the other?"

I turned to the administration.

"That I see Mr. Leonard today."

I held firm during the hubbub that followed, and then the tension broke, Amazo excused himself from the room, and I knew that I might soon have my wish. The others stood up to stretch; some stepped through the doorway. I gave short, distracted answers to those who addressed me. I remember the momentary illusion that I was seated in my old dining room, and that these people were the detectives, dusting the furniture for fingerprints, photographing the corpses. I heard Mrs. Cohen say again, "This is the victim. I care about the victim." Someone asked me if I wanted a cup of coffee.

When the warden finally returned and all of us except Mrs. Cohen began to move out of the room and along the hall, past the offices, toward the restricted area, I strove to focus my attention. I fought for strength. I tried to think of the sea and the gulls, but the gulls flew away and carried the ocean with them. I actually prayed—"Make me steady," I said in silence—and the prayer clarified things, as prayers often do, with a liberating simplicity. I suddenly realized that the object I was trying to block out of my mind in order to give courage to my heart was, in fact, the very thing I needed to face: My wife and son were dead. Alex Leonard was as powerless to touch them now as I was. I could make any blunder, he could make any threat, but they could never be hurt again by my mistakes or his malice. They were free; only Leonard and I were imprisoned.

So I stepped up to the metal detector with a lighter step and with what I thought was a clearer head than I'd had a few minutes before. Amazo, Rita, and the attorney had already passed through. The guard at the security station had greeted them; he knew who they were. When my turn came, he nodded so peremptorily that I wondered if he thought I was there to serve a sentence.

"Please place any metal objects—keys, pens, coins, or tie clips—on the counter before passing through." He spoke rapidly and somewhat unclearly, so that I hesitated for a moment. "Please place any metal objects—keys, pens, coins, or tie clips—on the counter before passing through," he repeated.

"Of course," I said, fumbling in my pockets to produce my keys and pen as quickly as possible, like answers to an intelligence test.

123

"Okay?" I said, poised to take another step.

He pointed at my neck. "Your collar?"

"Yes," I said, without a sense of what he meant. "I'm a clergyman."

"I guessed that." There was a flash of ire in his eyes, a black person's reaction to a white person's assumption that the black is stupid. The white person wants to explain, but the black person is already too bored and tired of the same old crap even to be angry.

"Does your collar have metal in it? That wrap-around kind usually has a pin in it."

At first I thought he said a *pen*, and I almost made matters much worse by pointing to the pen I had already laid on the counter, but then I understood.

"Oh, the collar pins, yes," I said, unfastening my collar. "Most people, unless they're priests or ministers, don't know what goes into our getup."

"We see all kinds go through here, with all kinds of metal." He offered me one brief, reassuring smile. "Pass through the detector, please," he said, stone-faced once again.

When the alarm went off, I froze on the step between the detector columns. I must have turned a ghastly pale. It continued to ring as I stood stock-still—like the call for the Last Judgment. Gradually, as those in front of me gestured to me to move backward, I became aware of the guard's voice repeating, "Step back from the detector. Step back from the detector."

As soon as the alarm was silent again, he

asked me, "What is in the box? Let's see the box, please."

"The box!" I exclaimed. After my exchange with the psychiatrist, how could I have forgotten the box? "This is a Communion set." I placed the box on the counter, but did not let go of it. "Please let me open it. This is very...sacred."

With trembling hands, I opened the latch on the black, velvet-lined case that held the miniature Communion vessels.

"This is a Communion set," I said. "This is the chalice, and the wine container—"

"This is a lot of metal," he said.

"—and the plate. And this here"—I found myself with tears in my eyes—"this is the Body of Christ."

2

No ascetic or holy man, not Simon the Stylite, who lived for thirty years on top of a pillar in the Egyptian desert, ever exercised more self-denial than I did, seeing Alex Leonard for the second time in my life and not tearing out his throat.

"Hi, Reverend," he called out, as soon as we'd entered the room. "I hear we're going to make a movie."

His eyes lit and his brows rose as if he were glad to see me. He'd worn the same expression when he first laid eyes on Cynthia.

He was manacled hand and foot and seated in a chair. He was dressed entirely in gray. Two guards stood on either side of him like attendants to a king. I noticed that his cuffed hands were also tethered by a short chain to a larger chain around his waist. The sight of him in bonds filled me with an indescribable outrage. There was an insinuation of justice that I found utterly obscene, as if by binding his hands and feet, someone dared to claim that our roles had been exchanged, that he was suffering what I had suffered. I wanted to scream out, "Untie him! Untie him! What right has he to wear restraints? Free his hands and his feet or chop them off, but spare us this mockery!"

"We're going to be celebrities, Reverend," he said to me. "They're going to be talking to us two on David Letterman."

"We still have some things to iron out," said Lincoln, while I stood speechless, no more than eight feet away from Leonard.

"Go home and do your ironing, Abe, nobody's stopping you, but we're making the movie. Hey, Rita," he said, jerking his head back over his shoulder, "tell one of your soul brothers here to get me a smoke, will you. A nice white Marlboro."

"They make your lungs *black*, Lennie. Black as your heart."

"Black as your mama's ass, you mean."

"Cut the shit, Alex," said Amazo. "I hear another racist remark like that from you, and the only way you'll smoke cigarettes in this place is out of *your* ass."

126

"Hear the language I have to put up with around here, Reverend? There's no fear of the Lord in this place. I dwell among a people of unclean lips."

"To get to the point, whether or not we make any movies depends above all else on this man's say-so. Any negotiations you have to do, you do first with him," said Amazo.

"Of course, absolutely. We're the main players, right? I know that. But I don't think we have much negotiating to do, do we, Reverend? You and me, we can understand each other. We have some common experiences." He paused. "I was a preacher's son, did you know that?"

"I did."

"Good. So you've already found out a little bit about me, have you? That's good, especially if we're going to work together, right? Just a sec." He winked. "Hey, Mr. Lincoln, do you think you might be able to represent me in the matter of getting a fucking cigarette sometime before Christmas?" He addressed me again. "Another thing you might want to know about me is that I'm a hardened nicotine addict with latent suicidal tendencies. I don't get a cigarette and I start getting this uncontrollable urge to bang my head on a super-hard object like a prison wall or an African American's skull. Counsel me, Dr. Polish. I'm in distress here."

"Shut up, Alex."

"My therapist," he said.

"Can he have a cigarette?" Lincoln asked.

"If you want to give him one," said Rita. "These guards are not getting him one, and I am certainly not getting him one, but if you want to get him one, he can have a cigarette."

Lincoln took a step back from Leonard, then exclaimed, "For God's sake, I have to stay here. I can't leave him."

"That's not really my problem," said Rita.

At the same time, Roth, the filmmaker, said, "Let *me* get him a cigarette. Tell me where the cigarettes are, and I will get him a cigarette."

"The only man of mercy in the whole multitude, and behold, he's a goddamn hippie. He looks like Jesus Christ, too, doesn't he, Reverend? If he got rid of the glasses. Don't you think he looks a little like Jesus Christ, Reverend?"

"I'm not sure what Jesus looks like," I said.

"Oh, you need to be sure of that, Reverend, especially you. Uh, Mr. Steven Spielberg, did I hear you say you were going for a cigarette, or is little E.T. going to have to die here?"

It was incredible. Bound hand and foot and lacking a gun, he was still able to control us. He moved us like marionettes. For just a moment, one of those recurring moments I have in which the horrors of my imagination seem to become the cold facts of the newspaper, as real as rape or murder, I wondered if Alex Leonard was God. I give thanks to Rita for breaking the spell.

"Wait. I think I have a cigarette here," she said. She produced a pack from her shirt pocket and extracted a cigarette with her mouth. She held it in her grinning lips for a few seconds before handing it to Roth. "You can give him this one."

"Just like kissing you, Rita," Leonard said, while Roth placed the smoke in his mouth and lit it under the watchful eyes of the guards. Roth took the cigarette away, and Leonard exhaled. "You know what they say about kissing a colored girl?"

"You know what I say about where you can kiss this here colored girl?"

"Would you wash it first? But—this must all be very distasteful for the reverend. I apologize for these people, Reverend. Stay here, Spielberg, and help me with the smoke. E.T. needs *heeellp*." He croaked the word like a Muppet in distress. "So what do you say, Reverend? It's all pretty simple, right? Like the warden here said, it's pretty much up to you. And I agree. You can talk to me on camera, or we can say our sayonaras here and return to our happy homes. What could be more simple than that? Because I'll tell you, Reverend, if you mean what you say about loving your enemy, which you probably still think is what I am, if you want to love your enemy, this movie is it. This movie is the love connection. The way, the truth, and the life. Because I am in this place forever, and because the person I love is busted broke. According to the government, she's not supposed to get anything out of this, but you're a charitable man, and where there's a will, there's a way. So much for the financial aspect. On top of that, there are millions of people out there in television land who think that I am some kind of Dracula or something."

All at once he dropped his persona as the sinister master of ceremonies, and grew earnest and angry.

"And they don't know a goddamn fucking thing about me! They sit on their asses in their little pink houses and pass judgment on me and they don't know a fucking single thing about what *I've* gone through, what *I've* suffered, what *I've* had done to me."

He banged his fists up and down on their rattling tether, and stamped his manacled feet, so that the two guards each laid their hands on his shoulders.

"You, at least you're a Christian, but these fans of yours got their heads up their asses as far as understanding anything about me. They think they know everything about the whole goddamn world because they can read a newspaper. You could probably teach a monkey to read a newspaper. Jesus."

He shook his head and laughed. "They *do* teach monkeys to read newspapers," he said to himself. He pulled what was left of the proffered cigarette from Roth's hand with a jerk of his head, dragged it to the filter, then spat the remains on the floor at my feet.

"So what do you say, Reverend, do we make a movie?"

"I guess we make a movie," I said.

"Goddamn right. And I will assure you of one

thing. I will make this promise to you. I want everybody to listen to me. This is going to be a top-of-the-line picture. Are you listening to me?" he said to Roth. "I want it done right. This is a once-in-a-lifetime opportunity for me—*his* whole fucking family is dead, for Christ's sake—and I want a quality motion picture. His family deserves it, and I deserve it. I want you to get people who know what the fuck they're doing. Professionals. You taking notes on this, Abe? I want it done right. You bring some assholes in here to do the job, and I don't shoot. I don't want any of this affirmative-action bullshit, either, where you got half a dozen NBA rejects staring into the wrong end of the camera waiting for the doughnuts to come. What are you doing for publicity?"

"Most of the publicity is really a long way off," said Roth.

"The film could be a long way off," said Amazo.

"You're all a long way off," said Leonard, ignoring Amazo. "Your dumbest asshole knows that a movie makes it or doesn't make it depending on publicity. You got to keep feeding it to the public like candy. What do you mean, it's a long way off? How much you putting up for advertising?"

"I think we're at the end of our meeting," said Amazo.

"Just a minute. Let me answer the question," said Roth.

"Yeah, let him answer my question."

"For a film of this kind, for a film of almost

any kind, it's too early to advertise. We haven't even begun filming yet. But we're not insensitive to the importance of publicity. Your point is well taken. Our best strategy now is to use the print and electronic media to generate public interest in the making of this picture. Right now, as we're speaking, Mr. Leonard, if all has gone as planned, a television film crew is preparing to get a shot of some of us leaving the prison with Reverend Pierce." He glanced at me. "That is, if Reverend Pierce doesn't object. The public is already interested in this whole wonderful coming together—"

"Hey, Reverend, in front of the camera already, huh? Better comb your hair at the door."

"We don't want to saturate them too soon," Roth continued without a break. "Right now, we want to keep their interest, but build slowly. Listen, this is a big opportunity for me, too. Trust me." "I'll trust you," said Leonard. "I trust just about everybody, really. Basic trust is a critical first step toward sound mental health. Isn't that what you say, Dr. Michelowsky? Doesn't the Bible even say so, Reverend? Doesn't God say somewhere in the Bible that you should trust your neighbor and you'll live longer or something like that?"

"I don't recall such a passage," I said.

I want to write a little more before I sleep. I have just turned off the eleven o'clock news—the first time I've had the television on in this house. I saw myself walking from the prison flanked by a filmmaker and a lawyer. A young woman appeared in the foreground and spoke about us into a microphone. The camera zoomed back to the prison steps as I broke from my escort and hurried to my car.

After the footage of me, the anchorman turned to a report on violence among teenagers, transition by way of contrast. An image of the forgiving disciple of Christ juxtaposed with images of Saturday-night specials tucked into blue jeans against flat, hairless bellies. In this way the viewer was invited to weigh the hopefulness of my life against the hopelessness of theirs.

I probably did not look as hopeful as was hoped. I have indeed grown very thin. My face has a gauntness that I never fully noticed in the mirror. I look like the Stylite, like one of the hermits of the desert. Still, I look much better than I did ten months ago. That is what I want to write about.

So far I have said very little about the weeks and months after the deaths of my wife and son. If ever a man was dead while seeming alive, I had been that man. If you made a graph of life states from the ecstatic to the comatose, I would have been at the last hairline demarcation before the comatose. One would think that the lowest point of my life was the day it all happened. Of course my heart says, *Yes, that was the lowest.* Yet in some ways, the following weeks in the hospital were even worse. While

Alex Leonard was rampaging through my life, I was still alive, with fear, with anger, with pain—with love and even hope. Afterward there was simply nothing. I felt indestructible and immortal in that awful, purposeless sense that defines hell. Sometimes I felt disembodied.

And yet I always remembered I had a body. Leonard had broken my ribs, my left arm, my jaw, my nose, and some of my teeth with his feet. As the doctors repaired each damaged part, I felt the jolts of my physicality.

I was amazed, and then horrified, at how my body could go on functioning when I had lost all desire to live. I could look up at the blank ceiling and wish to be as blank as that, and yet my heart still pumped blood to my temples. I sometimes thought I could feel the blood coursing through my veins, though perhaps that was merely the ghost of the IV. I lived when I did not want to live. What could be more obvious—we learn the difference between voluntary and involuntary muscles in grammar school. Still I think we always believe that life is somehow a function of our own will. "The will to live," we say. We rise and lie down, we eat, we walk, we recreate and procreate—but all the while life pervades us in spite of volition.

Life rapes us was perhaps my first intelligible thought. Life makes us vessels for violation. Strangely enough, the horror of that thought was not without some mitigating comfort. Anything that gave me solidarity with Cynthia or Jimmy was a comfort, though it always came at the cost of increasing horror. So I would lie in my bed in the hospital and imagine that I could know some of Cynthia's hell. We both had known the betrayal of our own bodies. We both had felt our flesh yield to the power of a force we did not accept.

It was much harder to conjure any solidarity with Jimmy. It remains much harder. For who can fathom a child's terror? To what moorings can a child fasten his frightened mind? Only to his parents. And if his parents are bound and helpless...I had always tried so hard to be an icon of strength for him, gentle strength, but strength. We were always wrestling—I was always inviting him to punch me in the stomach. Cynthia told me more than once that I was "too rough." But a minister fears emasculating his son before the boy is even old enough to choose whether or not he will become a eunuch for the Kingdom of God. That's probably why ministers' sons are such notorious bad apples. Alex Leonard was a minister's son, so we're back to him again. Never mind him. When I think of Jimmy sitting on the lap of his trussed-up father, hearing the cries of his violated mother, I am aware of a terror as vast and unknowable as the heart of God himself.

Through Andrew's mediation I was able to absent myself from much of Leonard's trial by videotaping my testimony. I gave no interviews. I refused counseling, most visitors, and all drugs except those prescribed for physical pain. I would not take antidepressants. In some ways my refusals became my own therapy— or at least a railing to grip. Still, as my body

135

began to heal and my discharge seemed imminent, I knew that refusal alone would not sustain me. I knew I needed a new spine, a new center, and that the generic kind of ministry I had practiced would no longer do. There was now only one significant "other" in the whole world, and that was Alex Leonard. Whatever meaningful decision I made about my life from then on would have to do with him. Even God seemed to step back from the resolution forming in my brain, like a father who has just given away a bride.

Around my new mission, I was able to re-form the old habits of bodily care, of self-maintenance, and then to refashion something approximating the persona I had once called myself. Gradually, perhaps more like a monster than a messiah, I rose from the dead.

Now I have at last come to the threshold of the room where I will have to face what my whole life means. Against incredible obstacles, every kind of societal and personal inertia, I have managed—how but with the providence of God?—to come face to face with the man whose face above all others I wish I had never seen, who makes me wish I had never seen my own.

So tonight I descend with a new confidence to the cellar where I have gone every night for months. I turn on the fluorescent light over my altar-sized workbench and switch on the Bach that now scores the wedding marches of my dreams. The great pipe organ fills and surrounds the house with triumphant, clamorous sound. Then, gripping the small .38 like a chalice and elevating my hands like a priest's to the man-shaped, target-inscribed shadow hanging before me, I open fire.

I like the way my gun recoils from each shot, as if it too feels the impact of the bullet, the piercing of matter or flesh. I like the way it gives off warmth and odor with use, like a human body. I like its little clicks and latches, its precise empty holes, the naive tap of its hammer over a vacant chamber—its simple material innocence, so unlike the duplicitous human heart.

Most of all, I like the way it is made of metal. Just like a Communion set.

3

Fall is in the air for the first time. Every year the season comes for the first time, as if it had never come before. There is just a trace of it today as I drive to the prison, in the gooseflesh on my arm because I have worn a short-sleeved shirt, in the open door of the hairdresser's shop, because they have turned off the air conditioner. The colors of the children's clothes have darkened a shade; I notice as they run past the shop and other stores up to the intersection, where the crossing guard, a gray-haired woman in a navy sweater, will hold up a red and white stop sign that seems clearer and brighter in the brisk, dry air. A few brown oak leaves skate over the crosswalk beside them.

Soon the gutters of this modest suburb will be piled with leaves, raked with a garnish of gum wrappers from the little lawns and over the sidewalks. The children will abandon the sidewalks and wade through the shushing mounds, flattening them to the height of the curbs. Some of the girls will appear in their Brownie caps, like the tops of the acorns that lie smashed in the road. Then the giant yellow leaf sweeper will begin its melancholy droning up and down the avenues. The cars will withdraw from the curbs to the driveways to let it pass. The white concrete saints, in the absence of flowers or shade, will grow starker and seemingly older on the raked-down lawns.

Soon, too, will come the anniversary of that supper when I sat down to eat with my wife and son and rose up to eat my bitter meals alone forever. I want to see Leonard dead before that day. That will depend, of course, on how long it takes me to soften the security procedures with my familiar presence. But even if my plans are postponed, I am likely to be spending my next autumn and all the autumns thereafter in a prison cell.

I wonder if the demonstrators I saw outside the prison today will continue to chant there, once it has become my home. Or will my actions have shamed them into silence? They will not be able to applaud me without sentencing me to death. Their signs read, BRING BACK THE DEATH PENALTY and TWO CHANCES

138

TO MURDER ARE ONE TOO MANY and PIERCE CAN FORGIVE LEONARD BUT SOCIETY SHOULDN'T and LOVE MERCY BUT DO JUSTICE—the last probably an edited allusion to the prophet Micah. They stood far down by the entranceway, about a quarter mile from the prison building itself, as close as they were allowed to come. I don't know if they recognized me as I drove through their ranks. I have leased a new car since my incident with the boys that night. I was wearing a clerical collar. Perversely, I smiled and gave them a thumbs-up gesture as I drove by. Rita, the warden's assistant, met me almost as soon as I had been buzzed through the outermost door. I carried my Bible, my Communion box, and two cartons of Marlboro cigarettes.

"Whoa, Reverend," she said, smiling. "You've taken on some bad habits since we last saw you. You're not planning to finish all those smokes while you're here, are you? What, are you trying to kill yourself?"

"No, no, I brought these for Mr. Leonard."

"I know why you brought them," she said. "And that's very nice, but you'll have to leave them with one of the security officers. I can take them now if you'd like."

"I'm sorry. Is he not allowed—"

"He's allowed to have smokes," she said, taking the cartons from me. She beckoned with her raised finger to a guard in the receiving area and handed him the cartons, saying, "Leonard. Alex Leonard."

"He can have them," she went on, "but he

can't just have them all at once. We regulate what they have." She enunciated the word "regulate" with special care. "You bring him any other little presents?"

"No."

"We will provide you with a list of the items you're allowed to bring. And the definite no-no's."

"Thank you. Will Mr. Leonard know that I've brought these?"

"He will know. We will inform him if you'd like. That way he will know not to say 'thank you.' Will you come this way, please?"

I followed her dutifully, like a patient in a hospital, past monitors and through steel doors and barred gates that she opened by speaking into a small intercom or nodding to visible operators at glass-enclosed control stations. We passed by the same burly guard who had sat at the metal detector a week and a half ago. This time I opened the Communion box for him before passing through the detector. He handed it back to me once I was through. I had worn a "Roman" tab collar, which required no metal pins.

"Mr. Hollywood is already in the visiting room, waiting for you," Rita said. "I think he's setting up his movie camera." She shook her head.

"The movie wasn't my idea."

"I know that. Nobody's accusing you of coming up with that nutty idea."

"But the other nutty ideas?" I said. We had stopped to face each other in front of a locked steel door.

"It's not my place to say what's nutty and what's not, least of all with a preacher. And anyway, I'm not even sure I *know* your idea. I see a lot of faces go by in this place, and when I see you, I don't know if I'm seeing religious or just clever."

"I'm anything but clever," I protested.

"Maybe it's your cleverness that says so. To tell the truth, I ain't so sure that you haven't arranged this whole business just to get a pop at Lennie's bad old head."

"I assure you—" I said, my voice quavering now.

"You don't have to assure me of nothing! I don't care if you kill the motherfucker dead. I'm just telling you, if you go to stomp him, you better be fast and you better do it with all you got. 'Cause when they pull you off him, you're out of here and you're not coming back no more. And I will say this, too. If you're not fixing to slam his head, I expect pretty soon you'll be raising your hand to your own. You're playing with fire, Reverend, and there's some kinds of fire even cleverness don't protect you from."

"The Lord is my protection," I said.

"I hope he is," she said, and opened the door.

Leonard was again manacled to a chair. There were three guards in the room this time, all of them white men. I wondered if Leonard had gotten his demand. In contrast to his jocular greeting last time, he did noth-

141

ing but nod when Rita brought me into the room. He seemed tense. He flexed and unflexed his bare arms, bending his head to scratch at them with his shaved chin. For some reason he had worn a long-sleeved shirt at our first meeting, though the weather was warmer then; today he was in a white T-shirt, and I saw again his two tattoos, the scorpion and the naked woman. The hair on her head and pubis was red, not blond like Leonard's, or my wife's. I was rescued from the chill that passed over me by Roth, who came out from behind his camera, where he had been standing with two crewmen, and shook my hand.

"We're just about ready," he said. "How are you?"

"Just fine," I said.

He introduced me to his assistants, two earnest, well-groomed younger men, and sat me in a chair facing Leonard. For a few minutes we said nothing, though Leonard kept his cold stare on me as he flexed and scratched. Only once did he glance in the direction of the camera.

"I brought you some cigarettes," I said after a few moments.

He raised his chin and grimaced slightly to indicate that he hadn't heard me. I think, now, that he merely wanted to make me repeat myself. I had spoken loudly enough.

"I brought you some cigarettes," I said again, in what I thought was the same volume. "Marlboros. I believe those are the ones you smoke."

"Those are the ones I smoke because those are the only fucking kind I can get in this place. They buy the kind the guards like so they can be snitching all they want, and the majority of the guards who aren't spics or coons are a bunch of rednecks, present company excluded, so that means Marlboros, which are the next best thing after shit. There's only one decent cigarette, and that's a Camel."

"Next time I'll try to get some Camels."

"Well, try to get them in the soft pack. The hard packs are for hard-ons. I like the soft packs." He winked. "They remind me of women. Hey, Spielberg," he called out, "how come you ain't got no fucking girls on your film crew there? What are you, a male chauvinist pig or something? What do I want to see these fag-boys for? I see all of that I want in this place."

Roth answered while squinting into his camera.

"We do have women working on the film, but the powers that be will not allow any women inside to do the filming."

"Sons of a bitch!" Leonard shouted. "Stupid ass sons of a bitch," he whispered to me. "Can you believe it?"

"I can believe almost anything," I said.

"All right, we're ready," Roth called.

One of his assistants stepped forward with a clapper board and held it before the camera. "*Love Your Enemy*, September twenty-first, take one," he said.

Leonard immediately locked eyes with me,

flexing both his arms. He inhaled and was silent.

"You can begin your visit," Roth said.

We were both silent.

"How are you today?" I said at last.

"Not too bad, how are you?" said Leonard.

"Okay. It's getting cooler out—feels like fall."

More silence.

Roth stepped out from behind the camera and stood just back and to the side of its vision. "I was thinking you two could talk a little about your backgrounds. You do have some things in common, after all."

"Yeah, I guess we do," said Leonard, smiling for the first time. I'm sure he glanced deliberately at the naked woman tattooed on his arm.

"Reverend Pierce is a clergyman, and you were the son of a clergyman, I understand. Isn't that true?"

"Am the son," Leonard corrected. "My daddy's still alive. Dear old Daddy. Probably still preaching, too."

"Well, why don't you talk a little about that? Do you remember anything from your upbringing? From being brought up as a minister's son?"

"I remember more than I want to remember."

"Can you tell us about that? Was your father an ordained minister? Had he gone to school for it and all?"

"Yeah, he was an ordained minister. He was a big-deal minister. His church was bigger than yours!" he said to me.

I nodded my acknowledgment. I even smiled at the familiar comparison: the vicarious, euphemistic way in which clergymen boast of their penis sizes.

"His must have been four times the size of yours. On Sundays the parking lot outside looked like Willowbrook Mall. He packed them in by the hundreds."

"What do you remember about those days? Was your father always a minister? Talk a little about that," Roth said.

"I could talk all day about that."

"Maybe we'll talk all day. Go on."

"I remember all kinds of stuff. What, do you want me to write a fucking encyclopedia? It's all in my head, still. The hymns, the scripture verses, salvation, sanctification, what we must do to be saved, all that shit. I bet I could get dressed up like you and go to your church and stand up there and carry on and nobody'd even know the difference. You think I couldn't do that?"

"You probably could," I said.

"What's the shortest verse in the Bible?" he challenged. "What's the shortest verse?"

"I'm not sure I know."

"You're kidding. You're a minister and you don't know that? Go on and guess if you don't know. Come on, guess." Then he shouted, "Guess, for Christ's sake!"

I was on the verge of shouting back, "Don't scream orders at me," but instead I took a deep breath and spread out my hands and shrugged. "I don't know. 'Behold,' maybe."

"Behold, maybe," he repeated in disgust. "See, he doesn't know. He's a fucking minister

145

collecting a salary and he doesn't know the shortest verse in the Bible. And it's not his fault," he said, appealing to the camera. He pulled himself up in his chair. He was growing more relaxed and more important.

"It's education. They don't teach nobody nothing anymore. People go to school, and they come out, and nobody knows the tools of the trade. That's why this country's in the mess it's in. You got carpenters who can't read a ruler and ministers who haven't been taught the Bible. You see it around here. Like now, they're saying we got racial tensions at the prison and they're using that as an excuse to hassle everybody and shake 'em down every two fucking seconds. Racial tensions! Yeah, we got racial tensions. What we've got is racial *people* who get jobs here and get paid—what is it you guys are making now? Fifteen bucks an hour? Twenty bucks an hour? And these people can't even spell or add or fucking multiply and divide or anything. Never mind knowing the first goddamn thing about being corrections officers. And they have to hire them because they're black and they have to pay them the same thing as these guys here, whether they know as much or not, because the law says you can't discriminate. It's bullshit."

He stopped talking. In a moment it dawned on him that he had lost his train of thought. I cued him, to avoid having to talk myself.

"So what's the shortest verse in the Bible?" I asked.

"'Jesus wept,'" he taunted. At first I thought

146

this was some fundamentalist way of saying, "Wouldn't you like to know?" or "Read 'em and weep," but he followed it with "John 11:35" and I realized this was the verse.

"Go ahead and look it up if you don't believe me," he said. "You got your Bible. John 11:35."

"I believe you."

"Look it up. Go on."

I sighed and looked it up.

"You're right," I said.

"What does it say? Read it." He was relentless.

"'Jesus began to weep.'"

"No, it's not 'Jesus began to weep'! It's 'Jesus wept.' Jesus wept. Only two words. What kind of a fucking Bible is that?"

"I guess it's a newer translation," I offered.

"Well, the answer is 'Jesus wept.' In the *real* Bible. In the regular Bible, that's what it says. Never mind the translation. Christ, now they have to translate the Bible or people won't be able to read it. Soon there won't even be Christians anymore because people won't be able to read the signs to tell them where the fucking churches are."

"What was your father's religious affiliation?" asked Roth, by way of redirecting the monologue. "What kind of a minister was he? Methodist, or Lutheran, or—"

"He was a Baptist."

"Uh-huh. And that was the faith you were baptized into as a child?"

"I never was baptized. I ran away from home before they could do it to me."

Roth seemed puzzled by this.

"You were older, then. So you hadn't been baptized as a child?"

"No, I hadn't. Baptists don't baptize children. You get baptized as an adult. That's why they're called Baptists. *You* know *that*, don't you?" he said to me.

"Yes."

"*Everybody* knows that. How come you don't know that? What, are you a Jew or something?" he asked. "You're a Jew, aren't you?"

"Well, not an observant Jew."

"But you're a Jew."

"Yes, I'm a Jew."

"I could tell by looking at him. After a while you can just tell. Well, Mr. Spielberg, there's something you didn't learn in Jew school. Baptists don't get baptized until they're adults. Now let's see if the reverend here can tell us why. You know why?"

"Because that's the age when a person is able to make the decision on his own." I was immediately disgusted with myself for attempting to have his approval. No matter, the answer was incomplete.

"Yeah, that's part of it, but there's a lot more to it than that. The first Christians only baptized adults. That's in the Bible too, unless your new translation fucked it up somehow. When Jesus was baptized, was he a baby or a man? You don't remember anything about John the Baptist showing up with the Wise Men and baptizing the Baby Jesus, do you?"

"No, I don't."

"Goddamn right, you don't. He was baptized as an adult."

And Leonard went on. After a little more sacramental theology, he entertained us with anecdotes from his religious upbringing, all of them variations on the story of the boy Christ in the temple, amazing his elders, with Leonard himself cast in the role of the precocious messianic child. He did not mention anything about his having been molested, though the word "abuse" came up at least once. I may have missed some of what he said, for to tell the truth I was distracted now and then, not by boredom, but by noting to myself the utterly outrageous nature of the exchange. He talked on about this and that, demanding responses from me when they were of service to his discourse, as if I were anyone else but the man whose wife and son he had slaughtered. It was as if we were neighbors, and he had once borrowed and forgotten to return a rake, but that was all in the past now. I cannot think of a more absurd, face-to-face in my whole life. He was more credible as an intruder in my house. At least then he knew he was outrageous.

And yet, on the other hand, our meeting was reminiscent of so many other times in my life when I'd been guest or host to a tedious, tactless man who talked on and on about himself and his opinions—one of those obtuse fellows whose greatest virtue is to be able to insult you repeatedly without meaning any harm. Later in the evening I'd be huffing and

149

pulling off my trousers when Cynthia, always more tolerant than I, always more capable of seeing the comedy than I, would lean across our bed and tease: "You two were having quite the little conversation tonight, weren't you?"

"Conversation!" I'd spout, to her great delight. "All he did for the whole frigging night was talk about himself. He didn't need a guest, he needed a tape recorder. I could have murdered him!"

How long ago that seems, and how carelessly I had spoken of murder then.

4 ✦

Dear Asshole,

I've been following your goings-on for awhile now and thought I'd write you a letter mainly to ask what the *Fuck* are you doing?!? The Golden Rule and all that is fine in its place but what your doing is sick, at least it makes me sick.

And now they want to make a movie about it? Give me a break!

I say I treat people the way they treat me. Your nice to me I'm nice to you. You fuck with me I fuck with you. You fuck around with my wife and kids and I'll eat your guts with your tongue for a pickle.

You know what I'd do if I were you and I could get close to Alex Leonard? I'd sell my house, my vehicles, everything I had just to bribe people to let me alone with him for ten minutes. That's all I'd need. I'd knock him out with a can of Mace. Then I'd tie him up. Then I'd wake him up. Then I'd pop out his eyes. Then I'd cut off his balls. Then I'd put one of his nuts into each drooly eye socket. Then I'd cut off his cock and stick it half hanging out of his mouth. Then I'd chop off two of his fingers and stuff one into each nostril of his nose. The Elephant Man. Then I'd walk out and treat myself to a big lunch.

Oh, first I'd ring an alarm or call the prison from a phone booth so they'd send a doctor and keep him from bleeding to death. I'd hate to have him die in his condition.

You know what I think? I think your the kind who feels so pathetic and guilty all the time that they want to suffer. You know what else I think? I think the only thing that'd make you any more satisfied than you are now is if Leonard had been a big black nigger and fucked your wife with his big black cock and then done the same to you.

They just had one of them over here who got a hold of a 16 year old girl. They don't just do it in the pussy anymore. Now its got to be in their mouths and up the ass too. Maybe if they catch the coon and you get a few free minutes you can come over and love him too.

Like the last president said, "Read my lips" ...

FUCK YOU!!!

151

This is an example of the kind of person who will want to canonize me if I succeed in killing Alex Leonard. I suspect the only threat he'd prove capable of carrying out is that of eating the big lunch. Asshole indeed.

I have not bothered to check my mailbox over at the church for quite a while. There has never been much but junk in it. Today I found it full to bursting, like the Apostle Peter's miraculous netful of fish. It seems I am becoming a celebrity.

Most of the letters were not in the "Dear Asshole" category, though there were a handful of those. For example, these closing paragraphs of a two-and-a-half-page, single-spaced, unsigned letter written entirely in Bible verses:

"The beloved of the Lord shall dwell in SAFETY" (Deut. 33:12).

"Thus saith the Lord, Behold, I will raise up evil against thee out of thine own house, and I will take thy wives before thine eyes, and give them unto thy neighbor, and he shall lie with thy wives in the sight of this sun" (II Sam. 12:11).

"Happy shall he be, that taketh and dasheth thy little ones against the stones" (Psalm 137:9).

"Remember, I pray thee, who ever perished, being innocent? or where were the righteous cut off? Even as I have seen, they that plow iniquity, and sow wickedness, reap the same" (Job 4:7 8).

"SIN NO MORE, LEST A WORSE THING COME UNTO THEE" (John 5:14).

For those who prefer their venom dripping from the secular tine of the Serpent's fork, here is a pithy summary of my shortcomings from a Ms. Astoreth Baker, who is also kind enough to provide her E-mail (but not her street) address, presumably because I cannot hurl my reply in the form of a brick through the screen of her computer.

Implicit in your attempt to "love" Alex Leonard, couched as it is in the language system of patriarchal religion, are several assumptions that I find completely offensive:

1.—that the victims of his crimes somehow belong to you, i.e., are *your* "wife" and "son," and thus that the crimes against them were primarily crimes against yourself;

2.—that as an adult white male you are somehow not implicated in these crimes, rather than being a co-perpetrator because of a co-beneficiary of terrorism against women and children;

3.—that crimes against women and children boil down to a matter best "settled" between men;

4.—that you (or anyone else) is entitled to forgive an offense that you (s/he) did not suffer (even if "innocent," cf. point 2 above).

On the subject of my "innocence," someone has sent me this clipping of an editorial from the *Great Falls County News,* the same paper that printed the first story of my request to see Alex Leonard:

GUILTY OR INNOCENT

It was the great English writer George Orwell who said, "All saints are guilty until proven innocent." He was writing about the Indian prophet of nonviolence, Mahatma Gandhi.

It seems we may have the makings of another Gandhi in our midst, in the person of Rev. Alson Pierce. The minister suffered an unspeakable tragedy in the rape-murder of his wife and the murder of his four-year-old son. He was tied up in another room when it all happened, and it's likely that the last sounds he heard before he himself was kicked into unconsciousness were the mortal screams of his family.

Now Pierce has embarked on a personal crusade to "love his enemy," the murderer Alex Leonard, who is serving a double life sentence.

And just lately we hear that all of this is going to be made into a full-length documentary movie.

It's here that the Orwell quote about saints springs to mind. Certainly Rev. Pierce qualifies, in appearances and according to the best Judeo-Christian principles, as a saint. He seems bound and determined to follow up an unimaginable crime with an unimaginable act of forgiveness.

Nevertheless, under the circumstances, the skeptic in us has to ask if what we are about to see is the supreme act of compassion or the supreme act of egotism. Will we be watching a philanthropist seeking to build a better world, or just another hustler seeking his fifteen minutes of fame?

Maybe all we'll be seeing is a terribly wounded man trying to fight his way out of a personal hell. And maybe, as with the rest of us, Rev. Pierce's motives are not so easily sorted out or so simply judged.

Whatever the case, the scenario that follows, on screen or off, promises to be of interest. Along with Orwell's dictum on Gandhi, we recall Lincoln's words at Gettysburg, the battlefield of a "great civil war, testing whether our nation, or any nation...can long endure."

We, too, are engaged in a great war of civil violence. It is being waged mercilessly on our streets, in our schools, and in our houses. Perhaps in the personal battlefield of Rev. Pierce we will find some way to peace for our own.

Don't count on it. What makes me curious about the clipping, which was by itself in an envelope with no return address, is that it is likely to have come from someone who knows me quite well. Who else would assume I had not seen an editorial in the newspaper that everyone in this area reads, except someone who knows I do not read a newspaper? The likeliest candidates are Andrew and Ellen Fabian, but I have a letter from each of them as well.

Andrew wrote via my P.O. box to tell me he is terminating his role as my spiritual director, an announcement he views as "no more than a formality in light of your recent actions." He is correct. "I must tell you, Alson," he says, "that however admirable your objectives, I sense you are in great peril. There is 'something missing' in your plan and in your own brief descriptions of it. I can't be more precise than that, I'm afraid. But when I reach out and rap my hand on this Leonard business, I find it firm but somewhat hollow. Can it be that the missing core is nothing more or less than those persons whose loss you've not allowed yourself to grieve sufficiently?"

He closes, "I'm not telling you to stay away from me. If anything, I want you to come by more often. But don't come as my directee, come as my friend."

Ellen Fabian also offers me her friendship—in "whatever form" I'll take it. For years, as a pastor, I had marveled at the kind of losers who seemed to exert an irresistible attraction for a certain kind of woman. Now I wake up to find that I have become one of those men.

Dear Alson,

I want to apologize for my behavior at your house a few weeks ago. It has taken me this long to write because I felt so ashamed. I still do.

I have to say that I was not just "coming on" to you. I would be a liar and I'd be taking you for a fool if I tried to deny that I was making you an offer of physical intimacy, but what I was really trying to offer you was my friendship in whatever form you could or would take it. Didn't you once say in a sermon that the Word became flesh because we wouldn't be capable of understanding it otherwise? So my words were ready to become flesh, and the words were, "I care about you."

You mentioned that you have another woman in your life—that's your business if you do—but I think maybe I was too slow to understand what you were really trying to say. If you meant that the memory of your wife is still very much with you, then I want you to know that I take that as a given. How could it be otherwise?

Alson, again I say I'm sorry. But don't shut me out of your life just because I goofed. If you can forgive a cruel murderer, can't you also forgive a well-meaning woman who's never been very good at looking before she leaps?

Maybe the newspaper clipping did not come from either of them. If it did, what was the intent if not to encourage me (probably Ellen) or to call me to my senses without openly criticizing me (possibly Andrew)? Hardly a malignant intent in either case.

As for the question posed in the editorial, the majority of my correspondents are inclined to turn in a verdict of innocent. For them, I am unquestionably a genuine saint. Leonard was right to speak of such people as "fans." Their letters are too embarrassing to copy down—but I'm not being honest. The truth is they are too *painful* to copy down because in their assertions that I am "a true disciple of Christ," "an inspiration to the country," "a role model for our troubled youth," and all the rest, they convict me as a blasphemer and a hypocrite.

But am I a hypocrite? Does a hypocrite yearn to be exposed? Is he even aware that he deserves exposure? I will utterly rejoice in the revelation that turns every appraisal of me upside down, that catches my judges in their own smug judgments, that makes every mouth gape.

Perhaps the only person in twenty-eight letters whose mouth I do not want to see gaping, and who may, of all my correspondents, think to pray for mercy on my soul, is this one. Hers is also the only letter that moves me.

Dear Rev. Pierce,
It's probably silly of me to send you this letter, but I've been thinking about you constantly and I feel I need to get some of those thoughts off my chest. Actually it was my husband who suggested that I try the letter. He is the most understanding man I have ever known, and I don't know what I would do without him.

I have been married to this same wonderful man for 23 years. We have two sons and a daughter, ages 18, 15 and 11. I am what they used to call a housewife and now call a "homemaker," and I'm not ashamed to say so. When people ask me if I work, I always say, "Yes, I have five jobs," that's one for every member of my family, and I don't forget to count myself. I have built my whole life around the people I love.

I also consider myself a Christian, and I try to practice my religion. We all attend church regularly. Bob, my husband, has put in many hours restoring the church building, and I have taught Sunday school for eight years on and off. Our oldest two are in Youth Group, and I expect the youngest to join in another year or two, when she's old enough.

I guess all I'm trying to say is that we're people who try to take our faith seriously.

So you're probably asking what any of this has to do with you. Since reading about your awful tragedy, and lately about your "turn the other cheek" approach to Alex Leonard, I have begun to wonder if I am a Christian at all. I try to forgive people who snub me or who are rude in traffic and things like that. Once I even forced myself to pray for a supervisor at my husband's place of employment who was giving him a hard time. Believe me, it took every ounce of strength I had!

I cannot even imagine myself suffering a loss like yours, but if such a thing ever happened, I know I couldn't love the person responsible. I'd kill another human being to protect my children, or my husband. Yet you're doing what Jesus said, to love our enemies. I just keep asking how could Jesus let such awful things happen, and then how could he ask us to do such an unnatural thing? I can almost accept the first better than the second. We can't know why

God does the things he does. But we can know what's inside us, and when I look inside, I find that I just don't have what it takes.

So I begin to doubt if I really believe in the religion I say I do.

Maybe this whole thing wouldn't weigh on me so much if I didn't feel like I knew you somewhat. I once heard you preach during an ecumenical service at your church. I wouldn't expect you to remember me, except that you just might because I have one eye that is slightly lower in my face than the other—the result of a car accident when I was a child. (Yes, years later, I was able to forgive the drunken driver who disfigured me.) Anyway, I'm sorry to say I don't remember much of your sermon, though I do remember it was about God loving the Church like a faithful spouse (that stuck with me for obvious reasons, I guess), and I remember how you said that heaven would be like their honeymoon by the seashore.

What I remember most of all is seeing your wife and son. He was just a baby then, and she nursed him during the service, and I remember how much I admired her for doing that in church, even though she had a blanket and was covered up. She was so beautiful. Because I'm not very attractive (though Bob happily disagrees), I'm afraid I've always been envious of very beautiful women, but your wife had something about her that almost made *me* feel beautiful. There wasn't *room* to be envious. She sat right up in front, and she looked straight up at you so confidently, with your son at her breast. I noticed that every so often when you were preaching you looked down at them, and you couldn't help smiling. Who could blame you? I thought to myself, what a wonderful thing it must be to preach the Word of God from up in the pulpit and to be able to look down at your lovely family and feel all the love you had for them as the words came out of your mouth.

I am not trying to hurt you with a painful memory. It's just that it is *my* painful memory, too. I'm in tears as I write this. When I think that they're gone, I want to kill, not love. I can't even think so far as to ask, "What if they were mine?"

I don't know if I'm in awe of you or angry at you or a little of both. I just know you're a better Christian than I am, and that you're trying to do what must be one of the hardest things a person could do. I will pray for you. Pray for me, that I'll have some of your faith but that I won't ever have to use it the same way.

Sincerely,
Sandra Veenstra

I think Sandra is telling the truth when she says, "I am not trying to hurt you with a painful memory." But how can such a memory not be painful?

I have had many like this one come washing over me lately, even before I read her letter. For a long time, I fought to suppress any memory or mention of my wife and son. Andrew is correct in saying that I have not allowed myself to "grieve sufficiently" over their loss. My refusal to do so is not the "hollow core" of my resolution to kill Leonard; it's the living heart of it. Without it I would crumble in a heap. Anyway, how could I ever "grieve sufficiently" for what I have lost? There is no sufficiency.

The memories do come back, stronger now that I am within reach of my goal. Looking at Leonard, seeing him in the vulnerable flesh, I can allow myself to look at Cynthia and Jimmy once again. Yes, Sandra, I remember her suckling him in that pew. I remember the honeymoon by the sea, which inspired that parable I told in my sermon, though like many inspirations it developed over time. Years later, when Jimmy was two, I wrote to Andrew late one afternoon in Maine, as my wife and son lay napping on the bed behind me, how I had glimpsed heaven in the vision of their living bodies on the windy northern seashore. I wonder if he still has the letter. I remember it as the truest thing I ever wrote, though I have forgotten most of what I said— a good thing, too, for its words would only mock me now.

My son is harder to remember than my wife. His mere four years are not the only reason. I took too little time for him. If any thought pains me after the thought of his and his mother's deaths, it is the scant attention I paid to him in his life. Oh, I affected all the mannerisms of the "new" father; I gave him quality time, I even gave him baths. But I was never fully *with* him, as I was with Cindy,

162

as she was with us both. He was a beloved little face floating like the sun on my horizon. I rejoiced in his warmth, I noted his rising and setting every day, but I did my business in his presence and gave him too little thought.

Nevertheless, I can recall his bare arms on the kitchen table, and his head resting on his shoulder, as his dollop of hand worked back and forth, coloring the world green and blue. I can still feel the weight of his sleeping body in my arms—I know that weight with the same precise certainty as a mason who's laid walls all his life knows the weight of a brick. I can see his legs running through grass or over sand, slower than a dog's legs or a seagull's flight, but faster than all my worries and warnings. I can hear all of his cries, the squeal of delight, the screech of protest at finding the limits of his will and the borders of his curiosity once again defined by a parent's fears, and the vague shriek of a terror without words.

I can see his stomach muscles flexing and relaxing above his submerged bathing trunks because he is attempting to pee underwater— we have told him, "There's no bathroom here, just pee in the water." And on his face is an expression of anxiety, because not having learned the subterfuges of an adult, he doesn't understand how no one else can know he's peeing if he knows, and he is embarrassed. What corruptions we make in a child's mind. Who knows but that my own ability to conceal a loaded pistol in a Communion box began a third of a century ago, when my father ordered me to hide my urination in a lake? On what other shore was the seed of evil germinated in a toddling Alex Leonard?

That is right, I can almost pity him—it is another privilege of the violence I have chosen. I can dare to remember my murdered family, and I can dare to pity their killer. I have more fellow feeling for him than for most of those who write to me. There is more genuine compassion in my heart today than in the hearts of those who skimmed the accounts of his atrocities over their morning coffee or who will editorialize on his death for the evening news—more genuine compassion in the toothless, gaping villeins who thronged to watch the brigand broken on the wheel than in our benign indifference, our professed willingness to "live and let live," which is seldom anything more than our cowardly unwillingness to suffer or to die.

Dear God,

I have not spoken to You with any regularity or reverence for a long time. Once in a while, yes, I have cried out almost in spite of myself, and I have always been surprised at my doing so, and at my palpable sense that You were listening. I suppose I have lost none of my faith in Your existence. In a strange way, the horrors I have known have strengthened rather than weakened that conviction. Somehow the presence of such evil in a world of mere molecules requires an agent both absolute and metaphysical. I don't say it requires a devil. But I believe You exist beyond a doubt.

All the rest, as You know, I do doubt.

It seems strange, too, that in this letter and in my ejaculations from time to time, I should have called upon You, "The Father," and not Your Son, who is a man like me and who suffered. But if he is not also God like You, then how can his sufferings connect me to You, or You to my sufferings?

I guess that in some subtle ways I have ingested the essentials of modern Christology, which is to say, I have pulled down Christ from the right hand of God with the dusty right hand of historical scholarship. If I could bring myself to admit it, I am probably an Arian, like Andrew and the rest of the pros. I do still think of Jesus as a provisional savior, but as the Incarnate Word of God to which Ellen alludes in her letter, "begotten before all worlds," co-equal with the Father and the Holy Spirit—I doubt him. That is the point where the rest unravels.

It then becomes impossible to believe that the Godhead has truly fathomed human pain, that my crucifixion in my dining room chair is connected to Christ's crucifixion in any way other than by intellectual analogy to the greater agonies of a better man. He got his, I got mine. Never mind any hope of triumphing over that pain in resurrection.

It also becomes impossible not to regard his teachings in the Sermon on the Mount as less than absolutely binding. "Love your enemies," he commands, but as who? The Son of God, or a first century Palestinian cult figure with an intriguing social program? And the fact that he was unmarried and childless (funny how we retain that orthodoxy after we've shucked off the others) doesn't help my faltering devotion.

So the Incarnation and the Trinity are important, I see—Father, Son, and Holy Spirit bound together as One Creator, and bound by grace and glorified protoplasm to the whole suffering creation. When you're young, you wonder why all of that complex architecture is necessary to house the mystery of faith. Then at last you comprehend the whole interlocking edifice—usually after yanking out a block that can never be returned to its essential place.

I don't know why I should be starting out this way. I suppose it's not unlike an estranged husband and wife meeting again after a year of separation and discussing the condition of their driveway. They talk about the house, not the longing and the bitterness that consume them, not the grim, irrevocable news that one has brought home to announce to the other.

I got the idea for writing to You when I went to hoe out the last two weeks' mail from the cardboard box the church has set aside for me in the office, and found all these letters. There were twenty-eight in all. I found myself wanting to read them out loud to You, to someone.

It's fun (a word that now seems as strange and remote as Your name) to imagine a whole sack of letters delivered after the killing of Alex Leonard. Don't many of them ask why? Don't they ask what good it was, seeing I could not bring my family back by destroying him? Wouldn't Cynthia, ever clearheaded and practical, have asked the same thing? Do I hear You asking it?

Somewhere deep down in myself, in a place You must know or else You are not God, I still believe You are ultimately good and I am ultimately mistaken. But to act on that requires faith, and can't You see how and why the little faith I had has been taken from me? First, it was choked by a comfortable life, in which I came to see Providence as nothing more extraordinary than a dinner out once a week, and by a professional ministry, in which I soon forgot to seek Your will because I was automatically and universally assumed to be doing it. What little faith I had was then utterly annihilated along with my comfortable life and my ministry and the lives of the only two people I ever really loved. What is there now?

All that I have left is determination. And I am determined that Alex Leonard know me, that I force that knowledge on him as he forced carnal knowledge from my wife, and that he die in the revelation of that knowledge.

That is all I have—all I *am*. I am no less in Your hands than I ever was before, but what I am is nothing more than this.

I want You to know that it was not my original intention to smuggle the gun into the prison in a Communion box. (Of course, I still might not succeed in doing so.) I had never been sure how I would do that; the first objective was simply to get in. The metal detector sounding off was serendipitous. Perhaps unconsciously I had already decided on such a ruse; it strikes me as peculiar that I should have brought the box that day—I think I told myself it improved my disguise—or that I was so insistent on keeping it with me when the issue came up. I can't pretend to know the mind of Alson Pierce any more than I can claim to know the mind of God.

No doubt all the saints in heaven will nod knowingly like students in a freshman English seminar at the deeply symbolic fact that I cannot find a way to fit a concealed handgun in a box of Communion vessels. There is not room for both. I will have to build a larger box. So much for symbols. So much for the saints.

I am truly sorry that this is the way that has presented itself. Though I fully intend to destroy another human life, I would use a different stratagem if I knew of one.

In any case, I promise You that when the time comes to carry my gun into the prison, I will have no bread or wine in the box, only the clean vessels. I will not defile the Body and Blood of Your beloved Son with my instrument of death.

Perhaps then I will in some small way have "loved my enemy" and been authentic in my disguise. For I will have shown You a favor, my dear estranged Lord, that You would not show to me.

Yours forever,
Alson Pierce

5

This time the church windows were ablaze with autumn scenes and colors. The sun shone through the crimson and mahogany glass as through the leaves of an ancient oak on a late afternoon in October. Some of the windows actually had pieces of leaf-shaped glass leaded together in motley clusters around the heads and bodies of the saints. Standing against such a background of foliage the Virgin Mary held a cornucopia of grapes and wheat, its sharp end pressed like a doctor's stethoscope to her womb. Beside her, in another window, a pilgrim husband and wife walked home from a tiny log church on the horizon above their heads. The woman cradled a nursing infant in her arms—a glass fragment of her breast was luminously visible in her dark gray dress—and her smiling husband carried a black blunderbuss on one of his broad shoulders.

In the next window a man in a powdered wig and tricorn hat stood holding a long, slender cross with a Revolutionary flag fastened under its horizontal piece—a coiled serpent and the motto "Don't Tread on Me." By the silver pistol held flat in the outstretched palm of his other hand, I recognized the man as Alexander Hamilton, shot down in a duel with Aaron Burr. I had played the part of this native son of New Jersey in a school pageant more than twenty years ago.

I felt as though I could have spent forever looking at those windows, which filled me with a sense of security and nostalgia. But as I leaned toward the Tiffany images of turkeys, pumpkins, and even ghosts farther down the wall, I became conscious of the voice of my wife calling my name. When I turned to her face, veiled for our wedding, I could tell she was distressed.

"Yes?" I said.

"The ring," she said.

"Alson, the ring," repeated the minister. His voice, too, was familiar, and I looked up to see Andrew Nelson, my former spiritual guide, ready as ever to identify himself as Cynthia's ally.

I looked down to thigh level to find our son, but I could not see him. I grew alarmed.

"Where's Jimmy?" I said. Maybe he'd gone to get the rings, or had sat down in one of the pews because his feet were tired. His absence was intolerably painful.

"He's all right. He's all right," Cynthia said softly. "He's over there, playing in the leaves."

I looked over toward the windows and saw his two-dimensional image spring out of a mound of scarlet glass leaves. The red shapes fell from his hands back to the pile with the sound of wind chimes gone mad.

"You're the one who's always saying he hasn't been born yet, right? Right, honey?" she said.

"The ring," Andrew said again.

"The ring," I said, turning slightly toward my best man.

"Never mind the ring. Did you bring my fucking Camels?"

I lifted my head to look into the sneering face of Alex Leonard. At the same time, the congregation at our backs began to laugh. I knew, the way one knows in dreams, that they were laughing because they felt Leonard was a wonderfully entertaining figure.

"What can you expect?" he said, addressing his audience. "The guy doesn't even know the shortest verse in the Bible."

"Oh, he knows that," I heard Cynthia say, but when I turned back to face her, the look in her eyes said, "You do know, don't you, Alson? Because if you've forgotten the ring and the verse..."

"We are lost." My mind finished her thought.

"No cigs, no wife," Leonard said, and whisked her up in his arms like a groom about to carry her over the threshold.

He stepped forward to the altar and "dipped" his partner, rapping her head hard on the wooden table like a gavel. Then, with a gleeful whoop, he began running up and down the aisles with my bride in his arms. Her face was turned in toward his shoulder and covered by her veil—I could not see it. But in one of the windows in front of me I could see Jimmy standing frozen, a look of horror on his face. "Momma!" he cried, and pressed his hands against the world of glass in which he was caught. Blood began to run down the panes from his hands.

"Jimmy," I called out, "don't touch the glass, Jimmy. Someone get him away from the glass!"

No one seemed to hear me, or to notice my son. All of them were seized with delight at Leonard's antics. I saw Cindy's parents, my mother, Leonard's girl Monica Zeller, the people at the prison, Amazo and Rita, Mrs. Cohen and Dr. Michelowsky, my parishioners—and all of them kept saying, "He just loves this guy. He loves that Lennie. That's why he's the best man."

Standing in a front corner of the nave, dressed in a black tuxedo, Roth, the film-maker, panned the scene with a video camera.

Then Ellen Fabian rose indignantly from her pew and went over to Jimmy's window, miraculously taking him out of the glass and into her arms. I turned to where Leonard stood, still clutching my bride. He half crouched in the center aisle, ready to spring. Cynthia's long veil was wrapped wildly around his arms and legs. He glanced back and forth melodramatically, raising the volume of laughter in the church, then shot me a look of daring. He bounded toward the door, and I followed.

Outside, I was met with the same pitch blackness and pelting rain as in my previous dream. I did not see Leonard or his captive.

Then a hand pressed my arm, and I was fixed by the sober gaze of Alexander Hamilton.

"I've waited for you," he said. "Take this and do not let go of it, no matter what happens."

He pressed the pistol into my hand. My fingers closed around it just as my eyes opened to the dawn.

It is remarkable how very little physical evidence I have that Cynthia or Jimmy ever existed. On a morning like this, after a night like the last one, I wish I had more. But all I have are several photographs, books inscribed to me from Cindy, a few other gifts, my wedding ring, and a handful of Jimmy's drawings that I'd stuck into various books. I find myself envious of those who lived when it was the custom to keep a lock of a loved one's hair. Actually, I think Cindy kept a few locks from Jimmy's first haircut. But I'm sure they're gone now.

When I was still in the hospital, her father had come to see me. He only came once, and he did not stay long, though I imagine they were permitting me to have only brief visits then. He wouldn't have stayed long, in any case. I remember how changed he looked, how feeble and formal he seemed, this man who had always prided himself on being the life of every get-together. He stood stiffly beside my bed, like the Ghost of Christmas Past in a wrinkled golf shirt. I remember a nurse on the other side of my bed, holding my hand. "Cindy's mother has taken this very hard," he was saying. "She's on heavy medication. I'm not sure she'll ever be right. For her sake, I really think it's for the best that you and I say good-bye now. I know this must sound very cold, but we need to get some distance from this—I do, too—and that means a clean break in your case."

"I understand," I had said. His altered appearance and demeanor had the effect of distracting me from the full import of what he or I was actually saying.

"I am willing, if you wish, to go over to the house and go through Cindy and little Jim's things. That's going to be tough for anybody to do, but it has to be done, and the sooner the better. It has to be soon if you want me to help. Ruth and I may be moving soon—got to get away from here. I doubt you're up to it. You weren't up to the funeral, so I'm sure you're not up for this."

"You're kind," I said, but what I'd really wanted to say was, Why are you so resentful of me? Are there any two men on God's earth who have more in common than we do now?

"Naturally there are a few keepsakes that Ruth and I would like to have. I can let you know what they are, in case you have any problems with any of it."

"I'll have no problems. Keep whatever you'd like. Give the clothes away." His promised abandonment had made me bitter. "Clear the place out. I don't care."

I did not expect to be taken so literally. The first thing that caught my eye, as I walked through the front door of the parsonage, was the empty banister columns at the foot of the stairway in our hall. Two painted wooden soldiers had kept watch there since Jimmy was three years old. Cindy's parents had sent them for his birthday, a sly grandparental challenge to his parents' prohibition of war toys. He wanted anyone coming through the front door to say hello to his soldiers, and he was as delighted on the hundredth day that someone did so as he had been on the first. Lately he had got it in his head that there ought to be a password. You had to confess to not knowing it, which would also delight him, and then he'd whisper it loudly in your ear— a daily inventory of an item on his mind. "Pasghetti," if that was for supper. "Ghosts," if it was close to Halloween. "Dead," he had said one day. No, not Dad, dead.

"I see they took away the soldiers," I said to Andrew, who had also had occasion to greet them on his visits. He had come with me to open the house, a precaution because of my "weakened state."

"I didn't take them," he said.

Surely someone had hoped to spare me such a poignant reminder of my loss. I did not want to be spared. After all, I had already resolved to buy a gun. I wanted to see the soldiers, wanted to take each of them in my hands and whisper "dead" in their faces. I also wanted to exhibit my returning strength to Andrew and probably to myself. It was I who had insisted on coming here. So I headed straight to Jimmy's room.

It was empty. Stripped bare. I threw open his closet door—the same.

"Where the hell is his stuff?" I said.

"I have no idea," Andrew said. "Really," he added when I glared in his face.

I walked to our bedroom. I had planned to delay going there for a while; I had planned to have Andrew gather up a few of my things from the dresser to take to my rented house. But now curiosity and outrage had gotten the better of my squeamishness. I passed through the dining room, where I found all the furniture, all the glasses and plates in the hutch, but most of the photographs gone from the sideboard. Only two remained, one of my parents and the other of myself on the day of my ordination.

I burst into the bedroom, holding my breath like a fireman or a grave robber. The drapes were drawn, the bed stripped. The top of Cynthia's dresser was empty; the top of mine still cluttered. A picture of Cynthia in her wedding dress was still there; so was a picture of baby Jimmy in my arms. Andrew softly called my name as I pulled open her dresser drawers, the doors of the closet, and even looked under her side of the bed to find nothing, not a shoe or a sock, not even those little calico sachets she kept in all her drawers.

I pushed past Andrew and back into the hall, seeing the dining-room chairs and table from the same angle as Leonard had seen them when he turned from the carnage he had made. I drew a deep breath.

"What have they done with all their stuff?" I practically wheezed.

"Alson, please calm down. The police have probably taken some things for evidence."

"Some things? Christ, there's nothing here!"

We were in the dining room now, and I brought my fist down feebly on the table, perhaps as much to make contact with a solid object as to express my anger—my dread.

"Is he out?" I said.

"Is who out?"

"Him, him, for God's sake! Have they let him out already?"

"If you mean Leonard, no. He's in jail, very likely for the rest of his life." He had both of his hands on my shoulders. "Alson, this was a bad idea. I'm very sorry we came. Let's just get out of here now. Please. Then we'll find out where all the stuff went."

"Wait."

I saw the letter on the dining-room hutch. I believe I had even seen it on my way into the bedroom, but had been too preoccupied to take it up. I had probably assumed it to be some busy little message from one of the parish ladies. "We've left some casseroles in the fellowship hall. If you'll preheat oven to 375, etc."

My first name was printed on the sealed envelope. Andrew's hands gradually brought me to sit down as I opened it. I'm sure he did not realize he was making me sit in the place, if not the exact chair, where Leonard had tied me.

I did as we agreed and went through the house thoroughly. I've left you all the photographs of you and Cindy together, all the wedding pictures, and some of little Jim. His are all together on your desk in the den.

I'll store anything that might be of value for ninety days. After that, I'll discard or destroy whatever we don't want. That's about as long as I'll be able to wait because I'll be paying for storage. It's out of the question to keep all that stuff around the house with Ruth in the state she's in. And we will be moving eventually.

I've taken the liberty of writing to your mother in Arizona to see what she might want of Jim's. Her sister has since written back to say that she is not well enough to handle any more upsetment.

I realize this is a hell of a way for us to be saying farewell. Of course there's a lot more we could say, but none of it would do any good, would it? You walk down the aisle with your daughter and you give her away to another man who's supposed to protect her and take care of her the way you did. I'm not saying there's anything you could or should've done that you didn't do, but it's extremely hard for me to accept the fact that my only daughter and little grandson are dead and you managed to stay alive. Something is wrong there, though I'm at a loss to say what it is.

We both have to live with this ugly thing for the rest of our lives. I think it's best we do it in our own ways and out of each other's ways. There's no way to wish you luck, but I wish you well.

C. Vandermeer

I never heard from her parents again. I can imagine what Cornelius must think of me now, in my new role as Leonard's "friend," though I'm sure he'll never tell me so. He was always a man of his word. Good-bye meant good-bye.

It turned out he had both bodies cremated and took the ashes home with him. I do not even have a grave. I just wish I had thought to ask for Jimmy's locks of hair.

It was always a thrill for me to find some trace of their bodies in the house, even to see Jimmy's unflushed stools decomposing in the bottom of the toilet, to say nothing of his eyelashes on my sleeve or a tiny pile of his nail parings left on the arm of the living-room couch. His mother's leavings were more frequent and abundant, mostly strands of her blond hair, lost on a car seat or woven in the bristles of her hairbrush, even caught on the hinges of my glasses or wrapped in the whorls of my pubic beard. Oh, let me have a moment with her away from that man. Let me write about the interest I took in seeing a few jots

179

of blond stubble on the pink plastic razor she left in the soap dish, or how, on one of those occasions when I was an insistent voyeur, she said, "If you have to watch, you might as well check my work," and raised her wet, soapy leg from the tub. For two summers she opted for the latest privilege of a blonde, and let the dusting on her thighs alone. The sight of it growing on her tanned legs so public and so late in our relationship filled me with a lust that was almost like terror.

Why can't I summon that lust now, and chase back the despair that threatens to overwhelm me?

The abrupt, pulsing whistle on the garbage truck sounds, warning children that the driver has just shifted into reverse. Then the truck accelerates as the hydraulic masher shovels the trash into its maw. I just went to the window to see the men work—for some reason, always a calming sight for me—and I noticed that they wore sweaters and denim jackets. I checked the thermometer, and it read forty-eight degrees, the coldest day of the month so far.

I think I'll go to the beach.

The Jersey shore is nothing like my beloved coast of Maine, but the cold day lessened the difference. I'm not sure why I had the impulse to ask Ellen Fabian to come with me, or why I followed that impulse. Perhaps

I needed to assure her that I was certainly as capable of "forgiving" her as I was of "loving" Alex Leonard. More likely, I was responding with unconscious gratitude to her actions in my terrifying dream. I don't think I was afraid to be by myself.

"Yes!" she said on the phone, without hesitating. "I'll bring lunch. And I'll drive if you want."

I said I would drive, mainly because I wanted the option of carting her back home as soon as I'd decided I had made a big mistake.

Ellen had packed a sumptuous lunch in a large open basket covered over with a coarse, tasseled cloth—it looked like something that came off a camel of one of the Three Wise Men. She had apples and bananas, pasta salad, breadsticks, cheese and salsa and tortilla chips and pickles and a bottle of wine. Since we arrived around noon, we began to eat almost at once. We had made our way over the empty boardwalk, past the boarded-up stands, and down the wooden steps to the deep, sandy beach, where cigarette filters are as much a part of the ecosystem as mussel shells and seagull shit. The beach was almost deserted; several young men in black wetsuits were struggling with their surfboards in the distant water. The day was overcast and raw, though on occasion the sun shed some light and warmth on us. We spread out a blanket on the cold sand. Ellen had worn a long, heavy skirt over bare legs and feet—she'd come prepared to wade, I guess. She rolled up her side of the

181

blanket over her toes while I opened the bottle of wine.

What a sight we must have made, this vital Celtic woman in layers of soft denim and dyed wool with a picturesque straw hat tied into her lush hair, and the gaunt figure beside her, in loose gray-black clothes, a tuque pulled over his ears and a threadbare blanket wrapped around his shoulders. I had not even bothered to shave.

"You're the only person I know who likes to go to the beach when it's practically winter," she said, shivering after her first sip of cold wine.

"I haven't been down here in years."

"You picked a wonderful day!"

I didn't respond, so she added, "I'm glad you asked me to come though."

I smiled and reached for a piece of bread, but instead took a piece of cheese. Bread and wine are no longer for me, though I accepted a glass of the latter to be polite. Already the food had gotten gritty from the wind. I washed the sand out of my teeth with a mouthful of wine, so cold and accusing.

The iron-colored ocean swelled and crashed, heavily it seemed, as if the surf were iron in more than its color. The sight of the waves was not as calming as I had hoped. They seemed a sluggish, oppressive parody of the frosty indigo and aqua waves I always tried to picture in my mind—lighter in motion as well as hue. I imagined that all of the ash from all of the cigarettes from all of the filters in the sand around us had been mixed in the brine of this ocean. I imagined small, pale sharks cruising relentlessly over seabeds of condoms and hypodermic needles.

"You like the ocean, don't you?" Ellen asked quietly. I realized I had scarcely looked away from it since coming onto the beach. "You used to go away to Maine in the summer."

"Yes, we did. It's always cold up there, near the ocean, but we loved it. Cindy and I did. She used to say that the rhododendron bushes ..." My voice cracked, and I finished by saying "I'm sorry."

"I'm sorry," Ellen said. "I shouldn't have brought up the past."

"You just asked if I liked the ocean. I was the one who started on my wife. You don't need to hear about that."

"Maybe you need to talk about that, and if you do, I'm perfectly happy to listen to you."

"Well, I don't."

I was growing uncomfortable. I felt like the young man laboring to swim his surfboard out to the cresting waves.

"I really appreciate this wonderful lunch," I blurted out. "My appetite doesn't do it justice, I'm afraid."

Now I was the one turned to my companion, and she was looking at the sea.

"I've missed you, Alson."

"Well ..." It was not true to say that I also missed her.

"When I sit here next to you, I remember what it was like to sit in your study once a month and talk about prayer and vocations, things like that. I could lay down all my baggage for one hour. It went by so fast—but I could still hear you preach on Sundays if I came to church, which I don't do much at all now."

"You should."

"It's not the same."

"It is the same. Everything that's important is the same. The worship's the same, the scripture's the same. The personnel don't matter."

"Okay, they don't matter, but it's not the same thing as spiritual direction. I've lost my guide, and I feel like I'm losing my way."

"You need a director, then."

"I have a director."

"Not anymore. I'm not capable of being anyone's spiritual director right now. I don't even have one of my own, and that's rule number one. The director needs a director. So I'm completely unfit."

For a dizzying moment I felt a powerful urge to tell her exactly how unfit I was, to confess my hidden purposes, not to have them approved or condemned, but to have them known by someone else besides Almighty God. I hoped that the wine hadn't loosened my tongue.

"You say that, but I almost feel as though I'm the one who's not fit. It's like you have bigger fish to fry now, with Alex Leonard."

"Now there's a subject I'm really not interested in talking about," I shot back.

"All right," she murmured, "all right." She

took my arm and laid her head lightly on my shoulder. "I just want you to have a good day, Alson. I don't want to argue with you. I miss you, that's all. You were an important part of my life."

Her cheek brushed mine as she took her head from my shoulder. It was so cool and soft. I glanced down to where a strip of her bare legs lay exposed between the fringes of the blanket and the hem of her skirt. Her calves were flattened against the ground, flecked with grains of sand and ginger-colored freckles. What did God ever make more lovely than human flesh? Was it only for our redemption, or also for some unfulfilled desire deep in his heart that the Word was made flesh and dwelt among us? We can feel the word "dear" tremble on the lips of God whenever we touch it. I found myself wanting to touch her legs. I looked up to the sea. The young man had succeeded in swimming his board out to the waves and in standing upon it. Like him, I tried to hold my balance.

"I am having a good day, you know. What you need now, Ellen, is a competent spiritual director."

She shook her head and smiled faintly.

"I already told you I've got one."

"You don't. And even if you did"—I rushed to beat the crest of her interruption—"even if you did, I stopped being your spiritual director when I asked you here. I crossed the line. If I'm your guide, we have no business being here."

"Why not?"

"It's just not appropriate."

She surprised me with her laughter.

"You mean we're on a date? Gee, I didn't realize—"

"You can call it whatever you like."

"We're eating lunch at the beach, Alson—in October, by the way—we're not in bed."

"Same difference," I said. "We might as well be in bed." I meant to explain the ethics, but she was quicker.

"Oh, really?" She took my arm and pulled herself close to me. "Well, in that case, Reverend Pierce, what have we got to lose?"

Her voice was a deliberate burlesque of seduction, devoid of all seriousness, but I refused to make any response. In a moment of dread, I realized that Alex Leonard was insinuating his way into my conscience. I could almost hear him saying, "Well, well, Reverend, what have we here? Who's the chick, huh? You do all right, Rev, really, for a guy who looks like shit on a Popsicle stick."

"Come on, Alson." She was calling me back. "Can't I make a joke? Am I so dangerous you can't let me make a joke?"

I faced her. Her eyes were moist and kind.

"You can make a joke," I said. "I could probably use a couple of jokes."

"Kiss me, then. Give me a kiss that says I can make a joke. Just a joke on my lips?"

She lifted her hand to keep her hat in a sudden gust of gritty wind, and I bussed her lips once. Immediately her other hand was behind my neck, drawing my face to hers. She looked into my eyes, then took the measure of my lips like a diver or an artist, someone hoping to execute perfection. I closed my eyes.

Her mouth was not Cynthia's mouth, no more than this iron sea was the ocean we loved. We had stood up to our knees in its cold surf one sunlit morning, after a night of love and stolen sleep, and I had kissed her deeply and pressed my hand against her warm abdomen, somehow knowing in that instant that we had already conceived a child. No, this kiss was like this ocean, slow and heavy, swirling back and forth with ponderous experience over the condom-littered shingle.

I was looking at the sea again, my heart beating fast and my lips almost bruised. As far as it was from the sea I loved, it was still a better sight than my rooms, my dreams, my hours spent in Alex Leonard's cell. The kiss and the lovingly made lunch were the sweetest things I had tasted in all these months of bitterness.

I got to my feet and asked her if she would like to walk with me along the water's edge. She took my arm, and we strolled in silence for several hours before heading home.

The sea air had intensified my appetite, as it always does, and I wished I had eaten more at our picnic. I asked if she wanted to join me for a pizza in some place or other off the parkway. Pizza is New Jersey's version of the Maine lobster, ubiquitous and delicious almost anywhere you buy it.

"Sure," she said, "whatever you feel like. Here comes the cellulite."

"Hmm?"

She slapped her thighs before getting out of the car.

I had not had a pizza in more than a year. This one was in the classic Jersey style, prepared by an enterprising Italian immigrant and his sullen teenaged son, with salty stretchable cheese and sweet sauce on a thin crust so pleasantly chewy it worked like a scratch to some hitherto unknown itch in the hinges of my jaws. As we tore each wedge from the disappearing circle in front of us, I thought how pernicious the love of life is. It grows like weeds and fat, it tastes of kisses and ripe cheese, it clogs up our intentions with compromise. One does not decide to start a new life, I thought; one merely decides to let a new life happen. It engulfs one like an aroma. One only needs to breathe it in.

But letting Ellen off at her door (without a kiss offered or stolen), and calling out to her through the open window that I would send her a list of possible spiritual directors in another day or so, I winced to hear her call back, "I love you."

I had called out those same words to Cynthia as she was torn from my arms, and she had called the same words back. The world is full of those words. You can scarcely get through a day without hearing them. There are not pizzas enough in Jersey or lobsters enough in Maine to equal the number of times one can hear *I love you*. It sounds over and over in the streets and on the airwaves like the knell of a terrible iron clock.

6

Today was my third visit to Alex Leonard. I carried my Bible and newly fashioned Communion box (no gun yet under the lid) from the front door of my house to the room where he waits. All the time and space in between were like a dream. I seemed to float in my sealed car from stoplight to stoplight and crosswalk to crosswalk. The children passed before my eyes in their crayon-colored jackets like a long train, endless and hypnotic, bound for some destination that had nothing to do with me. On the outskirts of the prison compound, the demonstrators for capital punishment had new signs that read, NO APPEAL FOR LEONARD and, LET LEONARD ROT IN HELL! But they were opposed by an equal number of counterdemonstrators with signs reading I WILL SHOW YOU A MORE EXCELLENT WAY (1 cor. 12:31), and LOVE CONQUERS HATE, and even WE ♥ REV. PIERCE! Reading my name on their signs was like reading my epitaph, so removed did I seem from their world, their thoughts. The silence of my locked car, which had made their pumping placards seem so surreal, was pierced by a mixture of cheers and catcalls as I drove through. A woman ran a short way beside my car holding up a crucifix. Was the gesture intended as a benediction or an exorcism?

Leonard was covered by three guards again, all white, two inside the visiting room and one outside the door. The latter held a pump-action shotgun. I wondered if the demonstrators had the prison authorities worried. Perhaps the question was on my face when I walked into the room; Leonard took it up like a thread of conversation.

"Did they strip-search you, Reverend?"

"Excuse me?" I said.

"I think Spielberg had to take down his pants. The fag boys didn't even wait for 'em to ask, did you?" He blew kisses in the direction of Roth and his assistants, who were already filming.

"Security!" he shouted to me, as if I were deaf or retarded. "The niggers in this place are getting entirely out of hand. They're worried we're going to have a regular fucking race riot. They better do more than worry. Sit down."

"I brought Camels this time. There are two cartons for you with the guards."

"Never mind that shit now. We've got more important things to attend to. Do you realize there are only sixty-three shopping days left till Christmas? That may sound like a lot, but you know how the time flies. Plus my attorney, old honest Abe, thinks he can have my appeal come up just before Christmas, which he thinks will be a good thing because everybody'll have baby Jesus on the brain and goodwill towards men and all that shit—you, too, Reverend, because to your fans out there you're like another Rudolph the Red-Nosed-Hark-the-Fucking-Herald-Angels-Sing Reindeer. Right? Ain't that what you are? Anyway, the thing is, I'm liable to be as busy as one of Santa's little elves come December, so we have to start thinking about our Christmas shopping right away. I've made you a list."

"Of what you want?" I couldn't believe it.

"No!" he sneered. "What do you take me for, anyway? What do you think, you're my daddy? You want to buy me any presents, you're going to have to figure that out yourself. Listen for the little hints, like everybody else. I'm talking about my girlfriend, Monica. You met Monica, right?"

"Yes."

"You been to see her again?"

"No."

"Well, you've got no reason to."

"I haven't seen her."

"She's got more to do with you than you think, though."

"Oh?"

"Uh-huh. Her and me had a major fight the day I came to your house. That's true. If she and I had managed to make up before I went storming out, maybe none of that stuff would've happened. Life is a funny thing, isn't it? But I figure by letting you help me with some of her Christmas shopping—my shopping for her, I mean—we're sort of bringing things full circle in some kind of weird way, you know. Like 'whatsoever ye sow, that shall ye reap,' and all that shit. What goes around, comes around. What do they call that, in religion, when stuff works out like that? What's it called?"

"I don't know."

"Of course you know."

"Alex, what had you and your girlfriend fought over?" asked Roth.

"None of your goddamn business! Just run your fucking camera and keep your mind on what you're doing."

"Where's the list?" I asked.

"They let me put it in my pocket. My shirt. Get up, come on, get it. I'm not going to hurt you."

I rose from my chair and diminished the space between Leonard and me by six feet. He smiled up at me while I reached toward his chest. I could feel the camera lens zoom to my trembling fingers. Just as they had pinched the folded paper in Leonard's pocket, he gave his handcuffs an abrupt shake and laughed when I jumped. The guards' hands were immediately on his shoulders.

I met his eyes and smiled. Oh, Lennie, I thought, almost hoping to relay the thought to his brain, they really should have their hands on my shoulders. But no one worries about me. I'm as harmless as a dove.

I backed up slowly to my seat, unfolding the paper and laying it on my lap so that I did not have to hold it in my hands. I read the items aloud as nonchalantly as possible.

"Perfume, yuppie chocolate, lingerie ..."

"Whoa, whoa, shut up!" Leonard snapped. "Spielberg, is this movie coming out before Christmas?"

"No, that's impossible."

"It better be impossible, or this guy just ruined my girlfriend's Christmas. You would've had to help me make up a whole new list of stuff."

"What's 'Merlin'?" I asked, ignoring him.

"Merlin! Merlin the fucking Magician. You know Merlin the Magician, don't you?"

"I do, but I don't know—"

"Monica loves Merlin the Magician. Don't ask me why. Every time we went out shopping, I had to wait while she looked over all the Merlin shit. She's just like a little kid with that stuff. And what they got for Merlin shit, you wouldn't believe. They got Merlin statues made out of glass, and silver Merlins with all kinds of crystals—those mothers cost a mint—and Merlin earrings and Merlin dolls, she's already got one of those, and games and posters, you name it. Can you believe this, she wants me to get a Merlin tattoo. I told her, 'Honey, I'm not even sure they *make* a Merlin tattoo.' I had a hard enough time finding my Zodiac sign. I'm a Scorpio." He lifted his arm slightly. "But I wouldn't be surprised if they made a Merlin tattoo. This is a fucking million-dollar industry, this Merlin business. That little fucker is hot."

"But what do you want me to get her?"

"I don't want you to get her nothing. We're

not to that step yet. I haven't even given you money, have I? Have I?"

"No, you haven't."

"Exactly. All you're doing is a little preliminary scoping out for me. I want to know what's out there, prices, sizes, colors, whether or not they gift-wrap. All of that. I want information."

"By when? When do you need it?" I was, as usual, struggling to control myself.

"Pronto. Halloween at the latest."

"I'll do my best."

"That's all any of us can do, Reverend. Now that we have that settled, it's back to movie-making. Christ, we're busy, huh? Where are we now, Spielberg? What's next on the agenda? Come on, the reverend hasn't got all day. He's fixing to shop till he drops. You know what they say, 'When the going gets tough, the tough go shopping.' I saw a woman wearing that on a T-shirt once, right across her knockers."

"We spent a good part of last time talking about your childhood, Alex. I'd like to spend a little more time with that, and maybe begin to work in some of your background, Reverend Pierce. For instance, I wondered if your father was a minister too."

"No. He was a plumber."

"Those guys make good money," Leonard said. "There's a guy in here was a plumber, says he grossed eighty-five thousand a year. Most of which went up his nose. You fuck with drugs, you're fucked."

"Was he a religious man?" Roth continued.

"No, not really. My mother was the religious one. They divorced when I was in high school. He wasn't religious, though. He tolerated religion as far as it supported his ideas." I was amazed, and somewhat appalled, at how easily this came out of me. "He was a very strict man."

"What do you call strict?" Leonard asked.

"He was a disciplinarian. When he said yes or no, he wouldn't change his mind, or let anybody try to change it. His word was final."

"You want to talk about strict, you talk about my old man. His word was not only final, his word was the word of Almighty God. And if you sassed him, he'd send your head through the fucking wall. He was a big son of a bitch, too. He was big and fat, you know, but solid underneath ..."

Leonard went on talking about his strict father and how he had managed to survive his father's tyranny through superior wit and spirit. I was relieved that the ball was back in his court. I knew that Roth would not hold him back. So Leonard's daddy was stricter than my daddy. Would they have liked each other, the porky Baptist patriarch and the macho agnostic reprobate—pointing to their fishing tackle and imbecilic sons as common ground? Or would my father have dismissed him as a fool, a man who wouldn't take a drink being on a par with one who would take "maybe" in response to an order or shit from anyone. Had I been a strict enough father? I had rebelled against my own in this matter and in so much else, but now I wondered if I hadn't gone to extremes. No more than a week before Jimmy's death, I remembered complaining to Cynthia, "That boy never listens. We might as well be a couple of mutes."

"Well, whose fault is that, Alsy?" she had asked. "You're practically thrilled every time he defies you."

"I'm happy he's got spirit, that's all. I don't let him get away with everything. I give him limits. I just want to treat him like a boy, not a pet."

And yet if he had obeyed me when he sprang from my lap that day and I called for him to come back, would he and his mother be alive? If my father had called to me in a tone of command, would I not have frozen in my tracks, then meekly returned to him, though my mother cried out in pain from another room? Could my father have burst the ropes that bound him? Could he have commanded Leonard himself and been obeyed?

"Did your father molest you?" Roth was asking.

"No," I said in unison with Leonard.

"He was talking to me, Reverend," he snapped. "You'll get your turn. No, he did not. But he as good as molested me by sending me to a Bible-banging summer camp that had a lot more to do with banging little boys than any Bible. We used to have a little song, me and all the other happy campers. 'In the Garden.' You know that hymn, don't you, Reverend? 'In the Garden'?"

"I do, yes."

"'He walks with me, and he talks with me, and then he looks both ways. And I strip to my socks, and he takes out his cock. Get on your knees and pray.' I can still sing all the verses."

"This must have been a deeply traumatic experience for you," said Roth.

"I survived. It happens to lots of people, especially in religion. Watch the news. They got the Catholic Church so scared, the Pope's afraid to take his weenie out long enough to pee. You know my lawyer, Lincoln? He was diddled by a Catholic priest when he was only ten years old. That's a fucking fact. That's why he took my case. He told me. I don't know if he'll admit it to you, but that's what he told me. This stuff is common, common. You didn't ever get into any of that kids' stuff, did you, Reverend?"

"No. How about you, Alex? You ever get into any kids' stuff?"

This was a breach in my disciplined meekness, but I wanted to nick him.

"No, fuck you very much. I leave that for men of the cloth. I get into pussy, Reverend. That's what I get into. But you wait, smartass, somebody's going to accuse you of boy-fucking before you're done. I'll give you that for a sure-thing prediction."

"How's that?" I asked, as if truly interested. I wanted to calm him down, calm myself down. I found myself clenching my right fist.

"Common sense. You got so many boy-fuckers running around, and all the kids are

197

so scared because their mothers are always telling them that if they talk to a stranger they'll end up with nothing left of them but a photograph on a half-gallon of milk, so then you got all these paranoid kids running around accusing guys of being child molesters who aren't even child molesters, and then the real child molesters start chucking the shit around, too, to keep the heat off their asses and pretty soon you can't tell the wheat from the chaff anymore. It's a matter of time. I got accused of it. Oh, yeah."

"Really?" I said, as if this were the most improbable thing I'd ever heard. "Who did that?" I sounded vaguely mocking, in spite of myself.

"It's a long story."

I said nothing, but kept my eyes fixed on his.

"My girlfriend had this little nigger boy by some black guy who took advantage of her, which is one big reason why I can't stand jigs, the other being that one of the guys who porked me was an old jig preacher with a pud like a leg of lamb. I ain't shitting you. Everybody at this camp I was telling you about couldn't bend down fast enough to kiss his old black ass because here we were a good Christian camp where everybody belonged to God irregardless of his color, except there wasn't a nigger kid to be found within a hundred miles of the place, only this old, black, blind-as-a-bat bugger who they must've brought in as a cover for the nasty goin's-on. There's your affirmative action once again. But that's another story. This little nigger kid of Monica's, and I really think she got raped but was afraid to tell me 'cause I'd go kill the father, who I probably would've killed anyway because he was a self-centered prick, but I bet he raped her. They'll always go for a white chick if they can—at least I went after my own color. Even my own hair color, for Christ's sake. But this little black bastard—and he was the dumbest fucking thing that ever sucked air, I mean it, six fucking years old and he couldn't write his name—he tried to accuse me of unlawful entry. Pecker-petting and all that. I'm sure his old bat of a grandmother put him up to it—he was too retarded to figure it out himself. She was always ragging on me. See, I was the problem, not her lazy fuck of a son. So, I fixed her. I said, 'Fine, lady, you got the little shit now.' I told Monica, 'Get him the fuck out of here. All he is for me is bad memories. Believe me, I don't want to touch him, I don't even want to see him. Out he goes.' He went too. Bye-bye, blackbird."

"Mr. Leonard, I'm going to ask you a hard question," Roth said.

"Don't make it too hard, okay? I ain't been to college or anything. What?"

Leonard glowered at Roth. His face and body had become tense with rage.

"Do you think your treatment at the hands of these religious fanatics, perverts actually, was what caused you to murder Reverend Pierce's wife and son? I mean, to choose a clergyman's family as victims?"

"I thought I made it clear that I do not want to talk about my family's deaths," I said emphatically.

"Nobody's asking *you* to talk about it. He's asking me."

"So can you answer the question?"

"Yeah, maybe I can answer the question. If you can ask the question. Because you don't even know what the real question is."

The rage in Leonard's voice was fanning the flames of my own rising anger.

"I'm saying it for the last time," I protested in a voice that made even the guards more alert. "I will not talk about the murder of my family!"

"And I'm telling you for the last time, nobody's asking you to talk about it, and it doesn't matter worth a fuck if they do. Your family's not here, they're dead. So whether we talk or don't talk doesn't do them any good or harm, one way or the other. And if I want to talk, I'll fucking talk. And if you don't want to listen to me talk, you can get off your bony ass and get the fuck out of here and stay out. You got it? I didn't invite you in here, remember? You want to pay your respects to your wife and sonny boy, go visit the cemetery. Instead of buying me cigarettes, go buy some fucking flowers. I don't give a damn. All you're giving me is lung cancer and a pain in the ass. But if you want to love your enemy, Reverend, then you act like two fucking cents' worth of a minister and you listen to me."

"I try to listen." He had calmed me—by reminding me of my purpose.

"In all fairness, Mr. Leonard, of the film

footage we've shot so far, the overwhelming majority ..."

"Will you shut the fuck up?" Leonard shouted at Roth. "Nobody's talking to you. Make your fucking movie, or you can get out too. I'm telling you"—he turned on me again—"I need you to listen to whatever I've got to talk about. I need you to hear my explanation, which I don't really owe to anybody because I'm paying my fucking debt to society, okay, but I'm telling you so you'll know."

He waited a moment for me to contradict him, but I said nothing.

"You and everybody else calls me a murderer, all right, and I am not a murderer. I *am* a rapist, I admit that, but I am not a murderer. I did not come into your house thinking to myself, 'I'm going to kill these people.' I was going to rape some people, but I was not going to kill them. This has all come out in therapy. This is documented. The rape was not what people think it is, either—what ignorant, prejudiced assholes think it is. They don't have a clue."

"What don't they have a clue about?" Roth asked. "What is it they don't understand?"

"The whole subject. They don't understand the whole subject. *You* probably don't understand it. *He* certainly doesn't understand it."

"Maybe you can help me understand," I said quietly, trying not to sound provocative. "I would really like to be able to understand. Can you help me do that?"

Leonard shook his head and laughed to himself. He lowered his head, smiling, as if to consider whether or not we were worth the trouble of his tutelage.

"I am what is called a power rapist. Okay? There are three basic types of rapists. They are not all the same. You can even ask my therapist. I mean, you can read this stuff anywhere, but you can ask her. Three types, and I'm a power type. The other types...wait a minute! Do you even know the types? Reverend, tell me the types. Tell me the types if you know them."

"I honestly don't know."

"You honestly don't know. You know, Spielberg?"

"Probably not."

"Probably not. He's a minister and you're a movie producer, the two of you together have probably taken more college courses than you've taken shits, and neither of you even know the three types. You know even less than I do, but you still get to play the human beings while I get to sit in my cage like some animal in Africa, and I do mean fucking Africa."

"We're all human beings, Alex," said Roth.

"Really? Well...give me a few minutes to burst into grateful tears for you letting me know that, cocksucker. Thank you, thank you."

"Alex, can you tell us the three types of rapists?" Roth was undaunted. "You were going to explain that. I would appreciate it if you would. Please."

Leonard took a deep breath, exhaling it as

a quivering sigh. He looked at me and half laughed. "You want to hear this, Reverend?"

"Sure," I said. "That's what I said."

"All right, here it is, and I want you to listen 'cause I'm not saying it again. There are three types. Three types of rapists. There's your fantasy rapist. This guy's in dreamland. He's banging some old lady on top of a garbage can with a gun to her head, and he thinks he's a regular Bruce Willis putting it to Julia Roberts or whoever. He thinks everybody he jumps gets a big charge out of it. He thinks he's the pleasure machine. He's probably some twerpy guy, no build, no teeth, for Christ's sake. Nobody's ever looked at him twice, so he lives in his fantasies. That's your type, Spielberg. Probably you too, Reverend.

"Then there's the sadistic rapist. This guy needs to be inflicting pain just to get it up. My own personal theory is, underneath it all he's probably really a fag. He's got to inflict more pain to get himself off. Then he's off, he doesn't feel so up no more, so he's on to more pain—more, more, till the chick's dead. Let me tell you something, when you start feeling sorry for yourself, you thank God I was not a sadistic rapist. We're talking major, major sick individuals here. You with me so far?"

"I'm with you." I leaned forward, feigning rapt attention—though by this time I was only feigning in part.

"Now there's the power rapist. That's what I am. I'm not a fantasy rapist, I'm not a sadistic rapist—and I'm not a murderer, and we're going to get to that—I am a power rapist. That means I rape to achieve a sense of power, the reason being I never had any power in my life. You stand up in church and you tell your followers to shit, they shit. I say to them, 'What's the time of day?' and they tell me, 'Eat shit.' Oh, if we're on the street, face to face, man to man, nobody's telling me to eat shit 'cause I might rearrange their face. But in church or in school, or any other place where you got a cop or you can call a cop, I'm a guy with zero power. All this fits in with astrology, which you probably don't know anything about either, because as a Scorpio the one thing I got to have is power. You can read that anyplace. I sort of freaked out my therapist because she's doing all this heavy-duty question-and-answer shit to tell me what I already know from a horoscope. So I'm teaching her at the same time she's teaching me. Anyway, whether you're talking astrology or psychology, the message is exactly the same: I got to have power.

"So how do I get power? I rape. I take your wife or anybody else's fucking wife and I rape. I point a gun at your face and you freeze like an ice cube. Power. I tie you to a chair and her to the bed. Power! It's power, man, fucking power. It has nothing to do with sex. I did not have sex with your wife. I had power on her. I tied her hands to the bed and I had power. What I did to her has nothing to do with my cock—it's my head! It's the stars and planets, even, but not my cock.

"You think that's how I get off? You think what went on between me and her was my sex life? Maybe *you* think so. Who knows, maybe she thought so. Maybe *she* thought she was having sex, I never thought that. I don't have to use force to get women, okay? If I had dollar bills like I've had pussy, I'd be the fucking president of General Motors. I've got a girlfriend. You met her. Is she a dog?"

"No."

"She's as good-looking as your wife, isn't she?"

"I don't compare my wife."

Again, I had relaxed my discipline. Like steel, I commanded myself, steel that looks like putty.

"That's right, you don't compare her. The lady's beyond compare. We ought to know, right? You're a funny guy, Pierce. You should be on Letterman. What are we talking about? Right, my girlfriend. Well, my girlfriend's not bad-looking. You know what she told me once? You'd never guess this in a hundred trillion million fucking years. She told me I was the gentlest lover she'd ever known. Okay, and she's been around a little bit, and I don't care about that, because she belongs to me now. The other guys she knew took advantage of her because she's so sensitive. God, she was just a kid when she first got spiked. It's *those* fucks who should be in jail. They're worse than rapists. Worse than sadistic rapists. Take advantage of a girl like that, who don't want nothing from life but somebody to take care

205

of her and a few Merlin geegaws. But she says to me, 'You're the gentlest lover I ever had.' And I know that's true. If she's tired or she's got a headache, I say 'That's all right, honey.' And she'd give it to me if I told her to. I'd just say 'I want this' and I'd have it, blowjob, up the ass, she'd do it, whatever I want. But I don't do that. That's my sex life, that's the way the terrible, horrible rapist treats his woman.

"No, I rape for power, not sex. Look it up sometime, you'll find it. My therapist can show you the book. And you know what else you'll find, Reverend?"

"What else?"

"Research has shown that you and guys like you get the benefit because of people like me. No shit. I make your life easier, I make you have more power, because so many chicks are afraid of me. So you guys aren't even doing me a favor coming in here, I've done you a favor. I should probably be getting a salary. Which means I still don't have power because I'm doing your dirty work for you. So what do you think of that, Reverend? What do you say to that?"

"Nothing."

"Nothing."

"I guess I'm still interested in hearing why you're not a murderer," I said. "I understand now about the power rapist. You've made that very clear. But you were going to tell us ..."

"Hold on! It's coming, for Christ's sake. I can't explain everything at once. You're not paying attention. You still think you can get more power over me and push me around. *I fucked your wife*, buddy, take a time-out! You can just wait a fucking minute."

"I can do that."

"Fucking right you can do that."

By this time he was sweating and almost glassy-eyed, in a near frenzy of self-under-standing. Above the incriminating screams of his victims, above all the courts of earth and the tribunal of heaven, he strained to hear the dumbstruck audiences in a thousand upscale movie theaters pronounce the words of abso-lution: "Life is so complex. Its shades of gray are countless."

"I am not a murderer because I had no intention of killing anybody. I killed in self-defense. Self-defense. None of your family had to die. Use your fucking head! When I came into your house and you came after me with that fireplace thing, like an asshole, I could have blasted you then, right? I mean, what were you intending to do with that thing, give me a backrub? I could have blasted you then in self-defense. When I had you tied up, I could have shot you dead then and there for the hell of it. I could have shot you and the kid. I wanted to rape, I needed to rape, but that's all I needed. You guys could be on your way to a camping trip in Florida right now, forgetting about the whole thing. *I'd* still be in jail, but you could be on your merry way.

"But no, your kid comes busting into the room—I tried to keep him from seeing what's going on in there, I got more concern for his fucking welfare than his fucking father who's supposed to be keeping him under fucking control—and he comes barging in there and hits me and then, when I try to get him under control, your wife hits me, I mean really punches me in the fucking mouth, and that is her big mistake, man. I mean, you would think a minister's wife wouldn't be so violent, but she's hitting me, and the kid's hitting me, and I don't like people hitting me, okay, and you know why? Because I am an abused child. You're looking at somebody who was hit every fucking day of his life till he was sixteen. You have any turd of an idea what that's like? What that does to somebody's self-esteem?"

Leonard was leaning forward with his cuffed hands extended in front of him as far as their tether allowed. His face was so angry, so earnest, so self-consciously pathetic that now, when I bring it to mind, it almost looks serene. The serenity is like the smooth white light heralding a seizure—his raving becomes my own ecstasy of disbelief. How can he say another word? How can the word-created universe allow another spasm of the obscene aperture that is his mouth? Yet his words form one after another like moments of time, like the beats of my heart.

All in all, this was a productive day. I left the prison with a feeling as close to satisfaction as any I have known since before the murders-that-were-not-really-murders. Not only did my new Communion box pass unnoticed; it passed unopened over the counter as I walked through the metal detector. I had even packed three rolls of quarters under the false lid to approximate the weight of the gun. If they had been discovered, and I almost hoped that they would be, I would have claimed them as the contents of a poor box on their secret way to safekeeping elsewhere. But the fact is, with security concerns rising, I am considered the only innocuous man in the compound. They probably wish they had a few more of me.

I also left the prison with two questions, unimportant now, save for my burning curiosity. The first one I have had all along: Why did Alex Leonard, self-professed power rapist, not tie up my son along with his parents?

The other question is new today: How could Cynthia have punched Leonard in the mouth with her hands tied?

7

I had hoped to have my questions answered this morning, but there was no chance to ask them. Instead there was the recognition that I might be running out of time. I must deal with Leonard soon.

I parked my car in the usual place at the

prison, and walked to the intercom beside the door. I spoke my name as always—no one needs to ask me my business—and waited to hear the buzzer sound and the door lock click open. Instead there was a pause, followed by the words "Please wait."

I stood there for what must have been five minutes in a chill wind, under a slate-gray sky. I turned and rested my back against the steel door. Brown leaves were falling in a flurry from the oaks bordering the chainlink-and-razor-wire fence beyond the parking lot. My heart was racing. In the past weeks I have come to know what must be the day-to-day doubts and reflexes of spies and smugglers: every change of routine, every bit of attention paid to you, suggests that your cover has been blown. Then you worry that you will be the one to blow your cover, by fearing you have been exposed, by overreacting with suspicious nonchalance. The advantage I have is that people expect me to act queerly because my pretended mission is the queerest thing they've ever heard. I try to remind myself of that. I don't have to "act naturally." I simply do what I do.

I tried the intercom again. "Just to remind you that Reverend Pierce is here," I said.

Another long pause. Then a squawk: "We know that. Just continue to wait, please." In the background I heard a woman say, "Should we just tell him t—?"

To go? What was wrong? Surely, if they had any suspicions about me, they would not keep me waiting at the door, allowing me a chance to get away. I had no gun with me. I had not yet tried to bring a gun. I just had to be patient.

I spread out my arms and laid my palms flat on the brick, resting my forehead against the door. I must have looked like a man about to be frisked. I don't know why I assumed that position—just that I was beginning to register a certain horror that I can only call metaphysical. If I was to be locked out of that prison, I was perhaps locked out of hell, too—but the resulting despair would belong to one locked out of paradise. I would turn from that door wearing the stony grin of the damned.

I felt I needed to walk away from where I stood for just a minute. I needed to shake these thoughts from my head. I could probably hear the intercom from a short distance when it spoke again. I walked to the farthest corner of my side of the building, heading for what I took to be the rear of the prison. As I was about to round the corner, I saw Roth and one of his assistants standing with their backs to me and talking loudly. I heard my name. I stepped back and leaned close to the wall on my side of the building.

"The thing about Leonard," Roth was saying, "is that he's genuinely funny. He's completely out to lunch, he's a total psychopath, but he grows on you after a while."

"I caught myself starting to snicker the other morning," his assistant began, but Roth had more to say.

"I mean, in a lot of ways he's becoming the center of the film. I keep trying to push Pierce into the foreground, but he just slips back to the outer edges."

"Well, he's obviously a very wounded man."

"Sure, I know he's wounded. But where's the blood? He's wounded, but does he cry? He doesn't get angry. He doesn't really show any compassion, either. And that's what this was all supposed to be about, for Christ's sake, love your enemy, right? Okay, Leonard tells him he likes a certain cigarette, and he gets the cigarette. He's going to go Christmas shopping for Leonard's little Mona—"

"Monica."

"But that's all, there's zero emotion, zero affect. He just isn't compelling. I think Leonard's the show."

"You may be right, but, God—a movie about *him*. He gives me the creeps. He's racist, sexist, homophobic. God, he was once a fundamentalist, not that there's probably any difference."

"There isn't. He's also an anti-Semite. He's a despicable subject. No argument. But that's still better than a boring subject. Can you imagine ninety minutes of mostly Pierce? Can't you just see the review we'd get from someplace like *The New Yorker*? 'By the close of Roth's movie, the audience feels entitled to gang-bang Pierce's wife and his mother. We've earned it.'"

The other man giggled. I heard several more bursts of his laughter as I turned and walked quickly back to the entrance where I had waited. I thought to ring the buzzer once again, in case I had missed an announcement during my time away, but then I noticed Roth and his assistant walking in my direction. They waved. I did not wave back.

"What's the holdup? Do you know?" Roth called out as they drew near. "We've been waiting for about twenty minutes at the east door where we usually go in. They just tell us to wait. We came around here to see if our luck'd be better at a different door, but it looks like you're having the same problem."

"I am. They've told me to wait, too."

"You usually come in this way?"

"Yes," I said.

"I wonder what's the delay. Guess we'll find out."

He began pumping up and down in the cold, though he didn't appear cold at all, just his toasty old eager-beaver self. He and his sidekick stood beaming through their beards at me as if we were waiting our turn on a ski lift.

"So what do you think of the project so far?" Roth asked me. "Are you reasonably satisfied with the way it's going?"

"It's of no concern to me," I said, but then added, "I think you do a good job of helping Alex to be more compelling. I can't say much more than that."

I didn't have to. When I turned to the door, the buzzer sounded and I heard the lock unlatch. Before I could put my hand to the knob, the door opened and Rita appeared. She had had her hair done.

"Oh, you're here. Didn't you hear me call you through just a minute ago?"

"No," I said.

"You gentlemen," she commanded, "not you, Reverend, but the movie people, have been instructed to wait by the east door." "We did, but nothing was happening," replied Roth, who, like Leonard, never knows when to shut up.

"There's plenty happening, sir, and what you need to do is return to the place where you were instructed to wait. That, or go home. Reverend, you can come with me."

"Is something wrong?" Roth called out, beginning to back away from the door.

"Nothing's wrong and nothing's right, except you're not supposed to be by this door and I am. Bye-bye."

We were then enclosed in a dimly lit tunnel between the outer door and an inner one. For the first time, Rita smiled. Her voice resonated in the chamber.

"That little man's about the busiest body I've ever seen. When he dies, he'll be trying to take Saint Peter's picture instead of just getting his raggedy butt through the gate, which he'll be lucky if he does."

"I like your hair," I ventured. It was cropped so close that it exaggerated the roundness of her head and thus the stoutness of her body, but she had what I guessed were new earrings and brighter lipstick, which, taken all together, seemed like an act of mercy in this hard setting.

She did not reply except to purse her lips slightly and brighten her eyes.

"You may not be having any powwow with Lennie today. And I'm pretty sure the movie boys are going straight home. I just didn't want you standing out in the cold."

"Thank you. Is there trouble?" I asked, as she inserted her security card in the second door.

"As long as there's a black man and a white man left in this world, there'll be trouble." She sighed. "Just a little scuffle during recreation."

She sat me down in the reception area near the offices. Others were there, professional-looking people, not the relatives of convicts, glancing at their watches and from time to time staring at me. A woman leaned toward a man with her eyes turned in my direction, and I knew she was asking, "Is that him?" I knew because after nodding his head decisively, he shook it slowly.

I looked away from them to where an attractive Hispanic woman sat behind her computer, moving her fingers rapidly over the keyboard. She looked up at me and flashed a smile, which I returned, before bowing my head. Cynthia had done much of her work outside the home at a computer. Many times I had gone to her office to surprise her with an invitation to lunch, and stepped as quietly as I could up to her desk, hoping for the pleasure of seeing her when she thought herself unseen, for the picture of her gazing at the monitor with a sibyline smile and moving the mouse in slow half circles like an uncertain lover's hand. I looked up at the woman again, wanting to lay my hands softly on her abundant dark hair and bless her with peace and protection all her life.

Rita motioned for me to rise and follow. We began to take my usual path, past the conference room where I had first met her, down a corridor toward the security station, where the bearlike guard named Preston sits by the metal detector, then through a series of other halls and chambers to the room where Leonard waits.

On our way through one of these, a guard met Rita and asked, "Where're you taking him?" Again I felt that dread in my bowels. If ever I am halted for good in one of these middle chambers, then I am in limbo the rest of my life.

"To Lennie. Right? Amazo said go ahead and bring him."

"Amazo's got his head up his ass as usual. They're still lining 'em up in Block C."

"What do I do, then, bring him back through?"

"Nah. Cut through this way and take him out the garage door. That'd be quickest."

"You sure?"

"Absolutely. They got enough buckshot in there now to roll an elephant on his ass and ride him all the way to the shore. Just move him through." He looked directly at me for the first time in the dialogue. "Sorry, Reverend, no moviemaking today."

It was on our detour to the outside of the prison that we came upon Leonard. We had turned toward a large garage door in what looked like the dingy loading bay for a trailer truck, when at our rear, two rows of convicts entered under a heavily armed escort. It was an echoing whoop from one of them that stopped us in our tracks and turned me around.

"There's your lover, Lennie," a man called out, and before I could distinguish him or see Leonard, his voice shot back, "Looks like your lover's with him, or is that fat coon not your mother?"

Then I saw him in the line. It was the first time I had seen him standing up since he took my wife away. Like the others, his hands were cuffed and tethered to his waist. His feet were manacled as well. He stood in his line, facing a parallel row of men, from which a short black convict had stepped forward to shout. At the same time, Rita ordered me to stay where I was, and headed toward the disturbance. If I had brought my gun, I might have been able to kill him then.

"I'd rather be a motherfucker than a baby-fucker," the black man taunted, and then after a guard had pushed him roughly back into line he added, "And I'd rather fuck you, baby-fucker, than wet my dick on that shit-cunt bitch you was living with. She shit out of her mouth too, or just from two places? Tell me the truth, baby-fucker."

As if felled by a seizure, Leonard threw his

body to the cement floor and rolled furiously, his manacled feet jerking upward like the stinging tail of a scorpion over to the other line, bringing down both a guard and his adversary with slicing blows of his legs. In an instant he was above the black man, choking him with his hands, and almost as quickly two guards grabbed him from behind and hauled him off. The other men were shouting and cursing, the guards were pushing them back into line with shotgun butts and truncheons, and Rita was running toward me.

We were outside in a matter of seconds. Strangely, the sun had begun shining through the clouds.

I must have looked a sight, because Rita wrapped her arm around my shoulders and insisted on walking me to my car. She asked me several times if I was okay, and I said I was. But I was trembling. I'm not sure why—except maybe that the sight of so many men in chains, and of Leonard thrashing on the floor, had reminded me of my own bondage, my own thrashings, my own beating at his hands, his feet. Somehow, too, there was the awful sense that our lives were merging. They had called me his lover. Even out in the parking lot, in the sunlight and the fresh air, I felt him all over me.

"This kind of thing happens all the time," Rita said soothingly. "That's what it's like in a place like this."

"It is, is it?" I said, trying to appear calm.

"Though it has been getting worse lately. Our friend Mr. Leonard has a lot to do with

218

that. His big racist mouth. Bragging about an appeal all the time. And that confounded movie. A lot of the men in there don't like that movie, you know."

"Really?" I asked, though I didn't care what they liked.

"Yeah, really," she said, raising her eyebrows. Her face was fully in the sun now. I was leaning on the opened door of my car.

"You got to understand the criminal mentality, pastor. Every single one of these criminals thinks he should be in a movie, too. He thinks he's a big star, it's just no one's had sense enough to discover him. They got the damnedest combination of zero self-esteem and egos the size of Jersey City. Plus, I can see their point in a way. They got no money in this place, no resources to improve the conditions for the men— that's what they keep telling everybody—but they'll bend over backwards for this little Jew moviemaker. They can always do something for him."

"You know how I feel—"

"I know. I'm just saying."

"Do I have to wait till next week to see Alex?" I added quickly. "Should I try tomorrow?"

"You can, I guess," she said, the pitch of her voice rising with incredulity. "Sure, try. My guess is they may want to wait a few days."

"Maybe I'll just wait till next week," I said. I did not like calling attention to myself by departing too much from our routine. I extended my hand to her. "Thank you."

She held my hand firmly for a moment and looked searchingly into my eyes. "Reverend, I'd say that if you have any words of salvation to give old Lennie, or anything else to give him, I'd give it to him soon."

In a few days, then—at most a week—I will go to give Alex Leonard what I have to give him. Now is the acceptable time, now is the day—if not of the Lord, then of my own decision.

If I am successful, and if at some later point, weakened by prison and fearful of death, I attempt to repent of my action, do not accept the gesture, O Lord. I shall have come to no realization that I do not already possess. Of my own free will and in perfect possession of my faculties, in defiance of all civil, religious, and moral law, I intend to murder another man. I deserve whatever punishment shall come to me in this life and the next, and I profess to the bitter depths of my soul that no punishment, no torture, no hell, can be worse than I have already known.

To those mortals who will undoubtedly pass judgment on me, allow me this one parting observation: Consider what our world would be like if the only responses we allowed toward a man like Alex Leonard—however opposed and "simplistic"—were absolute love or absolute hatred. What if the existence of a man like him were so intolerable to our sense of justice that we could only bear to convert him or destroy him? What would our world be like if all victims like me opted either for the absolute forgiveness I have pretended, or for the absolute vengeance I intend?

At this point a gray-bearded man in a loincloth comes forward from the pews of my imagination, with his palms pressed together in front of him, and answers, "It would be the same world we live in now, Sahib, for its inhabitants would still be subject to dualisms like the one you have just posed."

Sounds good, but I don't believe it.

My God, I take this step toward the throne of Your judgment, neither praising You nor blaming You, and with a perfect contempt for the praise and blame of man. Just as I am, I come, I come. I will not ask that "Thy will be done," because I know it will be done, whatever I ask. Just as You know I will do what I intend no matter what You will, unless Your will prevents me. I have one light on in this house, and now I am turning it off.

8

At first it looked as if everything would end at the metal detector. I have tried to visit the prison always at the same day and time in order to have the same guard at the station, and thus to be a familiar face. Neither Roth nor the prison authorities ever denied my request for a uniform schedule; in fact, it seemed to reassure all parties.

But this morning, when I came to the security station with my Communion box, empty of bread and wine but fully loaded, there was a new face at the desk. I tried with all my might not to appear nervous when I stepped up to the middle-aged black woman and set my box and Bible down in front of her.

"Where's Preston?" I asked. "The officer who's usually here. I hope he's not sick."

"He's not sick," she said without smiling. "They need him elsewhere. We're tightening security on some of the blocks."

I hoped to make an easy pass by distracting her with conversation, by appearing not to be in a hurry.

"I noticed on the way in today that at least you don't have to deal with my cheering section. They seem to have disappeared."

She looked at me as if I were beginning to come apart before her very eyes. Did I seem that nervous?

"The pickets," I explained. "I didn't see any people with signs."

"We have dispersed that particular activity," she said, riffling the pages of my Bible like a deck of cards. "To be totally honest, they're not sure you're going to be permitted here for a certain duration. There're too many security risks."

Just let me visit today, I thought.

"Please may I open the box?" I said, when she was about to do so. "This is very sacred.

They've allowed me to open it in the past."

"Maybe you hadn't ought to be bringing very sacred things into a facility like this. Go ahead."

I opened the box. She touched the chalice with two of her fingers.

"It's a Communion set," I said.

"Mm-hum."

She laid the box backward and lifted it up, still open, in both hands.

"Heavy," she said, and my bowels tightened.

"That's the way they make them," I said. "I'm told they're made to withstand fire, get run over by a truck, the whole bit."

"What do they use, rocks?"

"I think it's lead."

I suspect my remark was the nervous joke of a man who feels he's about to be apprehended, and whose pride requires a show of wit before the net falls. But she nodded without expression for me to close the box, and then passed it to me after I'd walked through the detector. I had told myself that if God wanted me to fail, he could stop me here. I was led to the room where Alex Leonard waited.

Again I was surprised. Along with Leonard and the familiar film crew and guards, Lincoln was also there. Leonard interrupted their conversation long enough to say, "Have a seat, Rev." They resumed their whispering, and I overheard the word "appeal." I could not understand why they would conduct their discussion, even in whispers, in the presence of me and the film crew. Leonard kept flashing me a conspiratorial grin, as if we had plans, as soon as we could get rid of the lawyer, to resume the next round of a checkers match on which we'd placed a friendly bet.

With Lincoln's back to me, and the film crew still involved in setting up, this would have been an ideal time to unlatch the box and open fire. But there was something I wanted to know first. Who knows, perhaps I also wanted the shots captured on film. There were six bullets in the cylinder. Head, chest, belly, groin, head, head.

"It's not going to be a problem," Leonard said out loud. "I'm telling you it's not going to be a problem. I'm going to ask him right now."

Lincoln whispered what seemed to be some kind of objection, and Leonard shouted, "I said I'm asking! Get over there and be my fucking attorney. Stop being my goddamn father."

Lincoln obeyed. "We're not filming yet," he snapped at Roth.

"We know," said Roth and one of his assistants in unison.

"We know," mimicked Leonard in a nasal, falsetto voice. "Don't you love those guys? They're just as sweet as come in a fairy's mouth. How are you today, Reverend? You get past the Watusi Gestapo okay?"

"Here I am," I said with more spirit and self-possession than I'd ever shown in this room before.

"Whoa, here he is all right. Listen to him! You look like the cat that swallowed the parochial canary. What, did you get laid last night?"

In spite of myself, I tittered nervously.

"Jesus Christ, boys, I think the reverend got laid. Which is more than I'm able to do these days, but I don't begrudge it to you, no sirree. Puts the spring right back in your step. Might even improve the old sermon, eh, Rev? Listen, if you can keep your mind off the poontang for just a minute, me and honest Abe the lawyer here have got a little favor to ask you."

"Ask and it shall be given."

"From the Good Book, right? Hey, you've read some of that. Good for you. 'Cause, no offense, but I was having my doubts for a while back there. Ask and it shall be given. Very good. Well, here's what we want to ask."

"Shoot!" I said, and once again laughed in spite of myself.

"Jesus, Reverend, let's not get too silly, okay? I've never seen you like this. She must have been something, eh?"

"She was something," I said, immediately squelching my laughter and fixing him with a stare. "She was something."

Now, I thought. Shoot him now. But I waited.

"Well, anyway," he said, glancing at his lawyer as if to say, *I hope the old nut isn't starting to crack on us.* "This is the thing. We might be having an appeal coming up for me before long, and we were wondering if you might want to put in a good word for your beloved enemy,

Alex. Tell everybody about the wonderful work we've been doing here, your Christian activity and whatnot, the movie plans. And so forth."

"I'd want to talk to you about this at another time," added Lincoln. "This is all in the planning stage."

"Your mother should have been in the planning stage, the family planning stage." This time Leonard laughed. "God, it's too bad the cameras ain't rolling, huh, Reverend? Between you and me, we'd have 'em laughing out their assholes. There's nothing to talk about, Abe. The reverend is here on a mission of Christian mercy. Whatever will show the tender love of the sweet Jesus to me is where he's at. For Christ's sake, he's even doing my Christmas shopping! What do you need to talk for? All you lawyers ever want to do is talk. Hey, Reverend, while we're on the subject, how's the Yuletide business progressing? What'd you find out for me?"

"Nothing really," I said coolly.

"Nothing?"

I could tell I'd flipped his switches with that one.

"I've been pretty busy these last couple of days."

"We've guessed that," he said, the menace seeping into his voice. "But still, man does not live by pussy alone."

"And besides, I've been doing a lot of thinking about our last meeting. I mean, you gave me a lot to mull over. Alex delivered to me what amounted to a whole dissertation on the nature of rape, not to mention the true definition of murder. Isn't that right, Alex?"

"That's right." He was wary now, his eyes like a snake's.

"There were just a couple of questions I had about what you said, and I was wondering if you'd answer them for me. If Mr. Lincoln has no objections, of course."

"That depends on the questions," said Lincoln.

"Shut up," said Leonard, his limbs seeming to slither and coil in anticipation. "Ask your question."

"Okay. Well, when you were explaining about the power rapist, which is the kind of rapist you are, you made a statement that to achieve power you had tied me up, which of course I know, but also that you'd tied up my wife—"

"Cynthia," he said.

"Yes…Cynthia." For a moment he had weakened my voice. "You tied Cynthia—to the bed, you said, I believe—but later, when you were explaining how you'd had to kill her in selfdefense—"

"And James."

"And James"—his tactic was no less effective the second time—"you said she had been punching you. I can't understand how she could punch you with her hands tied. That's the first thing."

I found myself very much out of breath.

"I don't think this is a thing we want to be discussing right now," said Lincoln.

"Oh, yes, we do," said Leonard. All his cocky air of command had returned to him, and I felt my strength sapping away.

"Alex—"

"Shut up!" he barked at his lawyer. "He asked me a question, and I'm going to answer it. We've certainly gone from somebody who had a weak stomach for certain subjects to a real curious son of a bitch, haven't we? Haven't we?" he shouted.

"I guess so," I said, weakly.

"What? I can't hear you."

I thought to shoot him then, while I still had the strength, but I was transfixed by the expectation of his answer.

"I guess so," I said again.

"Well, your guessing days are over, 'cause I have one or two things to tell you, Reverend. You want to know how Cynthia could punch me with her hands tied, right? Light me a cigarette, Abe, will you, and please don't offer any advice while you're doing it, because I might accidentally swallow your hand. Just a minute, Reverend."

He took a long, leisurely drag. Lincoln looked at me with an expression of annoyance thinly masking an expression of fear.

"Little Cynthia did not like the idea of being tied up. You two must not've been into any bondage stuff. I mean, she was really crying. These sweet little tears. 'Please don't tie me,' she says. Well, Jesus, you know, I've always been a sucker for a woman who cries. They cry and my heart just melts. So I say to her, 'How's this, honey? We'll tie just one hand. All right? We'll tie just one of these up to the bed like this, and if we like the things the other hand does, maybe we can let this one go, too. But we have to like the other hand a real lot. All right?' Christ, now we practically got the reverend crying. A real teary-eyed family, I guess. Anyway, Cynthia understood the deal. She was a smart lady. And she was good with that hand. Whoa! Over my neck, my hair. And she goes, 'Please don't hurt them, just please don't hurt them.' What a woman, huh? I tell you, Reverend, I was a little jealous of you. I mean, she looks after you, a good-hearted woman all the way, and she's got that magic hand too. I'll tell you, I was worried I was going to pop off before she did, all on account of that hand. I don't know how you must have done it."

I don't know why, but for some reason I glanced over at the camera. It was running. When had they turned it on? I stood up. At the same time my ears began drumming with sounds like thunder and metallic banging. I heard the shrieks of the damned. I was losing my mind.

"Stop that!" I yelled, advancing toward the camera.

"Oh, that hand," Leonard continued, "it was all over me—"

"Turn it off!"

"We have editorial privilege, Reverend," said Lincoln, his face now nothing but fear. "We have editorial privilege." His eyes were darting back and forth from the ceiling to the walls.

Roth and one of his assistants had stepped between me and the camera. They were telling me to sit down and saying things about "my response" and "editing." What was wrong with them? The red "on" light was still blinking in the camera's side, and the commotion in my ears grew louder. I turned back to face Leonard, who was jabbering on in a frenzy.

"My back, my arms, my ass—'Christ Almighty,' I thought, 'I'm going to have to tie up that hand just to calm her down a bit.'"

Two guards and Lincoln suddenly bolted from the room. I was sure that in a moment they would return to take Leonard away. Perhaps they would take me, too. I could hear reality falling apart around me as Leonard chanted and taunted. I fell back in my chair.

"Oh, sweet Christ, that hand—"

"Did you untie the other?" Roth called.

"I think we should have Communion," I shouted, over their voices and the rising noise in my head.

For a moment, Leonard was silenced.

"I want to give you Communion. I think it would be nice for all of us."

Trembling, I brought the box from the floor onto my lap. As the banging and howling increased, I wondered if I was about to usher in the end of the world. If so, the camera would capture it all. By this time, I intended to kill Roth as well.

"Communion for me, Reverend? I never had Communion in my life."

"All baptized persons should be entitled to Communion."

"But I was never baptized, Reverend. You know that."

"Keep filming, for God's sake," Roth shouted to his assistants.

My fingers had just touched the latch when an alarm rang out and the door burst open behind me. The last thing I remember of the room was the din that rushed through the doorway like a gust of wind, and the look of absolute terror on Alex Leonard's face.

I was in a room that appeared to be a gym of some kind, with barbells and benches and exercise machines. I estimate there were at least thirty other men there, most of them black inmates. Leonard was on the other side of the room, still manacled in his chair. Several other black and white men were tied or handcuffed to pieces of exercise equipment, with T-shirts pulled over their heads. Some of the inmates had knives and bricks. One carried a large wooden spatula of the kind used to take pizzas out of an oven, waving it over his head and behind and in front of his body like a batter warming up with a baseball bat. A few men had truncheons, and at least one held a shotgun.

I was seated on the floor, on a plastic mat. I was not tied. Not a soul in the room paid any attention to me whatsoever. I wondered if I was dead, and was fading from the scene, but gradually my awareness grew instead of diminished. I remembered not being able to see, and a thick arm wrapped like a python around my throat. I remembered the sound and the feeling of my heels dragging over concrete floors.

The men were milling around the room, which was the size of a basketball court, talking in small groups. As Lincoln had done, they moved their eyes anxiously over the walls and ceiling, though I could hear no sounds from outside. Veils of cigarette smoke wafted through the shafts of sunlight above me. The air reeked of sweat.

I glanced back to where I had seen Leonard, but instead I saw a tight circle of black men. One of them turned and looked at me, the first acknowledgment I had had, and I turned away. My eyes came to rest on another black man, lying on the floor about fifteen feet away from where I sat. He, too, was staring at me. It was a moment before I realized he was dressed in the uniform of a guard. It was another moment before I realized he was dead.

When I turned away from his corpse, the other inmate from the circle was standing above me. There was a crude knife in his hand, and I must have gasped.

"You got nothing to be afraid of," he said. "Nobody's going to hurt you if you just do what you're told. Come with me."

His words should have reassured me, but

instead they brought a lump of burning vomit into my throat. I turned my head and spewed it on the mat beside me.

The man squatted and placed his hand on my shoulder. Another stood near us.

"You okay?" asked the squatting man. His eyes were the only eyes of compassion I had seen in a week. I drank them into my own until he turned his head.

"He's gonna have to clean up his puke," said the standing man.

"That'll have to wait. Bingham wants to talk to him. Can you get up?"

"I think so," I said, reaching out my hand for support.

"Well, I ain't cleaning it up," said the stander.

"Nobody's asking you to clean it up, are they? All anybody's asking you to do is shut your fucking mouth. Can you do that?"

"Yeah, I can do that," the other said sullenly, sliding back a step. "Problem is, can I shut my fucking nose? We got dead bodies in here and now we got this puke. Shit ..."

He moved away, as the other man helped me to my feet and muttered at the back of the retreating man.

"There'll be another dead body in here if you don't shut your fucking mouth. Okay, then," he said, steadying me. "You feel like you're gonna puke again?"

"No."

"All right, then. Come along."

When the circle of inmates opened before

me, I saw Alex Leonard, still in manacles, his chair tipped back against the iron supports of a weight-lifting bench. His cheek was gashed, and blood ran from his nose and an eyebrow. His lips were swollen. Still, he managed to approximate a smile when he saw me.

"Hi, Rev," he gurgled. "What'd you bring him for?"

"To pray over your grave, motherfucker," said a short, very black man, who kicked Leonard's arm.

"Why don't you say the word 'nigger' just one more time before you go to hell." The man who said this cuffed him viciously across the face with the back of his hand. Although I identified more with his knuckles than with Leonard's bleeding mouth, I still flinched.

"Enough!" boomed the largest man there, who held a long-handled shovel upright beside him like a staff of authority.

"I say we do him now," said the short man. "He's gonna be done before it's all over, anyway. I say now."

"And I say hold on," said the man with the shovel. "You're not using your head. This here is a bargaining chip, a white movie-star bargaining chip, which is to say a blue chip for us."

Were they talking about me? I wondered. But the short man pointed at Leonard.

"I don't play cards with chips that dirty," he shouted. I recognized him as the man who had called Leonard a baby-fucker during the altercation the week before.

234

"Well, I do!" said the big man just as loud. "When there's crackers holding some of our people somewhere, I do. I play with any chip I got!"

"Do we know they got any of ours?" said the man who'd fetched me.

"We don't know nothing except we're here, and some of them are loose out there, and while we're here jawing, about a thousand motherfucking SWAT team boys is getting all dressed up for a turkey shoot with niggers for the turkeys. That's what I know. Even if whitey don't have none of ours, even if whitey's all locked up safe and sound and ready for his afternoon nap, we're gonna need bargaining chips with the powers that be, and I say we don't throw none of them away. You think I give a shit about him, or him?" He pointed to me. "I don't give catshit for them, but I do feel like staying alive right now."

"If I stay alive and he's the reason for it, I'd just as soon be dead." The short man appeared feverish now, and his shaking seemed to call forth a more deferential voice from his leader.

"You're personal with this, Bobby. You're thinking too personal."

"You're fucking right I'm personal," he answered in a fury. "If you could've seen that kid when my mother got him. My brother tried to kill himself when he saw him, his little boy like that. She was a whole month just washing his little busted asshole. That white cunt let him do that, and she was his own fucking mother. He got burn marks, he got—"

"But he didn't kill him," said the big man.

"It wasn't me," said Leonard.

"Shut up!" The big man rapped Leonard's ribs lightly with the back of his shovel.

"He killed this guy's whole family," my escort said, though whether to support or challenge the short man, I could not tell.

"And he comes every week just to love his enemy, don't you, Reverend?" the big man said to me. "Ain't that right?"

"That's 'cause his enemy is white," said someone else. "If it was a colored man done his wife and kid, he'd be asking to put the hypodermic into his arm. 'Find me a vein in this nigger.'"

There were nods of assent. Someone even said, "Amen."

"That's not true!" I said without thinking. "If he were black, I'd want to kill him just as much as I want to kill him now."

"Oho, you'd like to kill him now, would you?" the big man said. Then he snapped, "Bobby!" as the short man abruptly stepped forward and pressed a knife into my hand, forcing my fingers closed around it. Drops of sweat ran down his face.

"You kill him, then. You kill the motherfucker. I'm going in and out of here my whole life anyway, I'll tell them I did it. Here ..."

He grabbed the knife back from me and cut the left side of his shirt free from his body. He wiped the knife with it, then swathed the handle tightly. He shoved it back into my hand.

"I didn't mean I—"

"What didn't you mean, huh? You think he didn't mean it? He killed your wife and baby. He cut 'em up like a side of meat. Kill him!"

It was then that it dawned on me that my Communion box was gone. Very likely it was in the hands of guards, and my plot had been uncovered. It was now or never.

"Go on, man, go on."

The others, even the leader, seemed mesmerized by the drama.

"You know what he does, man? He talks about your wife's pussy. He talks—"

He jerked away from me and yanked down Leonard's pants so hard that the chair crashed to the floor. He stepped back to reveal Leonard flat on the fallen chair, with his genitals exposed.

"—about how he pumped that into her. You still want to love him, man? Go on and cut the motherfucker's balls off. Cut him, or I swear I'll cut you and him both!"

Leonard was whimpering with fear. "Oh God, oh God," he hiccuped. His penis lay shriveled in his groin like the worm of my own torment. I thought of Cynthia, begging for mercy.

"Cut him, you son of a bitch!" the man was screaming in my face.

Why was I hesitating? To have devised, rehearsed, and lived so desperate a plan, and then to have it altered, abbreviated, even improved all in a moment—I was moved almost to an ecstasy. I have never before felt a sense of God's favor overwhelm me like that. Had a dove descended from heaven and a voice pronounced me God's Beloved Son, I could not have felt more favored.

There was Leonard, tied and beaten as I had been tied and beaten, exposed and humiliated as Cynthia had been exposed and humiliated. There in my hand was the weapon—not just any weapon, not the gun I had intended to use, but the same kind of weapon Leonard had thrust into the bodies of my wife and little boy. And it had not been smuggled sacrilegiously into this room, it had been placed in my hand, provided in place of my damning "communion" no less so than the lamb on Mount Moriah had been provided to Abraham in the place of his son.

I looked at Leonard's face, bloody and almost fetal beneath me. "God have mercy on your soul," I said as I knelt beside him. The short man backed away.

I wrapped both my hands around the hilt of the knife. I raised it over his chest, as high as my face. I took a deep breath and closed my eyes. There was a period when my hearing ceased.

I thought, *This is what it feels like to be dead.*

The rest is a dream for me, and a few minutes of television news for everyone else. It seems I was swept to the outside of the prison building in less than a minute, though it probably took longer. I see the short man who had handed me the knife, pierced with a bullet, his eyes blank before his knees hit the floor.

I see lines of flak-jacketed men unfolding along walls and catwalks like ribbons of icing on a wedding cake, each one dropping into position behind the other.

I see lines of other men with their hands behind their necks trudging in the opposite direction from the one in which I am running, with a voice behind me barking, "Let's go! Let's go!"

I see reporters scurrying between the police cars in the parking lot like rats over a battlefield, snapping their black cameras in my face and asking questions to which I answer not a single word.

I hear a voice wailing among the sirens like the sound of a man who has lost his wife and child, and I turn to see Roth collapsed on the ground over the tangles of his ruined film and broken cameras.

And I see the woman from the station by the metal detector advancing toward me with my Bible and my Communion box in her hands. I can feel once more the sinking sensation of judgment, and then the elation of escape when she hands them to me and I am not arrested.

"You owe this to Preston," she says, her voice ready to break with grief and condemnation. "You know how you said to me before that you hoped he wasn't sick? Well, he's sick now. Got maybe nine or ten stab wounds all over his chest and arms. He grabbed hold of this here thing like it was a football or something, and he's shouting like a wild Indian, 'The Body of Christ. The Body of Christ.' I seen him when they put him into the ambulance. He *looked* like the body of Christ. Jesus!"

Nothing I see, however, can surpass or eclipse my last sight of Alex Leonard as he is borne in his chair deeper into the prison from which I am being sucked like an abortion. He is shouting above the gunfire.

"Baptize me!"

Part Three

1 ✦

I sat on my living-room floor in a shambles of old newspapers and cried. It was the day after the riot, and I had not yet slept. I had walked the streets almost until dawn. I came home and seized the newspapers, hurling them in a fury from the closet. Leonard's words still rang in my head; nothing could drown them but my family's screams.

There was actually little new to me in the news. I had come to expect accounts of mutilation, torture. People had discouraged me from reading them, calling them graphic. The accounts were graphic, though not nearly so much so as my suspicions and dreams. "Bound and raped... stabbed repeatedly in the chest and abdomen...cut the child's throat." Still the words struck me with all the horror of the worst things I'd expected. There was no difference. Stabbings sound like venial acts of violence to our jaded ears—we use them in our clicheaas, our friends stab us in the back, bad news cuts like a knife. But when you have kissed the punctured breasts, when you have buttoned the last button of the snowsuit around the sliced neck, and stooped over the crib in the darkness to listen for the pufflike breaths of the delicate tubes severed and choked with blood—then you know the meaning of the word *stab*.

Even the one detail that would have been news was no longer news. LEONARD CLAIMS LOVE-STARVED MINISTER'S WIFE BEGGED TO CARESS HIM DURING ASSAULT. "An answer was offered today in the Alex Leonard double-murder trial for a question that has long puzzled police: Why was only one of victim Cynthia Pierce's hands tied to her bed? According to the defendant ..." He called out for me to baptize him. There was really no conversion on his part or mine, was there? I had opened up the newspaper, in part, to open my own heart, to see if I had actually undergone some soul-transforming experience in those last moments of chaos during the riot. But what struck me now was the essential sameness of Alex Leonard. Beaten, rescued from death, perhaps even repentant according to his own light, he was still pure audacity, calling out his latest whim with no thought whatsoever for the sufferings he had caused. "Baptize me!" he'd cried out. Not "Forgive me!"

And he had been who he was for some time.

Cynthia and Jim were not Leonard's first victims.

In 1985 he had raped and sodomized a twenty-eight-year-old single mother in her home while her infant son lay screaming in his crib. He had choked her with a belt until she lost consciousness, then fled the apartment. For that outrage he had served a total of seven years in prison, less than half of his original sentence of fifteen, before being released on probation.

So Alex Leonard did not burst into my

home like a meteor bursting through our atmosphere from the depths of a chaotic universe. He was not a symbol of how "you never know." The murders of my wife and son were predictable, and preventable. Alex Leonard himself had prophesied their doom. But no one had cared to heed the prophet.

I could not believe this. I could not believe that a society that will not allow a package of cigarettes to leave the factory without bearing a warning of the dangers every imbecile knows to be facts, that will not allow uninspected apricots to cross its borders, would allow a man like Leonard to walk free and anonymous under the sun.

And yet I knew, and at last I admitted to myself, that I was overdramatizing my disbelief. Had I been called to serve on the review board for Alex Leonard's parole—in which case I would not have suffered at his hands—would I not, on general "Christian" principles, have been among those who voted to give him another chance? And would I have done so without a doubt that he would never rape or attempt to kill again? Would I have been completely sure that my neighbors were completely safe? No. The only thing of which I would have been completely if not correctly sure was that Leonard's next victim would not be one of my family. There was only a one-in-a-million chance of that, and I would have professed to be willing to take it, only because I believed I was not taking it.

Was that not the whole substance of my for-

mer so-called liberalism? A conservative is someone who sits down to his own dinner at his own
reserved table, and asks the waiter to remove
the empty chairs for fear that another human
being will join him and ask to share so much
as a crumb of the feast he is devouring. A lib-
eral calls out to the waiter, "Bring those extra
chairs to me!" and proceeds to call in people
from the sidewalk to dine with him, all the while
devising a plan to be off to another table or
another restaurant by the time the check
arrives.

My thoughts, as I sat there among the newspapers, were not so involved as the ones I now
write. I crushed the yellowing pages of
newsprint in my hands, and beat them against
my skull, smearing my temples and forehead
with the color of ashes. I groaned, and I waited, as I have learned to wait, for the breaking
point that inevitably delivers us from the
intolerable, though sometimes what breaks is
the precious skin keeping us alive.

My breaking point came with the sound of
frantic knocking at my front door.

I opened, and Ellen Fabian poured in like
a deluge of arms, bosom, and smothering
hair.

"Oh, dear God, you're safe," she said,
embracing me, kissing my neck. "I knew you
were in there. I thought you'd never come out."

I was disoriented at first. I thought she

meant the house and my slowness at answering the door. Then I realized she meant the prison.

"I called last night. I even drove over a couple of times, but you weren't home. I thought you might be sleeping. I didn't know what to do. But you're safe, safe. Oh God, you look awful."

"I'm just tired."

"Of course you're tired," she said, out of breath, closing the door behind her, pulling off her coat and throwing it over a chair. "You've been to hell and back. But you've won! I'm so proud of you."

She took hold of my hands and brushed my hair away from my brow with a furtive gesture, as if she'd committed a sacrilege by embracing me so boldly before.

"Won what?" I said, still dazed.

"Leonard. He's asked to be baptized. It's in this morning's papers, it's on TV. It's true, isn't it?"

"Yes, I suppose it is. Can we sit down?"

"Sure. Do you want me to fix something for you?"

"No, let's just sit down."

She scanned the mess of newspapers on the floor, but said nothing.

"I wonder how it got in the news so fast," I said. "This all happened during a riot."

"Leonard's lawyer said it on the news. He said they'd beaten Leonard half to death and people had tried to force you to kill him and you'd led them to believe you would to stall for time, and it worked, and now Leonard wants you to baptize him."

"That's what I told them, yes."

"I guess they had to take Leonard to the hospital. He says there might be a press conference later in the week. Did you know about that?"

"No."

"That didn't sound like your idea when I heard it."

"No, that is definitely a lawyer's idea. He wants to get all his pieces in place for an appeal. Leonard's going to appeal."

"Do you think he's sincere about the baptism? You don't think it's all a trick?"

"Who knows?" I sighed. "Probably not. He would have played the trick earlier if that was the plan. He probably means it. I'd bet my life he means it."

"And it's you who did it," she said, taking hold of my hand again. "Alson, I think you just may be a saint. With newsprint all over his face." She licked two of her fingers and rubbed my forehead, still holding my hand.

"There was another woman," I said.

This time it was she who lost her bearings. She stopped my spit-bath and loosened her grip on my hand.

"What do you mean? A woman with you?"

"No," I groaned. "Another woman Leonard raped. Another victim."

"I know. Oh, I guess you didn't. You've read your papers, I see."

"Yes, I've read my papers."

We sat quietly for a few moments, without touching. I like silent companionship—something I had only ever known in an empty church or with my wife. I wished we would be still for a longer time than I knew we would.

"So, now what?" Ellen said.

"There's no 'what,' I just...I guess I'm just blown away by knowing about this other woman."

"Many women get raped, Alson," she said.

"What's that supposed to mean?"

"It's not supposed to mean anything."

We were still for another moment.

"So can I do something for you before I go?" she asked. I should have answered no, and let her be on her way, but as before, I found myself needing her and all too willing to use her.

"As a matter of fact, there is. If you're still willing to give me some assistance."

"You know I am."

"I need someone to go to a library and find out what they can about this other woman. It says here she was raped in 1985. They call her 'a New Jersey woman.' It may be the papers in 1985 give more information."

"What is it exactly you want to know?"

"Anything. Anything about her. I just want to know what there is to know." Her face was still quizzical. "It's for my own peace of mind. Then I can clear all these papers out of here and go on with it. And I can't walk into a public place now—I'd never get out. Can you do it?"

"How soon do you want it?"

"As soon as you're able. I'm sorry, Ellen."

"For what?"

"For everything," I said, with a sense I had lived this moment before. She kissed my cheek and left without a word.

When she had gone, I sat down once again in the middle of my newspapers to see if I could find out anything more about the woman. In part, I was trying to distract myself from what I had just read of my family's deaths. Also, I didn't want to acknowledge that Leonard's request for baptism had forever shattered my illusion that I could act apart from a God I chose to ignore but not to hate. Now God seemed aligned with any choice I made, though doubtless this had always been the case. He was either at my back, sending me forth with the waters of Baptism, or in my face, receiving the gunshots of my defiance.

As I leafed through the papers, Ellen's words came back to me: *Many women get raped.* In the papers I had stockpiled, I read of rape after rape, and murder after murder. I read for the first time about crimes that all but the smallest handful of people had by now forgotten. I read of a woman who came home to find her house ransacked and her daughter missing. She opened a closet and saw the dazed child, raped and bleeding. A tap came on her shoulder, and she turned to see a man holding a machete. The sentence that followed read like a joke in its context: "She decided to submit to him."

The victim in the closet emerged as a sort of leitmotif—another woman was left tied in a closet until her husband came home to hang up his coat. A stranger had knocked at her door, feigning illness, and when she'd opened it, he had punched her full in the face and dragged her to her humiliation. What were the first words said from spouse to spouse, I wonder. "What happened?" "I'm glad you're home"? "Are you okay?" A hundred possibilities, and all of them ridiculous.

There were schoolgirls so viciously savaged with bottles and sticks that they could barely crawl from the alleys where they had been thrown down. There were mementos taken: dollars, underwear, snapshots, locks of hair, severed ears—and mementos given, written on, scratched on, stuffed wickedly into the orifices of the victims.

These, and as many murders: children shot for having no change in their pockets, shot to facilitate an easier removal of their sneakers, stabbed for no reason anyone could determine—old women strangled to death with their pocketbook straps, old men choked to death on their own yarmulkes.

Above the headline of one atrocity, and below the newspaper's masthead, I read the motto, "The Herald of the Garden State," and by association remembered a song from a children's play performed at my grammar

251

school when I was in fourth grade: "My Garden State, I'm So Proud of You." All of our dearly beloved and dissonant voices sang about New Jersey to our parents as papier-mâché floats of the Passaic Falls and the Holland Submarine were towed around the aisles of the auditorium by children dressed as Edison's lightbulbs, Jersey tomatoes, and even as little silkworms in commemoration of Paterson's former title, "Silk City of the World." How many of those girls have been raped since then? How many killed? What happens to a people who wake every day and go to sleep every night to the news of horrors repeated over and over? How do they survive, not the crimes themselves, but the constant soundless screaming of the victims?

For a while, as I had walked restlessly the night before, I had entertained the thought of never going back to the prison, of dropping the whole insane business. Maybe I should just start my life over, I thought. But where could I go? Out of the prison, out of New Jersey, then out of this world? There is no escape for me. The only way out goes in—to him.

Ellen returned in the middle of the afternoon without having learned much. The papers from 1985 also mentioned the details about the woman being single, a mother—an "unemployed" mother—and twenty-eight years old. The only thing new was her town of residence, and some information about how Leonard had entered her home, at what time, and so on, which Ellen said I could read for myself. "I don't care to read it out loud," she said, "but I made copies of everything they had."

When she said "unemployed," it occurred to me that Ellen might have had to miss work to visit me in the morning and to run my errand. I asked her about this.

"I haven't worked since June, Alson."

"Did you quit?"

"I wish I had, not that it would make any difference except I'd have had the satisfaction. No, I was laid off. I've been collecting unemployment and reading lots of books I can't remember a word of two weeks later."

"You were working at the bookstore, right?" In fact, I had helped her to obtain the job through someone in the congregation.

"Yup."

"And they laid you off?" A pause. "Why?" I was trying to show some interest, and was growing irritated by her implication, or what I took as her implication, that I couldn't care less. Looking back, I don't know why I bothered. The fact is, I *wasn't* interested. What were such details to me at that point anyway?

"They were slowing down. They were starting to open these big Barnes and Nobles all over the place, and these guys didn't have a prayer, or a clue, or whatever. They just couldn't find enough work for me. I hear the place is for sale now."

"Did you like the job? You were pretty excited when we found it, remember, a change from waitressing—at least something to pass the time till you applied to grad school. That was the plan, as I recall."

"That was the plan. I must've been dreaming."

"Why do you say that?"

"Because I'm not going to graduate school. All that would do for me is give me a few extra bills to pay while I'm unemployed. That and remind me of how old I'm getting. It'd be like working in a bookstore—sounds good, but just a big, time-consuming bore."

"You didn't like the job, then?"

"I hated the job. Don't let that hurt your feelings. What difference does it make which dumb job I do? I'll survive. I'm not so sure about you, though. What are you going to do with this information I found? Or is that none of my business?"

It wasn't her business, but I wasn't going to tell her so. In fact, I would tell her my intention even as it was just then taking shape in my mind. I'd noticed an edginess in her that made me want to accommodate her in a way I had seldom wanted to before. Human relationships are peculiar things. One person follows the other, gives up, and then the other turns and follows the one. The most contented persons are those who have managed never to move in any direction but their own. The world follows at their heels.

"I'm going to take a walk to Beaumont," I said.

"You're going to try to find her?"

"No, of course not. There's a good chance she doesn't even live there anymore. I just feel a need to go over there. I'm not even sure why."

I stood abruptly, my way of turning heel in the chase. Of course, she changed direction, too. I could hear it in the familiar solicitous tone creeping back into her voice.

"Why are you going to walk? It's freezing out there. Do you want me to drive you? You look like you can hardly stand, let alone walk all the way over to Beaumont. At least take a bus."

"It's not that far. I could drive myself if I wanted."

I suppose the movements of a relationship are never as predictable as we think:

"I tell you what. Why don't you drive me over and I'll walk back. Would you be willing to do that?"

"I'd be willing to drive you both ways," she said.

"I'll keep that in mind."

The drive to Beaumont only took about ten minutes. I showed her where to turn off Veterans Avenue to the recreational field that lies at the heart of this small, blue-collar town. I intended to sit there for a while before beginning my walk.

She pulled to the curb behind a row of interspersed maples and benches that line the field. I thanked her for the lift. She looked so warm and vital in her emerald green coat, but harried and somewhat older, too. For the first time I noticed a strand or two of gray in her mane of reddish brown hair.

"Don't walk back in the dark," she said. "Call me. I'll be home."

"I'll be fine."

"They'll jump a minister as soon as anybody else."

"I've noticed," I said.

"Oh God, Alson, I didn't mean—"

"I know. I know. You don't have to pussyfoot around me. I can even read my own newspapers now."

She returned my smile.

"I hope you find whatever it is you're looking for," she said.

"I guess that's up to God," I said. "We just need to pray we'll know it when we find it."

She looked at me strangely as I got out of the car—I suppose because I had not used such pious words with her since the days before the atrocity. Like Alex Leonard, I appeared to be getting religion.

I took a seat on one of the concrete-and-wood slat benches facing the rec field. Nearby a group of elderly Turkish men in black overcoats and gray wool fezzes had formed their daily coffee circle at one of the benches by the Knights of Columbus building, in the corner where the American flag flies above the war monument. Out on the field, two coaches

256

were drilling a team of junior-high football players. They slammed the padded bumpers when the whistles blew, as snatches of foreign conversation drifted over from the old men with the intermittent aroma of their coffee. I could hear the flag snap in the chilling wind. A red setter barked, chasing a stick in the other corner of the field. Once I'd felt at home in this world.

Back at the house I had hastily gone to my room and changed into clericals while Ellen jiggled her car keys in the living room. My hope was that I'd be easily recognizable in my black shirt and collar—hadn't cameras been in my face for more than two months?—that someone in town would accost me, and that from there I might learn more about the woman I was searching for.

I'm not sure what I wanted to learn, or why I wanted to learn it. I certainly didn't need an additional reason to kill Alex Leonard. I think I needed to do something purposeful in between the riot and the next time—if there would even be a next time—that I saw him. I needed something to take my mind off his unsettling request, and the no less unsettling way he'd been delivered from my hands. Maybe I was also looking for some respite from the protracted loneliness of my bereavement and my secret plan. Why do people go to such lengths to search out information about their runaway fathers or siblings separated from them at birth—years later, when they would seem to be happy enough without it? I knew why. This woman was the closest living relative I had. The same man had brought us into the world, and the world already seemed less lonely with the knowledge of her existence.

I got up from my bench and took a deep breath of crisp November air. "Time to go hunting," I whispered.

My father was a lover of blood sport, cursed with an only son who aspired early to be a fisher of men—though in the end he would be a hunter of them, too. When I was around ten or eleven years old, he took me with him to visit the uncle of a fellow plumber who maintained a ramshackle "farm" in northwestern Jersey, more a menagerie than anything else. "The goddamned groundhogs" were "raising hell" in the man's two or three pastures, which were decadent with burdock and milkweed, and our morning diversion was to help him cull the population. I was handed a .22-caliber rifle, "the ideal gun for a boy," and a box of "hollow point" ammunition, the virtue of which is to explode on impact. Off we went, three men and a boy, to exterminate groundhogs in Jersey's last recognizable fragment of Eden.

I'd be lying if I said I wasn't up for the task. True, I had already begun to exhibit the traces of a scruple about impaling worms on hooks or watching a bass die belly-up on the shore, its gills clawing at the hostile summer air. I had found a way to beg off the one or two deer-hunting expeditions on which I'd been invited. In one case I had faked a fever, preferring lies to blood. But when I'd been told how the dazed pony and the burdock-matted cow I petted would surely stumble and break their legs in the groundhog holes, I felt I had a good reason to kill.

Everything went well at first. I reveled in the country air, in the company of these tough men who seemed to regard me as an equal, and as responsible, having armed me with my own gun and ammunition, and not least of all in the implicit approval of my ever-disapproving father. It was agreed at the start that the first groundhog to show its odious head would be mine.

I put the bead on the hog and in the sighting notch; squeezing the trigger as I'd been told ("just like a woman, son, you hold her tight and squeeze her"), I fired. I hit him.

Then, as my father and the other men urged me and then hollered at me to eject the spent shell and chamber a new one, I watched in horror as the wounded creature loped and dragged itself several yards into the hole of its burrow.

"It'll die, you hit him solid," the farmer said, trying to soothe my ego in the face of my father's obvious displeasure. "You got him for sure."

For the rest of the day, during which every man shot at least two groundhogs, and I was allowed to ride the ancient pony and listen to the dirty jokes, I thought of the wounded groundhog seething in pain in its underground burrow, perhaps wondering with its blunt animal mind why another creature had treated it so. Silly as it sounds, for many years I met Groundhog Day with a deeper sorrow than Good Friday, and when I first came to terms with the redeeming act of the latter, I thought of my rifle shot as the most grievous of those sins Christ had borne for me.

As I walked the parallel avenues of Beaumont, crisscrossing down the residential streets that ran between them, I felt the sorrow and the sickness of that morning of hunting up in Sussex County. Somewhere in one of those houses once lived and perhaps still lived the human being who was now more fully connected to me than any other person on earth, and I would never find her. Surely she had heard of me by now. Had I added a wound to those she already suffered? Did she curse me for my seeming forbearance or reproach herself for lacking the same? Was she married now? Did her infant, now an adolescent, know of his mother's ordeal? If so, did he wish he were me, so he could kill Alex Leonard? Did he wish he could kill me?

I passed banks and hardware stores and what seemed like at least a dozen corner taverns, and wondered if she glanced at me from their windows. I peeked at the women chatting under the hair dryers in the beauty salon, and at the sullen-faced LPNs and chambermaids driving home from work in their uniforms and used, ungainly cars, and wondered. Was she the black woman glancing up from her pile of wash in the Laundromat? The papers had said nothing of her race. She might be one of the Turkish women who whisked past me in the same colors I wore, a black dress and a white head covering, or one of the Korean twins who run the gift shop around the corner from the rec field. She could be any shape or hue. Was she even alive? I used to try to estimate the very longest time my groundhog could have lived with his wound. Past a certain point, the animal was no longer lingering, but surviving. I was never sure if I was comforted or even more horrified by that possibility.

No one addressed me so much as a word—except for one man who said "Excuse me, Father," when he walked in front of me from a go-go bar to his van on the curb, which identified him as "Jack the Roofer." Finally I stepped into a nondescript grill and ordered a cup of coffee. I was at last beginning to feel as though I could sleep. A little ceramic tippler with a red light for a nose blinked on and off on the counter, and for a while I drank my coffee watching its reflection in the window.

I was startled by a woman standing beside my table. She was not the waitress.

"Excuse me," she said.

"Yes."

"You don't know me," she said. That introduction always comes as a relief to a minister. We are usually accosted by people we are supposed to know, but have forgotten, at least by name.

"I was just wondering ..." She looked up and down the aisle of the restaurant as if she did not want to be overheard. She wore her blond

261

hair in a ponytail, but she was at least a little older than I. Her skirt and jacket were a deep Advent purple. "Are you Reverend Pierce?" she said.

"Yes, I am."

"I thought so," she said, looking away from me toward the street. Then she looked at her hands. She did not wear a wedding ring. Finally she looked back into my eyes.

"I was just wondering ..." she said again.

"Can I help you?" I asked.

"I don't think so," she said.

She remained standing by the table, albeit furtively. I could tell there was something she wanted to say, but could not decide if she would say it. I still cannot believe what I said to her.

"Are you the woman Alex Leonard raped?"

"God," she said, twisting her face and then touching her hand to her cheek. In a moment she had hurried to the sidewalk. I'll never know how long the groundhog lingered underground, or whether this woman was the one I sought, or a friend of hers, or the victim of another rape, or as is probably the case, only someone prone to react with horror to a horrible question.

2

I decided to phone Ellen and ask her to pick me up near the diner. I was now feeling very weak—the coffee had only made me queasy—and I was aghast at my behavior with the woman inside. It was the worst loss of self-control since I had confronted those two boys in the parking lot, and then I had at least had some purpose, some provocation. When Ellen offered to come into my house and make me a snack, I did not refuse, sleepy as I was. I found myself wanting to confess to her what I had done, perhaps hoping that in her unqualified acceptance of me I would find absolution. Instead, her response was cold.

"Alson, what if that had been the woman? Has it occurred to you that she wouldn't want to talk to you or to anybody else about what happened? Can't you see the obvious fact that the whole reason you don't even know her name is that she wouldn't want you to know it?"

She tried then to soften her voice and expression, but I could tell it was an effort.

"Alson, what possible reason could she have to want to talk with you?"

What she said hurt. I managed to say, "Maybe because we have more in common with each other than we have with most people."

"Maybe," she whispered.

We were quiet for a minute. The wind rattled a pane. The stove ticked as the heat left its coils. Finally I said, "Well it wasn't her anyway. I think I should go to sleep now, Ellen."

I could feel her studying my face, though I was not looking at hers.

"All right," she said, again softly.

"Ellen, I don't want you to think—" I stopped, wondering what it was I didn't want her to think. She spoke before I could continue.

"I was raped, too," she said.

I turned to face her. I almost asked, "By Alex Leonard?" but I had the sense to say instead, "When was this?"

"Years ago. Oh God," she said, with tears coming. "I don't know why I said that. You don't need to hear that. I'm sorry."

"You never mentioned anything. I would never have involved you, Ellen—"

"Stop." She sniffed. "It happened before I met you. Just before. I never mentioned it because I didn't want to mention it, and I wish I hadn't mentioned it now. I'm leaving. You need to go to sleep."

"How do you go to sleep after somebody just told you a thing like that?"

Her arms lay limp on the table. I feared to take her hand, but wanted to.

"It's over now. It was no big deal. It was a big deal. But I'm not thinking about it most of the time. I can't believe I just told you."

"You should have said something to me in direction. You make me wonder if I was as helpful to you as I'd like to think."

"The helpful part was not having to talk about it. You know me—with my big mouth, every friend I had knew about it in three days, and I went to a woman's crisis, rape crisis center, whatever the hell it was, so I had all the opportunities in the world to talk about it. I even told my ex-husband, probably to make him feel guilty, you know, not there to protect me. That was a waste. You'll never know what a relief it was for me to sit down with you once or twice a month and talk about spiritual stuff—it made me feel like there was more to me than my vagina. Believe me. I'll always be grateful to you for that."

"Did they catch him?"

She shook her head and bit her lip. "I never reported it. Bad move, right?"

"That's not for me to say."

"I just couldn't deal with it then. And I was lucky, everybody made a point of telling me how lucky I was. I mean, the way these things go...he didn't hit me, he didn't *kill* me, he didn't make me do...all the things he could have made me do."

For some reason, the thought of her "good luck" made her cry all the more.

"That was what nobody understood. Like I was lucky, but that made it awful in a way, too. If he'd been a maniac or something, or real mad...instead he was just so calm. It was nothing to him. *I* was nothing. Absolutely nothing. It was just like an everyday thing. Something to do."

I offered her my handkerchief. People reveal the God-appalling truth of their lives to us, and we do or say something we saw on television.

"I had these boxes," she sobbed after wiping her eyes and nose. "I had these cardboard boxes at the top of my stairs. I'd just cleaned my whole place, and I put all this junk in these boxes. I figured maybe I'd give some of it to the Salvation Army or maybe I'd have a yard sale. I worked for three days cleaning out all that crap. I remember thinking to myself, 'Hey, Ellen, you're getting your shit together now.'

"And then one night I come home from work and there are my boxes at the top of the stairs, except this time when I get to the top, a guy jumps out from behind them with a knife and tells me not to scream, and tells me to unlock my door, and that's what I do, and then he sits down on my couch and tells me to take off all my clothes, and I do that, too..."

Here her voice broke, and here I got up and moved to her side of the table and held her upper arm in my hands. Was I giving comfort or taking it? Had we locked the front door?

"And he didn't hit me, he didn't threaten me, it was like I'd invited him over. He couldn't have been more than twenty years old. He had an accent, I don't know if he was Spanish or an Arab or what he was. And this is the part that really killed me. I'm standing there, and I've got my top off and my hands are shaking so I can't unfasten the button on my skirt and I worry that if I stall he'll hurt me, which of course makes me shake all the more, and then I just stop right there and I think, 'This is another human being.' And I say to him, 'You're such a nice-looking young man. You don't have to do this to get a girl.'

"And he doesn't even say a word. He just smiles at me, and then he gives his head this little nod like 'Keep undressing, honey. I know I'm good-looking. Just take off your clothes.'"

She took a gulp of air.

"It was like a comment on my whole life. Like this is me, this is what it's all been like, laying down on the rug and opening up my heavy legs and getting fucked over."

I was crying with her by then, and she took one of my hands from her arm and held it to her cheek.

"I didn't mean to tell you all this," she whispered, her tears subsiding now that she saw mine.

"I'm glad you did," I said.

"No, you're not. I just—it's taking you over there to look for this rape victim you'd never even seen ..."

"I never would have asked you—"

"You don't understand."

"I do."

"No. You don't. You think I'm freaking out because of bad memories or something. Would I hang around with a guy like you if I couldn't deal with the subject? Huh? Alson, I've always liked you a little bit. It was partly the guru-and-groupie thing, okay? And you never played that game, which just made me like you more. I never would've acted on it..." She turned in her chair to face me. "I haven't exactly been a nun in my life, but I've never gone after anybody's husband. Not

267

after the way my husband cheated on me. I've always liked men, Alson. I was never promiscuous, but you know, I had men. We never talked much about that, but I let enough slip between the lines for you to know what I was about. Well, it's not easy to give yourself to any man after you go through a thing like that. I mean, however much you and Cynthia loved each other, don't think that if she'd lived she could have just climbed back in bed with you and everything'd be like before. Well, when you came to the church that morning, I got this idea in my head, 'This is a man I can relate to. His wife was raped, I was raped. And he can see beyond the rape, he has eyes for spiritual reality, he can forgive...'"

I waved for her to stop as I turned away.

"I'm not the saint you think I am!"

"Okay," she said, touching her finger to my cracked lips. "I don't care if you are. I don't care if you can forgive Alex Leonard or walk on water. I just wonder if someday you can love me, and I can enjoy being loved. Now I've said it all clearly and I want to get into my car and drive home."

"You're nuts," I said, gently.

"That's right," she said, patting my hands, which were now folded in my lap. "I'm nuts. And maybe you're right, maybe you're not a saint after all. I'm beginning to wonder if you're not just as nuts as I am. Just don't shut me out, Alson. Let me think there's one person in the world I can fuck up with, even if we can't fuck, and I don't have to worry about

268

getting written off, and don't tell me that person is God, because I'm the type who needs to be able to pinch it once in a while to see if it's all real. Go to sleep."

"Ellen..."

Without thinking, I put my arms around her and kissed the tears on both her cheeks. She smiled—gave a short, sobbing laugh—and then I kissed her full on the mouth. But she only wiped her lips across mine with the shaking of her head. She took my hands in hers, standing up, still shaking her head, fighting the urge to cry again.

"Not like this. Not tonight. I've shown you my heart. Please don't pity me."

I rose with my hands still in hers.

"I want to show you my heart, too," I heard myself say.

Then I walked to my bedroom, where I kept the Communion box.

I laid the black box on the kitchen table. The thin cross etched in the lid faced us where we stood like a bride and groom. I thought how much my imminent revelation would be—as I had promised Ellen—a "showing of my heart." Indeed, it felt as if my heart were in that box, more so than in my chest, though it was beating hard there now.

I also remember thinking, with that vague and specious logic that accompanies so many of our spur-of-the-moment surrenders, how

I was about to bring all the loose ends of the day together. I was going to join the male and female ends of two separate wires and light up the darkness. I was going to attain a preliminary peace before doing my last terrible deed.

"You've probably never even seen this," I said.

"No," she answered quietly.

"Most people, even most church people, haven't. Even people who go to church all their lives sometimes never see this, especially if they die suddenly."

I extended the fingers of one hand toward it, an embarrassingly sacramental gesture.

"A minister or a priest uses this to take Communion to people who are too ill or otherwise unable to come to church. I take this with me when I go to the prison. Even though Alex Leonard does not receive Communion, because he hasn't been baptized, and because, until now anyway, he hasn't wanted any part of such things, I take this with me every time I go to see him. A man at the prison risked his life to save this, during the disturbance there, because he believed it contained the food of salvation."

Except for the last remark, during which my voice dropped and trembled, I spoke with evenness, authority, and—to my ears at least—a touch of irony. By now Ellen was looking at me instead of at the box. She was no longer crying or sniffling. Her sadness had given way to anticipation—and probably to surprise. I spoke with none of the inaudible listlessness and morbidity that had characterized so much of what I had said to her in the days since she had met me at church. Through her shoulder and arm, now touching mine, I could feel her willingness to follow my lead— an awful sensation from which I recoiled.

That reaction, I suppose, made me eager to proceed, to join the wires.

"Let me open it for you," I said, bending over the table. I opened the latch and revealed the polished vessels in their niches of black velvet.

"This container normally holds the wine we have blessed in our services, this is the chalice, and this little plate is the paten," I said, naming each piece as though she were a small child. When I straightened up again and looked into her face, her expression was actually like a child's— though perhaps she was merely reflecting what she thought she glimpsed in me. It is here, I think, that the fissure began to open.

"These things are made of real silver. They have been in our church since the turn of the century. Even though ours is a very Protestant church, we still treat these material things with respect because of what they contain, what they help us remember. Close to Jesus, you see. The women of the church polish them from time to time. They're often the last nonmedical instruments that people see before they die."

"Yes," she said, but with a question in her voice. And though I felt the fissure widening, I said the next words.

"But in this box, Ellen, there is a terrible secret. A terrible secret in my heart."

I faced her, and she grasped my hands to support me in what I was about to reveal. I noticed a small flake of dried mucus dangling in one of her nostrils. It was not funny or repulsive. Once you become a father or mother, the secretions of human bodies are not the same as before—especially in those you love. And I think I had begun to love Ellen, in some way. Her eyes were still puffy and her hair disheveled. Her cheeks were blotchy and livid. Her palms were moist in mine. She was weary. I might have been looking at her on the evening she'd been raped. Her arms, hanging to where her hands held mine, felt the way she had described her legs as feeling on that night—heavy, helpless against the world's meanness.

The veil was altogether torn now. I saw how false and wicked my impulse had been. How dare I draw this poor woman into my scheme! It was as selfish and cruel, no doubt, as my question to that anonymous woman in Beaumont, as my hope of finding Leonard's first known victim. I saw my dreadful, shameful folly, but with hardly less dread and shame I saw the only sensible way out of it.

"So there is a secret here...in this box," I said, still wavering, but she tightened her grip on my hands again, and I was resolved. "Though it's not such a secret if you have eyes to see. All this lovely silverware, this plush little box, like a gem case, all this is made to hold...blood, brokenness. 'This is my body, which is broken for you.' Your heart, Ellen, my heart—all the brokenness and blood, Jimmy ..." I was flailing, and beginning to choke up. I took hold of myself, pulling my hands gently from hers.

"Ellen, I want to give you Communion," I said. "It's the only thing I know how to do right now. It's the only thing I can share with you. Will you take it?"

She nodded her head—baffled, or moved, I am not sure.

Of course, the set was not "loaded"—though the snub-nosed vessel hidden under the lid was. Fortunately I had both bread and wine in the house—both cheap, both white, neither blessed. I sent Ellen to my bedroom for my prayer book and pieced together a service. She stood at my side reverently, with her hands folded as I read. When I placed the bottle of wine back on the table after filling the chalice, I accidentally brushed the empty box, and it fell backward with a dull, unsettling thud, but I proceeded without a pause.

I lifted the small plate of bread, the sign for Ellen to take a piece of it, or to open her hand for me to give her one, but instead she opened her mouth. She took the bread from my hand with her lips—and then lifted a second piece of bread from the plate and brought it to mine. Some years ago our church had done one of those Communions where the participants feed one another, so her gesture was not exactly an innovation, but it had not been my intention to receive. I found myself trapped in the momentum I had started. What could I do now but open my mouth?

If there had been any way to hold the bread there and expel it later, I would have done so. But it dissolved when, after drinking from the cup herself, Ellen trickled the sour wine onto my tongue.

I offered to let her sleep on my couch if she was too tired or upset to drive home, but she said she was feeling very good just then—I think she sensed that I was not feeling very good myself. I believe she asked me if I wanted her to stay. I remember her thanking me warmly, kissing my cheek before she left. I was very distracted by then.

You see, I felt as though I had been poisoned. I felt like one of those plotters in an Elizabethan play, compelled by an ironic twist of events to drink from the deadly cup he has prepared for someone else. I had gone to drug Ellen—mind you, with salvation and the love of God—and had been forced to swallow the dram myself. I felt as if my days were sorely numbered. I could feel the warmth of the wine filling my body as the echoes of Alex Leonard's supposedly repentant outcry filled my head. There was no point in my crying out for mercy because, to my great dismay, it was mercy I had just received.

3 ✦

I've called Andrew and persuaded him to assist me in preparing Alex Leonard for baptism. I don't know what else to do. Following the riot, the prison authorities have banned nearly all visitors except physicians for at least ten days. When the doors do open, security will be tighter than ever. If I don't play along with Leonard's request, I may never be able to see him. But actually to teach him the catechism when I plan to kill him is more of a pretense than even I am able to manage. I suppose it's no better to involve Andrew. But who knows? I could die unexpectedly, and then Andrew could just carry on. Maybe that's what God has in mind.

I keep going over my last moments with Leonard. The exact sequence of events is no longer clear to me. I remember the inmates shouting at me to kill him. I remember taking the rag-wrapped handle of the knife in my hands and raising the blade over his chest. Later, during the interrogations that followed the riot, I said that I had been stalling for time, playing along, hoping to prevent the other inmates from killing Leonard or me. Even Rita appeared willing to buy the story.

It was a lie, of course. I had no such intention. But did I hesitate? Did I take longer to raise the knife than I remember? Those moments were so feverishly unreal—my senses were overwhelmed with shouting, the smell of sweat and vomit, and the sight of blood. Did Leonard cry out to be baptized because he saw me hesitate, or did I hesitate because he called out? Was that his purpose in calling out, to stay my hand? Or was he actually converted somehow, perhaps by believing I was ready to spare him? Did he see me smile at the imminent fulfillment of my revenge, and mistake my expression for one of love?

I suppose none of this matters. I am still resolved to kill him if I can. I only wish I did not have this sense of directing my violence against God himself. Before, I had felt myself estranged from God, acting under his disapproving eye, but not face to face with it. Then, for a few moments during the uprising, I had felt a sense of his favor and forgiveness, as if he had said, *I was prepared to grant your wish all along, and now, in my own way, in a better way than you could have imagined, here it is. Take it, my child.*

Leonard broke the spell when he pleaded to be baptized. Now I must break more than the commandment to love our enemies. I must be willing to cut down someone who would, in the name of Christ, become my brother and friend. I must defy salvation itself. Of course, Leonard may be no more sincere in his request to follow Jesus than I have been in mine.

I also keep thinking of Preston, the guard at the metal detector who rescued my

Communion box and me with it. If God is pulling all these strings, then didn't he arrange this also? If God meant only to thwart my plans, why did he have someone nearly killed to prevent their detection? In any case, God has acted with all of his proverbial willingness to use and abuse an innocent creature. I am told Preston is in stable condition. I have sent him flowers and a card. I simply could not bear to visit him. I wonder how he will feel when he finds out that he risked his life to rescue a gun.

All of this speculation disgusts me. Religion is not the opiate of the people; it's the needless headache of the people. It's the best reason on earth for taking an opiate. What are all these questions to me? I will cling to what I know for sure. I know my wife and son were ripped open and stabbed to death by a man who now dares to ask me to wash their blood off his hands in a basin of holy water.

In fact, the anniversary of their deaths was the day before yesterday. I had hoped to kill Leonard by then, but the anniversary was an artificial deadline. Without a calendar we would have no way of knowing that the earth has orbited the sun since some important event, and what difference does it make if we know? What difference does it make if my wife and child died on the eighth or the tenth of November, or in October or December? Every day is an anniversary, every time I put my head to a pillow in an empty bed is an anniversary, every clean square centimeter of porcelain sink not marked by the toothpaste droppings from Jimmy's toothbrush is a day on the calendar not marked by the sight of his smile. God damn the anniversary. It is of no use to me.

Nevertheless, I still noted it with a foolish ceremony. I cut a jagged lock from my unkempt hair and burned it in the dry concrete bird-bath in the backyard. I have no idea what this pagan gesture was supposed to mean. I could not keep a match lit in the wind. Finally I used a splash of whiskey for lighter fluid. I took a mouthful and let my throat burn as my hair did. My little sacrifice gave off a bitter stench. No doubt there was a trace of that odor in the air when the Church condemned a woman to be burned alive as a witch, following a very thorough spiritual and physical examination.

We saw Leonard today. He still calls me Reverend. He says he was born again during the riot. He says that God used me and my wife and son to win him for Christ. He says he wants his girlfriend to be present for the baptism, and he wants me to marry them shortly there-after. He said all this without once using the word *fuck*. He has the sequence all very clear in his head: baptism as soon as possible, an appeal under way before Christmas if possi-ble, a formal engagement to Monica Zeller on

Christmas Day (Lincoln's past references to Zeller as Leonard's fianceé were apparently euphemistic), wedding bells (recorded, of course) on the first day of the new year. He made no mention of the knife I had held poised over his chest.

I explained that Andrew was going to assist me with the catechism, that in fact he would do most of the catechizing. The reason I gave was the necessity of making his baptism an act of the whole Christian Church and not just a personal matter between him and me.

He said the catechism would probably not take long to do, because he knew just about all of "that stuff" anyway. Who did it or how long it took was not important, because he knew he was saved.

I wonder if what we see in Leonard is a conversion or a regression. He seems to have flipped an internal switch that replays every canting formula of his upbringing. I have to say I found some grim amusement in listening as Andrew attempted to give Leonard a dreary "contextual understanding" of the Apostles' Creed, only to be slapped with a backwash of fundamentalist malarkey.

Andrew tried to explain that the bodily resurrection of Christ might be no more than mythological embellishment of an event "which nevertheless happened." The early Church, he said, had found no better way to express this ineffably subtle experience than in the "resurrection language" already available in pagan mystery cults. This proved too much for Alex, who felt compelled to draw upon some available language of his own.

Andrew set him off when he suggested that "the Church may not even have *begun* to fully grasp what the Resurrection means."

"What it means!" Leonard spouted. "What it means is that Jesus Christ's dead body got up and walked out of his fucking grave, you peckerhead!"

Then he turned to me in dismay that was almost precious.

"Reverend, why do you have to bring these people in here? For God's sake!"

"Now, Alex," I said, "I know Reverend Nelson's views are a little unorthodox, and a little hard to understand sometimes, even for me, but it's important for a Christian to be open to different points of view. And I really think you should apologize for calling him a peckerhead."

Another memorable moment came when Andrew told Leonard that the renunciation of evil in the baptismal examination included a renunciaton of all racial prejudice.

"That's one thing I've never been is prejudiced," replied Leonard, without so much as a trace of irony in his voice. "I've always treated people the way they treated me, irregardless of race, color, what-have-you."

Was it the voice of the resurrected Lord or of his Adversary that whispered in my ear, "Leave these two to their folly and come away from this place"?

I said to the voice: "At least the movie camera is gone."

Not for long, though. Roth was waiting for us when we finished our session with Leonard. He says the baptism is to be the new center of the documentary, that and "the process of healing" at the prison. He hopes to recoup his losses by using news bites and snapshots. He kept talking about a documentary history of the Civil War that did the same thing. Daguerreotypes of Alex Leonard with a cavalry saber.

I told him that my father-in-law had all of my photographs, and that I had no idea where he lived. It was so strange to find the truth so useful.

Ellen invited me to have Thanksgiving at her house, and I could find no good reason to refuse. Any reason would appear to mask some repulsion at what she had confided to me the other day. I must at least let her know that if I turn away from her it is not because she was a victim.

I asked her not to make a heavy meal, at least not on my account. She compensated with variety and elegance. The diminutive turkey was wreathed on its platter with small roasted apples, sprigs of parsley, and cranberry clusters. A dozen or more little soup bowls held modest double portions of mashed potatoes, gravy, salad, rice pilaf, chutney, pickles, stuffing, even pasta. She announced as she set it all out that what we did not eat she could freeze for herself to thaw as lunch later on, so I should feel no obligation to try or to finish anything. She offered me the gift she herself could rarely enjoy—the way lovers offer each other their own bodies—food without guilt.

As she bent her face over the table, lighting the candles and smiling in their radiance, I could not help but feel ashamed. I can do nothing in return for this woman's kindness— except, when all is revealed, to make her look and feel like a fool. Nevertheless, I go on enjoying the kindness. I have suffered an infamous crime, I have devised an unusual revenge, but neither seems to have spared me the common fate of reaching that age when men act as though life owes them an indulgence.

Ellen did not ask if I would say the grace. Had I said one anyway, I would have given thanks for that omission above all.

She had even rented a movie for us to watch afterward, three in fact, so I could take my pick.

As it turned out, something was wrong with the VCR. The screen was full of snow. She tried all three movies without luck. I found myself looking at her body as she bent over and then kneeled to fiddle with the machine. In a different age she would have been considered voluptuous, beautiful. The screen full of visual static quivered above her head like some techno-idiot's virtual beehive; below it her hair rested on her neck, and her bottom on her heels, with actual loveliness. I winced to feel a betrayal in these thoughts, to remember Cynthia sitting fashionably trim and utterly absorbed by her computer screen.

Nothing worked with the VCR. Ellen asked if I would like to drink some sherry and listen to some music. I remembered the "plan B" a teacher always wants to have in case the audiovisual equipment doesn't work—a million years ago, it seemed.

We listened to music for a while. She told me she wanted to play me her favorite song, "Imagine" by John Lennon. I had heard snatches of it before, but had never listened all the way through.

"It is something to imagine, really," Ellen said when the song was over, "people just living for today and for each other, without heaven and hell hanging over them. I'm not saying I don't believe in any of that, I just wonder if our lives wouldn't be more focused and practical the other way."

"The question of heaven and hell and whether there's a life after this one is the only thoroughly practical question a person ever asks," I replied, not quite to the point. "Maybe Mr. Lennon has the right answer, but he couldn't have afforded not to ask the question. It determines everything."

"I guess I see what you mean," she said.

"I see what you mean, too," I said, though I think neither of us saw anything but that we were touching on a subject we didn't feel like arguing about.

I was somewhat amazed by what I had said. For the past year I have given little thought to any world beyond this one. If there is a heaven, Cynthia and Jimmy must be there. If there is a hell, Alex Leonard certainly belongs there, though one never knows with God, whose ideas are characteristically more outrageous than any Beatle's. As for me, I have acted as if I am above the question. Removing Leonard from this world has seemed more pressing and important than my destiny in any other one. Recently, however, I find it takes more effort to suppress the fear of divine judgment.

But we have television, thank God, or else we would go mad from such thoughts. Ellen and I watched on into the night, stupid sitcoms mostly, though in the end we did find a movie, riddled with commercials. We sat on her well-worn couch like an old married couple and watched the comic misadventures of a single mother who falls in love with the guardian angel sent to protect her undeserving boor of an ex-husband. Most of the humor centered around the angel's miraculous ability to bring the woman to orgasm telepathically, and her nine-year-old son's even more miraculous ability to parent both himself and his mother.

For Ellen the boy, and everything else in the movie, was charming and hilarious. Her laughter sounded to me as her dining room table had looked: full of a nourishing, sensual generosity that I found appealing, but of which I could partake only in niggling portions. I was not always like this. I was not always so bitter and self-absorbed. Once I was a man that a woman could love without pity, that she could shout at and laugh at and run away from and shamelessly seduce, because he was a man. Now I am like one of those invalids I used to visit in the days when my Communion box held nothing but Communion, a person whose sickness has become his sin, who has no joy in life and who passes his sour judgments like phlegm or gas on all of those souls who do. It occurs to me that after putting Leonard out of his misery I ought to do the same for myself. Ah, but then I'd miss seeing our wretched movie, and reading what outrages my lackluster performance entitles the audience to inflict on my wife's corpse.

Near the end of the show, as Ellen's laughter changed to sentimental tears, I lifted my hand from my lap, and through her dress and opaque stocking I massaged one of the legs she had been forced to open to the meanness of the world. The gesture strikes me as a bit adolescent. I wonder if my best excuse lies in the wine, the woman, or the song.

It snowed the next day, about ten inches. Snowstorms are like little apocalypses in northeastern New Jersey. We suddenly discover that we have displaced so much of the earth's surface with our human presence that we literally have no place to put what drops on us from the sky.

285

I turned off the television news and went outside for a few moments to stand in the falling snow. I caught the flakes in my hand—as fragile as embryos or civilizations, as fragile as happiness. Two winters ago I was towing Jimmy in his sleigh and lobbing snowballs at his mother's behind, the three of us laughing louder than the sirens that were, even then, converging relentlessly upon our lives.

I have missed two sessions with Leonard now. I missed the first when I remembered his Christmas list, which he had mentioned again at our previous meeting. I thought I ought not to show up without some work done on Monica's Christmas present. Now today there is this storm. Andrew phoned and said neither of us should drive out of his way to pick up the other. If I couldn't make it to the prison, he would go by himself. It's all highway from his place, and he had the garage put chains on his tires.

He is worried because another minister has suddenly appeared on the scene, an evangelist of some kind. A few days before Thanksgiving, I received a letter asking me to endorse "Alex Leonard Ministries," should the venture "be anointed." Apparently, Leonard hopes to take his "testimony" on the road if his appeal goes through. No matter. If he succeeds in living until the new year, I'll go on the road with him. I'll mousse my hair and come on stage night after night and wrap him in my arms to rounds of cathartic applause. In the meantime, this newcomer is not my problem. Leonard still needs me for his movie, and he needs me to make his fairy tale complete.

The snowstorm gave me an excuse to work on the Communion box. The latch was always tight; now the whole business seems to have shifted so that it's nearly impossible to close the lid. I think it may have been damaged during the riot. So I fussed with it in the basement until I grew frustrated and came upstairs again. I'm tempted to build yet another one, but am fearful that a third box is certain to arouse suspicion.

I went shopping in the evening. The snow had stopped, and the main roads were plowed by then. The malls were as bright and eerie as palaces on Mars. I walked between two points of a million-megawatt snowflake as shoppers scurried in and out around me like black ants. I walked for quite a while without entering a store, testing my nerves against the loudspeakers. I can stand most carols, but I hate secular Christmas music, the sole purpose of which is to evoke a mood that its very existence makes impossible. If there is music in hell, it works like that, and it plays without ceasing.

I finally stopped at an electronics shop and bought myself a pocket-sized tape recorder, one of those that take a microcassette. I find myself wanting to capture a small sample of Leonard's voice before I kill him. I could preserve it like that last remaining specimen of smallpox virus frozen in a research bunker somewhere. I could play it if I ever began to feel remorse.

I also bought a pewter Merlin with a small prism at the end of his wand. He stands about four inches tall and cost fifty-nine dollars. I brought him into the cellar and hanged him from a lightbulb string. He turns slowly in his noose as his wand spatters the concrete walls with chips of colored light. He would make a good target.

"Reverend, where have you been?"

"Home, just a little under the weather. How are you, Alex?"

"Fine. It's awful nice of you to ask! I thought you'd died or something. Jeez, what are you doing, singing in a rock group? You need a haircut. You represent the Master, remember? You got to look the part."

"I brought you a Merlin."

"A what?"

"A Merlin. For Monica. It's pewter. I saved the receipt if you think she has one like this. I would have forgotten it was in my pocket except it set off the metal detector. Gave everyone quite a scare. I'll have to bring it back to the desk, of course, but they said I could show you. Think she'll like it?"

"She's not even going to see it! Didn't you know that Merlin is a satanic symbol?"

"Him?"

"Yeah, him. I don't even like having that thing in here."

"I'm so sorry. I really didn't know."

"Well, now you do. Get thee behind me, Satan. It's probably all right now. Stick it on the floor and put a newspaper over it or something. Lucky you saved the receipt. Just put it in the corner, never mind. So are you going to baptize me, Reverend, or what? There are some people showing a real interest in this, you know. You've been my first choice all along, but if you're not interested anymore, just say so."

"Of course I'm interested, Alex. You know I'm always interested."

"That's not exactly how things have looked."

"We must be careful about judging things by how they look. Appearances can be very deceptive. I've stayed away awhile, that's all. I've given you time by yourself and me time by myself. It's part of the preparation. Each of us has spent some time in the wilderness."

"So you're doing it for sure?"

"I wouldn't miss it to save my life. Besides, if anyone else did it, we'd just about be ruining Mr. Roth's movie, wouldn't we? And I think it would look better for the appeal, too. Don't you?"

"That's another thing. If you're going to help me with that, you need to see Lincoln."

"We'll take care of everything, don't worry. The baptism first. Do you feel ready? Has Reverend Nelson made everything clear for you?"

"Mostly I've made it clear for myself. My personal relationship with my Lord and Savior is what makes everything clear. That guy I don't know about. He makes me wonder if he isn't a wolf in sheep's clothing."

"Not Reverend Nelson."

"Yeah, Reverend Nelson! Don't be so naive. You didn't know about Merlin, either, right?"

"That's true."

"Right."

"Well, do you have any questions? Is there anything left I could answer for you?"

"Not really. How about you? Do you have any questions? Well, do you have any? My heart is an open book now. The whole world can read what's there, and the whole thing's been written by Jesus Christ. Isn't that what the Scriptures say? 'Thy word hast thou hid in my heart, that I might not sin against thee'? What's on your mind? Ask away."

"This isn't really important..."

"Ask me something important, then."

"Well, I guess this is important, but only to me. It's just a thing I've always wondered. In fact, I was all ready to ask it on that day when everything blew up here."

"The day you faked everybody out with that knife, just to save my life? That day?"

"Yes. That day."

"I was born again on that day. So what was your question?"

"It was about...the crime."

"Go on."

"Well, not to make a big thing out of it, but I always wondered why you tied my wife and me up, but didn't tie up Jimmy. My son. I just wondered about that. Maybe you don't even know yourself."

"Oh, I know. You know, Reverend, you are a person with a lot of curiosity about things, aren't you? I used to be like that before I gave myself to Christ. Now I know that most things are best left in his hands. But you'd like to know?"

"Only if you feel like telling me."

"It's not a question of feeling. I do what the Lord wills. And maybe he wills for me to answer your question. Thy will be done, then. Why I didn't tie up little Jimmy. Well, Reverend, before I was saved, I walked in darkness, you know? I just figured there was no sense tying up Jimmy in case I had a use for him later on."

"A use?"

"Oh, Reverend, Reverend, nobody knows the troubles I've seen. There's an old Negro spiritual that goes like that. You know that one?"

"I think so, maybe."

"Pastor Davies told me about it. You haven't met him yet. You will. A wonderful Christian with a full Gospel message, not like your Reverend Nelson there. A real family man, too. Four kids, all beautiful girls, you should see 'em. He showed me their pictures. You should be getting a letter from him. Did you get anything from him yet?"

"I don't think so. No, I didn't. You were saying—"

"Reverend, one day something happened to me that I will never forget as long as I live. In its own way it's probably a worse thing than what happened to you. I was about as old as your Jimmy. How old was he again?"

"Four."

"Maybe I was older, then. I think I was about eight. And one morning, when my mother was still in bed, my father started to get after me. I knew what he wanted because he'd done it to me before, when my mother wasn't around. So I went tearing into my parents' bedroom and I jumped into my mother's arms, hollering like a son of a gun. And then my old man busted into the room. I can still hear him shouting at me, 'Don't you ever run from your father!' and shouting at my mother, 'Don't you ever stand against me, woman!' He was wild. Wild! And we just lay there holding each other and shaking like a leaf, like a couple of leafs. And then you know what he did, Reverend? You know what he did?"

"What?"

"He climbed onto that bed and got on his knees. For a minute I thought he was going to pray. But he wasn't going to pray. What he did instead was he stuck his fat fingers into the both of us, one hand for me and one hand for my mom. And we didn't do nothing. Not a thing. Just laid there together. You ever hear anything sicker than that? Hmm?"

"I guess not."

"Neither did I. And for a long time that was in my head. That was my sickness too. That day you first saw me? My sickness too. But not anymore. Because I can honestly say, Alson,

I have forgiven that man what he did to me, to me and my mother. Just like you forgive me. Praise the Lord."

4

When I knocked at Ellen Fabian's door, I realized for the first time that the entrance to her apartment was not up an enclosed stairway, but straight through the front door on the open porch, the other apartment being at the back. So she had moved since her rape. I was glad of that for her.

She was surprised to see me, of course. She answered the door with her hair disheveled. Her voice was huskier than usual; she had not been long out of bed.

"Alson. To what do I owe this surprise? This is the first time you've come to my door without an invitation. You got your hair cut." She brushed my ear with her fingertips. "You look nice."

"I've come to see if you have any more of that turkey still in the refrigerator."

"Gee, I don't, but—"

"Can I come in?"

"Sure. Of course you can come in." I could tell she was uneasy. She sensed some kind of announcement.

"Are you really hungry?"

"No, I was just fooling."

"So tomorrow's the big day," she said, taking my coat and scarf. "Are you nervous?"

"A little. But I'm ready. Got everything but the water."

"Well, don't forget that!" She poked my arm and laughed, still uneasy.

I sat down on her couch and she did the same beside me.

"Ellen, after I see Alex Leonard tomorrow, I'm going away. It's become very clear to me—spiritually, even—that once I've done what I have to do inside that prison, I can't remain here. I will go right away, not without missing some dear people and places, which is a pleasant surprise to me, because for a long time I was past missing anything. I owe most of that to you. Anyway, I've come to say good-bye."

This last seemed so blunt. Yet what other way was there to say it?

"I don't want to say good-bye."

She was upset, but also relieved to know why I had come. Was a part of her also relieved to have my burdensome presence passing from her life? How could she have felt otherwise? It is a measure of the affection she has for me that she would so readily forfeit that relief, that unburdening, to keep me with her.

"Why do you have to go? And do you have to go now? Aren't you deciding all of this too soon?"

"It's decided."

"Where are you going?"

"Far away."

"Aren't you the one who used to tell me how

294

people in our culture always think they can solve their problems by changing their addresses or their hair styles?"

"I am. And it turns out I'm one of them. As you noticed, I've just been for a haircut." I sighed. "Ellen, I've thought about this carefully. Maybe you'll understand later..."

"Oh, for God's sake, Alson, don't do *Casablanca* with me."

I was taken aback for a minute. She reassured me with her hand and spoke quietly.

"There are other ways to fade out of circulation, if that's what you want. I think you should live with me."

"I've been underground for a long time now, or I feel like it anyway. I want to be above ground, but out of sight, if that makes any sense."

"Take me with you, then. I've never been a burden to you, have I?" I shook my head. "And I could help you. I'd get a job, I'd keep you away from any...scrutiny, I'd..."

"I can't take you, Ellen. I won't say it isn't tempting."

"But why not?"

I had not intended to go into specifics.

"They won't allow women where I'm going." Pause. "I'm going to become a sort of monk."

"A sort of monk? What, like a hermit or something?"

"Yes, like that, but in a community, too. I don't have this worked out exactly, but I can't take a woman."

"It's hard for me to think of you as a monk.

I'm not sure this is the right thing for you. Maybe it is. You'd be free to seek God."

I turned to face her. We'd been sitting side by side, facing forward, the way men are said to communicate, like two monks.

"We're always free to seek God," I said.

"What about Alex?"

"What about him?"

"Isn't he going to need you around to look after him and all after he's baptized?"

"No, I don't think he will. My work will be done, in any case."

She looked straight ahead. A tear ran down her cheek.

"Ellen, this is a selfish decision that I'm making for myself, but really I think you're going to prosper from it, too. I am not a healthy or an enriching part of your life. You need to be free of me. I wish you'd think more about going back to school."

She was shaking her head. She still did not look at me when she spoke.

"Please don't talk about what's going to be best for me, okay? I won't try to talk you out of anything anymore, but don't talk about my welfare. I'll be the judge of my welfare from now on. You're not my spiritual director anymore."

"No. I talk too much. Maybe I should have written you a letter."

"I would've killed you."

She faced me now and smiled.

"I'm sure you would have found a nice way to do it."

As if to suggest to me how pleasantly a

man might die, she kissed me—a long kiss like the one on the beach, but not so oppressive or coaxing. This was a kiss of resignation.

"I should go," I said, though she must have read the question in my eyes.

"So this is how we're going to end our relationship, Alson? You're not even going to give me Communion?"

"We can say good-bye any way you wish," I said. She looked into my eyes for a moment, fathoming my sincerity. Then she led me by the hand to her bedroom, and I followed like a small boy.

The bed filled the tiny room. No lamp was on, but in the oblique winter sunlight I could see clearly. The patterned curtains and coverlet were done in rich swirls of burgundy and brown. There were scarves over the lampshades and afghans on the chairs—this was a room where you could leave your clothes unhung and almost not notice. On the dresser, among the lipsticks and crystal atomizers reflected in the mirror, was a small jade Buddha. Next to him, in a miniature black frame, I saw my own face, the photo that had accompanied my published article on world disarmament. I was surprised to see both of us there, like two substitute Christs.

She kissed me again, and I brought my hands lightly to her breasts, more to be certain that we were about to make love than to begin making it.

"I have to go to the bathroom for a minute," she whispered close to my ear.

"Don't undress in there—away from me." My voice sounded so loud.

She shook her head and smiled faintly. It meant "No, I won't," and "You are a man after all."

I sat down on the bed while she was gone, but I stood as soon as she crossed her arms to pull off her sweater. I was aroused at once. I had expected she might be one of those people who look better with their clothes on than off, one of the majority. She was not. When she turned to unfasten her earrings in the mirror, I was surprised to find her buttocks narrower and firmer than I'd imagined. With Cynthia it was always the opposite: she was so compact in her jeans or swathed in a skirt that I was continually amazed by the swell of her naked hips, and the fleshiness of her behind as she moved—that breathtaking slope down the small of her back.

How, I asked myself, with Ellen showing her back and the mirror showing her front to me, how could a man have known the body of my wife, of this woman, or of any woman in an hour of violence? He could not, though he had a lifetime. Her very nakedness clothed her. There is indeed such a thing as rape, I told myself, but no such thing as violation. Only revelation.

"You're beautiful," I told her.

"No, I'm not," she said. She turned to face me again. She was beautiful.

I added words from the Song of Solomon, which, I am ashamed to recall, I had once quoted to Cynthia in a moment like this one: "Your navel is a rounded bowl that never lacks mixed wine. Your belly is a heap of wheat, encircled with lilies."

Then she removed my clothes, and we were side by side again, this time under the blankets. We held hands, almost as if the love had already been made. For a moment I thought that perhaps it was so, we had done all we would do. I was not very disappointed. I find myself wondering now if we were in that bed because Ellen wanted to be, or because she had offered herself so unflaggingly before that she felt obliged to follow through now that I was ready to accept, if only as a farewell. I think maybe the kiss would have been enough for her.

In any case, I lay at her side, hoping words would not be necessary to tell her that I wanted her on top of me. I would not let her open her legs lying on her back.

She soon understood, though the condition of my penis might have made her doubt if her move above me was the right one. Watching her undress with my pants and underpants serving as a tourniquet, I'd managed the necessary blood; now I was flaccid. What if I could do no better? I thought of how I'd missed the chance to stab Alex Leonard when my hand rose over his bloody face. Will I prove just as impotent tomorrow?

She came down my skeletal chest and hollow abdomen like a slow avalanche of breasts and loose hair, cheeks and kisses. In her tenderly working mouth I could feel myself grow hard again.

She was so careful as she straddled me. Not like my wife, who swung her nimble leg over and rode close to my chest like a jockey. I was a durable enough horse in those days. I think poor Ellen was afraid of crushing me. I had wanted her to be dominant in order to reverse the position of her rape; perhaps all I did was make her feel conspicuously heavy. Perhaps all she wanted to do was take me atop her body and feel my ribs tossing safely on her breasts.

She pushed gently but steadily, deliberately squeezing me with her vagina on every pull. She kissed and caressed my neck and face. She did not make me talk, and she did not attempt to move the arm I kept pressed against the headboard as if it were fastened there.

When I saw she was laboring, I took that hand and brought it to her pumping behind. I moved the other from its resting place between her shoulder blades and into her hair. Quite soon her rhythm quickened—with her neck arched above me, she called out an enigmatic "Oh God," and in the cries that followed, so evocative of birth and death, and of my dear lost wife, I surrendered myself also.

I had not planned to stop at a church, and my first reaction to the impulse to stop when I saw the cars parked at the little Episcopal chapel just up the hill from Ellen's was an emphatic *no*. It smacked too much of a man trying to give his life "closure"—that word people use for their contrived inability to think any further about a broken promise or an unfulfilled dream. Of course my visit to Ellen smacked of this very thing.

I was not going to stop at the church. But when you have a reactive personality, as I obviously do, you sometimes suspect and then defy your own reactions. If there was no reason to stop at the church, there was no reason *not* to stop, either. I pulled over to the curb.

The building was one of those stone edifices intended to duplicate an English parish church of the nineteenth century: dark wood furnishings, the same dark wood ribbed overhead to suggest the upside-down hull of a ship; brass cross, candlesticks, eagle for the Gospel; whitewashed walls, maroon carpets and kneeling cushions, Advent purple hangings at the pulpit and altar; and vivid but somberly translucent stained glass. The priest and a handful of worshipers scattered about the nave were reading a litany of some kind. I stole quietly to a seat at the rear. The priest paused in his reading to announce the page number for my benefit; it was probably this unexpected courtesy, combined with my lateness and the lingering tingle of my hour in Ellen's bed, that kept me from realizing for a few more moments that I had stepped into a place uncannily like the church interiors of my worst dreams.

When I did note the similarity, I felt no

nightmarish sensations. Rather, I felt a kindly reassurance. Here I was, in that eerily familiar setting, but wide awake, with Leonard locked up tight, waiting to receive my bullets. As long as I found the correct page in the prayer book, I could anticipate everything that happened while I was there, every word and the rubric for every gesture.

I did not join in the prayers, however. I looked around at my pewmates: several old women; a dark-skinned young matron and her young son; a tall, white-haired Anglo-Saxon in a tweed sportcoat; a gaunt young man with a patchy beard and a worn corduroy jacket—a handful of misfits defined by faith and the lack of an eight to five job.

I also looked at the windows, most of which depicted scenes from the life of Christ, that great misfit, who lacked a job, a family, and a place to lay his head. My eyes were especially drawn to a window showing the Crucifixion. Christ hung with his bloody hands outstretched, his crowned head bending like a sunflower's. Clustered around the cross were the faces of mocking soldiers and mocking priests, the agents of physical and intellectual cruelty. Kneeling in the foreground, Mary Magdalene covered her face with her hands, while the victim's mother, in fathomless blue, stood gazing in sorrow at his face.

Oddly, what struck me about the window was the luminous whiteness of Christ's loincloth. It stood out like a word of graffiti, like an all-too-obvious idea that had never occurred to me before. Jesus was in his underwear. The reflex to cover himself with his hands, to draw his knees up over his loins, was stayed by the implacable nails. At first the detail seemed to be mocking me with its effrontery, but of course it was Christ who was being mocked.

There was suddenly a lull in the service, like the vacuum that follows a power outage, when all the humming machinery of our comfort dies at once. The priest was no longer reading. People were murmuring the names of persons and places: "William," "Carlos," "Aunt Beulah," "Bosnia." Was it "Alice" someone said then, or "Alex"? I knew that in less than a minute the priest would resume his intonation.

"Cynthia!" I cried out, startled by the exaggerated volume of my own voice—and then, more softly, "James. Ellen."

I rose up. I glanced once more at the broken and defiled body of the Son of God in his underwear—a glance that held more love than any I had ever cast him from pulpit or altar, or beside the swelling sea—and walked away from his church.

And descended into hell.

It is between two and three in the morning, and I have just awakened from my worst nightmare.

It was the wedding dream again.

303

This time there was no one in the church but me and the minister. He sat obscurely in the shadows behind the altar, but his vestments trailed out from his chair, across the floor, and filled the church with an undulating carpet of aqua-colored silk. I kept lifting my feet to let the ripples of cloth move under them. On the altar in front of where I stood was my Communion box. I knew it held our wedding rings.

As in past dreams, the stained-glass windows were charged with light—but never more than here. In one of them Ellen stood naked in a field of wheat and lilies, so frank and sensual that I turned away my eyes.

I saw Monica Zeller in another—in hell, I thought at first—but then I noticed the thick black stake to which she was chained like a martyr in the fire, her eyes gazing toward heaven and her palms pressed together in supplication. She too was radiantly naked.

Finally, in a window nearest the door and the baptismal font, with an infant at her breast and her yellow hair tied in a ponytail, her eyes slanted and her nose and lips broad and full, a third woman rose like a rocket toward the heavens as pairs of disembodied hands fell away from her throat and bare flanks, and a bloody saber from her loins. Great hands, much larger and more vivid than those she shed, opened to receive her.

What stupidity to believe that our minds can crowd all of this detail, all of this junk, into a few moments of REM sleep and not to believe that our lives are eternal!

The organ began to play, though there was no organist. It was the same Bach piece as always. Then my bride appeared, veiled and graceful at the door.

She too was alone, no bridesmaid or father. No son. Suddenly the emptiness of the church filled me with desire. I sensed that its sunlit enclosure was to serve as our honeymoon suite also, perhaps even our home. I longed for her to come forward.

The minister moved toward me as she did. The light of the nave revealed him as Preston, the guard who had saved my Communion box. His face was as inscrutable as a pharaoh's, but I was not afraid. I knew we were in good hands.

My bride halted beside me. The music stopped. The minister nodded, and she raised her hands and lifted her veil from her face.

It was Alex Leonard.

He looked at me with squinted eyes and pursed, rouged lips, with longing and beseeching, and an expression so acquiescent that I felt a single finger touching his face would puncture his skin and rot would erupt from it as from a corpse.

He whispered, "What's in the box, Alsy? I can't wait. You know what a surprise does to me. Tell." He moistened his lips with the word. "Tell. I'll let you tie up both my hands if you tell."

I turned away in horror and lifted my eyes to the minister, who stretched out his arms and pierced, bleeding hands, raising his head to where the cross hung on the beam above him.

On it, Jesus writhed alive like a worm on a hook. Though both of his hands were nailed outstretched from his body, it seemed he held to his chest the body of my wife, also writhing and also crucified, who at her chest held our only son, the three of them head above head together on the same cross.

She cried out: "My love, my love, why hast thou forsaken us?"

"Don't look at that," Leonard breathed on me. "Look at me, Alsy. Look at me always." I held my breath and blacked out into my mortal life.

So this is how it shall end. The reality of hell, which used to float fancifully on the edge of my belief, like a painted dragon in the corner of an antique map—now I see it opening its gory mouth to me.

I am married to Alex Leonard. I have joined my destiny to his. If I kill him, I follow his soul to hell. Even if I baptize him, will I not follow him likewise to heaven? The knot is tied, it was probably tied before we were born. I have only drawn it tighter.

Should I cry and grovel before You, Lord and Creator? Merciful Redeemer? Should I beg for mercy? You promised that none of us would be tested beyond our ability to resist. Yet You have tested me, and toyed with me beyond my ability to so much as grasp. You have lured me like a rat through a maze, only to have me find Your cold, calculating hand ready to seize me at the end.

Can You honestly say that You have any love for me whatsoever?

Do You honestly mean to say that by killing Leonard I will have defied not only You, but the very victims of his malice? I will never believe either without proof. And what proof could You possibly give me?

Nothing is impossible for You, we are told. Then let me put my enemy under my feet and let me *never* see him again in this world or the next. Can You do that? Can You untie Your own knots? Supposedly You can even raise the dead. You can untie death itself.

Fine. Praise the Lord! *Then give me back my family.*

Oh, dear Christ, just give me back my family.

EPILOGUE

By the Rev. Andrew S. Nelson

The day of Alex Leonard's baptism was a cold one, in the low teens when I woke, and no higher than twenty with a biting wind at 11:00 a.m., when the ceremony was to take place. The sky was nothing but leaden gray. Heavy snowfall had been predicted for the afternoon and evening.

I knew that the night before had been a hard one for Alson. He called me in the wee hours of the morning, very distressed, saying he had just awoken from a terrible nightmare. I assume this is the same nightmare recorded above, though on the phone he would not tell me much about it. I remember— I will not easily forget—what I said to him.

"Dreams are just dreams. They don't come from heaven or hell. They come from our own human desires and fears. You've struggled for a long time to do what you're going to do tomorrow. You've let nothing stand in your way, including me. No dream should stand in your way now."

He was silent. "Alson?" I said. He muttered something and hung up. I tried to call him back, but he did not pick up the phone.

I then called Ellen Fabian, the person who

was probably closest to him during the past several months. She had checked in on him now and then, and I thought she might be willing to do so that night. Ellen informed me that she and Alson had parted company that same day. She would not trouble him further. "We have set each other free," she said.

In retrospect, I should have wondered at this farewell. At the time and at that late hour, I thought little of it. I had done what I could. I fell back asleep. As it turns out, I never saw or heard from Ellen Fabian again. Her landlord tells me she is somewhere out west, going to school.

That leaves me, as Alson's only remaining friend, to tie up the loose ends of his story. Even if Ellen were here, she was not a witness to the events I am about to tell. Of course it is tempting to analyze and make judgments about those events, and many have already taken it upon themselves to do so. I want no part of that. But I do want these discussions to rest on as many facts as possible. That is the only reason you are able to read this story, and the only reason I have consented to "finish" it.

Anyway, Alson was standing at the curb when I stopped to pick him up. When I asked about the night before, he simply said, "I'm all right."

There were reporters on us as soon as Alson and I drove into the prison compound. They were tapping on the car windows even before I'd turned off the ignition. Alson seemed unaware of them. He said to me, "Say a prayer for us, Andrew. Pray for strength. Pray for Cindy and Jim."

I suppose I was a little less than forthcoming. For one thing, this was an unusual request, coming from him. (He notes that I never opened our sessions with a prayer, but he had never asked me to.) And for another, the crowded parking lot seemed hardly the right place.

"We'll keep our eyes open," he said when I objected. "They'll just think we're having a conversation. We have to learn to ignore them."

And so I said a prayer as he had asked. I waved back the reporters first. I don't remember much of what I said. I do remember that he heaved a sigh when I mentioned the names of his wife and son.

He looked especially tired and careworn that morning, even for someone who hadn't looked healthy for more than a year. Perhaps his untidy appearance in the weeks past had distracted me from how much he had aged. Now the lines and hollows, and those terrible suffering eyes, stood out as if for the first time.

Just before we got out of the car, he made a curious remark.

"Andrew, have you ever thought about when Christ is in the praetorium, when the soldiers hit him and make the crown of thorns and all of that—that part of the mockery must have included some form of sexual abuse? They disrobed him, all of the soldiers there together..."

His voice faded.

"I guess I never thought of it," I said. "Maybe that's what happened." I was waiting for him to get to some point. The windows had begun frosting over, and I felt cold and confined.

"I think it is what happened," he said. "I'm sure of it. God the Father had to watch that."

The next thing I knew, he had opened his door and stepped out of the car.

He said nothing to the reporters on the way in, except, "You will know everything when it's over." Perhaps "everything" was meant to include his notebooks, which I found stacked in order on the workbench in his basement the following day. To some of the reporters he also said, "God bless you." He held up his hand, as a sign of benediction or simply to refuse further questions—it's hard to say. His other arm clutched his service book and Communion box. I offered to carry both, but of course he refused. He had insisted, though, that I carry the vessels for the baptism.

It was a relief to be inside the prison, away from the press and away from the cold, though I cringed at the sight of wreaths and candy canes hung in such a place. We were told that with our permission a few journalists would be allowed to accompany us to the room where Leonard waited. I felt this was Alson's call; he simply smiled and nodded.

We were almost a procession by the time we got to Leonard. I felt like we should have carried hymn books and sung. Besides Alson

312

and me, there were three reporters, two armed guards, the warden, a commanding African-American woman who served as his assistant, a representative from the community, and the prison psychiatrist.

When we came to the security desks, Alson halted and locked eyes with the guard there. The two were silent for a moment, and continued to be so for a few seconds after the warden called from his place on the line behind us, "What's the holdup, Preston?" I remember a small ceramic Christmas tree that blinked on and off on the shelf behind the guard; somehow the quiet accentuated the blinking.

"Today's the day," Preston said to Alson.

"Today's the day," Alson said to him. "It's good to see you back at work."

Alson placed his Communion box on the counter.

"I don't know about your religion," he said, "or what your beliefs are about what's in this box, but God will never forget what you were willing to risk for him. That's what counts."

The guard averted his gaze and passed the box back to him. Alson was visibly surprised.

"You take this on through. When the bell goes off, that'll be your church bells. You get in free today, Reverend. All others pay admission."

There was good-natured laughter from those standing behind me as Preston turned to me and said with mock sternness, "You! Place any metal objects, keys, pens, coins, or tie clips on the counter before passing through."

I placed my car keys and the box containing the baptismal vessels on the counter as Alson passed through the detector and rang the bell. Even without knowing what he carried, I winced at the sound.

Others were waiting for us in the room with Leonard: his lawyer, his girlfriend, the evangelist who had been trying to usurp the whole affair for weeks, more guards, and of course the film crew. Had they not scheduled the proceedings for a bigger room than usual, we would never have all fit.

The room was apparently a meeting place of some kind, with a large, cafeteria-type table in the middle. There were no television monitors. I asked to have the table moved up to one end, and covered it with an altar cloth I had brought. The cloth was a good deal smaller than the table, which now stood between Pierce and me and the rest of the gathering. Of course, Leonard stood facing us at the center of the witnesses.

He had his hair cut. He'd gone from what I'd call a "James Dean style" to something much shorter and softer looking, almost downy, like the body of an Easter chick. He wore prison clothes, but impeccably pressed, the shirt tucked neatly into the pants. I was glad to see he had worn long sleeves covering his tattoos. I also remember thinking that their being covered would steady Alson. I had noticed on our few visits to the prison together that he seemed to make a point of not looking at them. And if I am not mistaken,

Leonard knew this, and sometimes made a point of positioning his arms so it was difficult *not* to look at them.

As I have resolved not to analyze my friend, I suppose I shouldn't analyze Alex Leonard either. I will say that I had my doubts, and will always have them, about how sincere Leonard was. Once he engaged me for what seemed like an hour in an absurd argument over whether he ought to be baptized as Alex or Alexander, the latter being his full name. He insisted vehemently that he must be baptized Alex, and just as vehemently that his real name was, and would always remain, Alexander. Back then I told myself that his "conversion" was probably full of twists and kinks, but that he had turned to God according to his own flickering light and we had no right to expect better. At least this was my rationalization for not questioning him more intently, for allowing Pierce to discourage me from doing so, for allowing myself to be carried along by the public momentum of "the lovely Christmas story" that seemed to be unfolding.

It was Pierce's request that Leonard not be handcuffed during the service. Leonard stood before us with one hand clasped over the opposite wrist in front of him, his head bowed and his legs apart. There was something humble but also decidedly macho about the stance. His girlfriend held his left arm with both of her hands. His only words before the service began were "Let's do it, Reverend."

I had left the details of the service to Alson.

After all, I was there as his assistant. He'd asked me to read the lessons and the examination. We had forgotten to ask for chairs, and so we had to stand throughout the service. I was most concerned for Alson, who seemed very tired.

That is probably why at first I thought he had fainted when he went down beside me. I was reading the baptismal examination, and when I said "'Do you renounce Satan and all the spiritual forces of wickedness that rebel against God?'" and after Leonard responded, as instructed, "I renounce them," Pierce disappeared.

He was kneeling when I looked. He raised his eyes to Leonard and said, "I renounce them also."

I was shaken, but decided it was best to go on.

"'Do you renounce the evil powers of this world which corrupt and destroy the creatures of God?'" I read.

And again, after Leonard had said, "I renounce them," Pierce said, still kneeling beside me, "I renounce them also."

No one else seemed startled by this bizarre turn—I suppose everyone thought this was a part of the service. Also, I think everyone was mainly concerned with how he or she looked to the camera. No one so much as slouched.

Alson echoed Leonard throughout the remaining questions of the examination. "Do you turn to Jesus Christ and accept him as your Savior?" "Do you put your whole trust in his grace and love?" "I do," and then "I do."

When we proceeded to the covenant and prayers, Alson stood up again and said his part. I was relieved, but still worried. His voice trembled, and his hand was unsteady. When the time came to pour out the water for blessing, I said—and I shouldn't have said it, but I was hoping to relieve some of my friend's tension—I said, "At this point, it's all right to have a brief break. I noticed there are a few chairs at the back of the room. Perhaps someone would like to bring those forward. We've all been standing for a while. Maybe, Reverend Pierce, you'd like a chair?"

"I'm fine," he said, pouring out the water and rolling up his sleeves.

My announcement had the effect of calling an order of "at ease." Everyone relaxed at once, as if they'd been posing for a Civil War photograph, one of those that took whole minutes just to be impressed on the primitive film. I can remember taking in air and feeling a certain buoyancy myself. Leonard's girlfriend kissed his cheek. A guard looked at his watch. Someone in the background muttered something I couldn't hear and the microphone never caught, and the rest laughed. Leonard looked over his shoulder and laughed, too.

"Almost," he said.

It was then that Alson fixed his gaze intently on Leonard. At first Leonard did not notice the stare, but after a moment he did. He stopped laughing, but continued to smile.

"So, we ready to move to the next step, Reverend?"

Alson was quiet—then he said, "Only you and God know that, Alex."

"Of course," Leonard said, not smiling now. "Well, *we're* all ready."

Alson cut in just before Leonard finished. "Only you and God know if you have truly repented of your sins."

I was almost not listening to what he said. My surprise at this change in the script was not my only reason. There was, suddenly, an energy apparent in my emaciated friend, a ghost of the forcefulness of an earlier time in his life. Everyone in the room was dead still.

"You are a sinner, Alex Leonard. You're not a wounded child, or a power rapist, or the gentlest lover in the world, you're a sinner. God loves you, but you"—he pointed at Leonard—"are a sinner. You raped two women. You murdered two beautiful human beings. You have sinned against God. And you have sinned against me."

The film shows some of the guards and officials exchanging worried looks at this point. At the time, my eyes were fixed entirely on Alson and Leonard. The convict gave a slight shrug of his shoulders.

"If that's how I've made you feel, I'm sorry," he said.

"Good for you, Alex!" I heard a woman say—his psychiatrist, I think.

"We're not talking about how you made me *feel!* I'm talking about what you *did*. I'm talking about how you made them feel when you stuck a knife into their bodies. This isn't some...some *feeling* in my head, it's the blood of my wife and son on the ground that we're both standing on."

"Gentlemen," the warden called from behind us, while at the same time I placed my hands on Alson's shoulders. But the filmmaker stilled us both. *"Please* let them finish this dialogue." A director always outranks a warden and a clergyman, I guess.

Leonard had by this time unclasped his hands. His girlfriend still clung to one of his arms. He glanced from side to side, and exhaled loudly. The other minister was whispering something behind him.

"If you don't repent, Alex, baptism is meaningless," Alson went on. "'Alex Leonard Ministries' is certainly meaningless. What are you thinking now, that the two of us ought to go on the road together? Be a happy twosome for Jesus?"

"I guess we could, Reverend." Leonard forced a laugh. "That wasn't exactly the plan—"

"The only road you and I belong on is the road of penance." It was then that Alson placed his hand on his Communion box, a movement followed immediately by Alex Leonard's eyes.

"You know, Reverend, you're starting to preach at me here—"

"Yes, he is," said the psychiatrist.

Alson drew a breath and exclaimed, "I'm a preacher, for God's sake. What do you want me to do instead, juggle plates? I'm a preacher, Alex, a wifeless, childless preacher, and I'm

319

telling you that if you do not sincerely repent of your sins, you will go to hell."

"Tell *him* to go to hell, Lennie," the girlfriend muttered, but Leonard shot back, "Shut up. You be submissive." He pulled free of her hold on his arm and faced Alson.

"I heard all I need to hear of that stuff from my daddy, minus taking the name of the Lord in vain." Now Leonard was pointing at Alson and nodding his head, though his tone of voice was almost glum. One of the guards moved closer to us. "I heard all I needed about hellfire from that guy."

"And you're hearing it again. And you're hearing it from somebody's who's very close to going there himself—who's seen it! Haven't you seen hell, Alex? Don't you remember what it looks like? Do you know why I got down on my knees before, Alex?"

"I have no idea." Now Leonard was playing the part of the self-controlled schoolboy, unjustly reprimanded. His head was lowered, his fists clenched at his side.

"Do you know what's in this box?" Alson said, unlatching it. "Do you know what this Communion box contains?"

"I don't much care at this point, Reverend."

"Oh yes, you do care. Yes, you do. The vessel that holds Christ's blood, which you and I have shed. The little container"—he tore the items out of the box like a thief ransacking a glove compartment—"that holds his broken body, which you and I have both broken, because here, Alex, right here—"

320

Nothing of his emotional outburst had prepared me—had prepared any of us, I'm sure—for the sight that followed. When Pierce writes about his reality-warping first impression of Alex Leonard standing in the doorway of his dining room—that must have been something like what I felt, seeing him hold up a handgun no more than a yard from where I stood.

Only one guard, the one who had already moved forward, showed the presence of mind to act decisively. Perhaps he shouldn't have announced his maneuver by saying, "Reverend, we need to have that," as he rushed forward. Leonard sprang at him with preternatural speed, knocked him to the ground, and seized the gun from Alson, discharging it once in the process. No one was hit, though we all froze at the sound.

At the same time, his girlfriend screamed, which served to freeze us further—all of us except Leonard. He aimed the gun directly at Alson's head. In a flash he had moved to the side of the table.

"One person, just one person makes a single fucking move—or says a single fucking word—and I blow out his brains."

Alson turned to face Leonard, so I could see only the back of his head. He said nothing, neither did anyone else. It was one of the most awful moments of quiet I have ever known.

"Now, I want all the guards to step forward, one at a time, and place their weapons on the table here, right next to the holy water. One at a time, real slow, not too slow, and nobody try to be a hero or you're the one they'll blame for killing the saint for our times."

"Do what he says," I gasped. The warden echoed my words so that everyone heard them.

In several moments the altar was covered with guns and truncheons.

"You!" he called to me. "Back around the front of the table with the rest."

"Lennie, let me come by you," the girl shouted.

"Shut up and stay where you are," he said. "It's just me and him, just me and him and not a word out of anybody. This is between us, isn't it, Reverend?"

"Yes," Alson said, and it was reassuring to hear his voice.

We stood at an altar covered with unblessed water and weapons, behind which Alex Leonard and Alson Pierce faced one another. I was the person closest to them.

"All right, Reverend," Leonard began. "I've been answering all kinds of questions this morning. Now it's your turn. What's with this?"

"It's a gun."

Leonard laughed and shook his head. "Now don't be shittin' me, Reverend—"

"It's a gun," Alson cut in, "and I'd planned to kill you with it. But I decided to baptize you instead."

Needless to say, all of us were still stunned. You could feel the disbelief, even though no one so much as moved.

"Then what'd you need this for?" Leonard almost snarled. I felt he'd shoot Alson right then.

"I came here not knowing which I was going to do. I'd been planning to kill you for months. Then I wasn't sure. Then a few minutes ago I was sure."

"Well, Jesus Christ, Reverend, if you wanted me dead, why didn't you just ask? I mean, you could've come to me with tears in your eyes and said, 'Alex, would you please kill yourself?' A crying clergyman or a crying cunt, you know me—I have a hard time saying no to either one. You didn't have to go to all this trouble. But, Christ, you are a clever one. You are a fucking clever man. You want me dead? You wanted me dead in that race riot too, didn't you? You weren't stalling for time. You just didn't have the balls to do it."

He held the gun to his own head.

"You want me dead?"

He immediately aimed the pistol back at Alson—a warning to the rest of us, I think—then touched the barrel to his own skull once more.

"Is that what you want, huh?"

"No," Alson said, in a louder voice than any he'd used that day.

"'No,' he says." Leonard turned to us as if appealing to a jury. "Well, then, what do you want?"

"I want to baptize you. And I want you to live."

"And why's that, Reverend? Because you love

323

me, right? You love your enemy, just like Jesus said. Is that it?"

"No. Because I love *them*. Because I love Christ, even. Isn't that incredible? Maybe because I finally got laid. You'd go for that one, right? I don't love you, Alex. God loves you. I couldn't love you if I tried. And I admit I never tried. But neither did you! If just once..."

Alson shook his head, his face full of bitterness.

"Go on," Leonard taunted.

"If once you'd done something, besides make outrageous demands and talk on and on about yourself or shown an ounce of compassion...but even then. I could never love you."

Suddenly Alson cried out, "I wish I'd never *seen* you. But I'm stuck with you, you bastard!"

"Whoa," said Leonard, appealing to us again. "Listen to his mouth. And this guy wants to baptize *me*. I don't think, Reverend, I don't think you're in any position to be calling anybody any names."

Leonard still held the gun to his temple.

"Alex, listen to me—"

"Oh, listen, huh? You know, as far as that goes, if you'd said all this to me right from the start, instead of all this bogus bullshit about loving your enemy—"

"I know, I know. Just listen, damn it."

"The language!"

"God, just listen, and then you can kill me for all I care, just don't kill yourself. Please. Just listen."

"All right, I'll listen. I'll listen. But time's

a-wastin'. And the movie's starting to drag, right, Spielberg? People don't have a little action soon, they'll be throwing their popcorn on the floor and asking for their money back. What? What? Tell me what. Go ahead."

"You're right, I don't have a right to call any names, you're right. I should have said this to you right away. You see what I am. You see what I was willing to do to get revenge. And what are you, Alex?"

"Nothing you need to be concerned about."

"Oh yes, oh yes. When you broke into my house, you became something I had to be concerned about..."

"I thought my sins were supposed to be forgiven. You keep bringing up all this shit from the past. He even told me"—he pointed at me—"that sin is an old-fashioned way of saying that stuff. That's what you said, right? Old-fashioned language, you told me. Move your head or something, will you, asshole?"

I nodded my head. As terrified as I was, I did not miss the irony of having my theology quoted by a man who'd once dismissed my nonreductive view of the Resurrection by calling me a "peckerhead."

"See?" Leonard said when I'd nodded. "You know, I really lucked out with you, Pierce. I mean, of all the fucking ministers in this world, I go after the one who doesn't know the shortest verse in the Bible, because his Bible's not old-fashioned enough or some goddamn thing, who doesn't even keep himself up to date in the sin department—I guess there he is old-fashioned—and who packs a gun with his Communion! I mean, at the very least, the Lord should give me some extra credit for bad luck. Don't you think?"

"Maybe. Maybe we both get extra credit for bad luck, Alex. God only knows. Who knows why God lets the things happen that happen? You got hurt as a kid. You hurt other people. You hurt me. I wanted to hurt you, you've got my gun aimed at your own head, look at all these guns on this table—for Christ's sake, Alex, renounce it! Give it up! Renounce evil. Renounce destruction. But *mean* it. If you can't do it for love, then do it for spite. Spite the evil, Alex."

"Don't preach at me, Reverend. I don't even like looking at you, let alone hearing your voice ragging on me here."

"Too bad," Alson said.

"What?" Leonard was incredulous.

"Too bad! Too fucking bad. You're stuck with me, Alex. I don't like it any better than you do. You kill yourself or you kill me and we resume this conversation in hell. Or you get baptized, you forgive me, and maybe we go to heaven. Together either way. Tough luck for us both."

"You forgive me?" Leonard said.

"Yes, I do," Alson said. "As much as God gives me grace, I forgive you. Only Cynthia and James can—"

"Never mind them," Leonard snapped, still holding the gun to his head, but glancing at us aggressively from moment to moment.

"They're dead. Anyway, you said I sinned against you, right? I hurt you too, right?"

"I said I forgive you," said Alson.

"Say you forgive me for raping your wife and killing her and your son. Get on your knees and say it."

Alson hesitated and then obeyed.

"I forgive you."

"Say the whole thing, damn you. Or I blow out my brains." Leonard was building to a frenzy. "Repeat after me. I forgive Alex Leonard."

"I forgive Alex Leonard."

"For raping my wife, Cynthia."

"For raping my wife, Cynthia."

Alson's voice cracked, but he did not lose it.

"For killing her."

"For killing her."

"For cutting my son James's throat."

"For cutting my son James's throat."

"For wanting to fuck his little ass. Go on."

"For wanting to fuck his little ass," said with tears.

"So help me God."

"In the name of the Father, and of the Son, and of the Holy Spirit. Amen."

Leonard paused for a minute, breathing hard now, seeming unsure what to do next.

"It's done now, Lennie," the psychiatrist dared to say.

"It's not done!" he screamed. He jerked the gun from his head and aimed it in our direction. A few of us cried out. He just as quickly aimed it at Alson.

"Say you're glad I did your family. Say you're glad because now I can come to Jesus."

Then the most awful pause of all.

Leonard raised his brows, impatient for an answer, and thrust the gun back to his own temple. Alson lifted his eyes to Leonard for the first time since going to his knees. He took a hard breath through his nose.

"I can't say that."

"What?"

"I can't say that. I won't say that."

"Why the fuck not?"

"Because it's not true."

"Not true! You've been telling everybody nothing but lies ever since you showed your pricky face in here. You're nothing but a goddamn liar, what do you care if it's not true?"

"I won't say that. If all this...torture has been God's will"—how he fought for these words!—"then I accept God's will. But I'll never say I was glad. Not in this world."

"You wouldn't say it *to save my life*?"

"I wouldn't say it to save my soul."

With some difficulty, Alson got to his feet.

"Who said you could stand up?" Leonard demanded.

"God did," Alson said. There was a glimmer of a smile on his lips. "I've made my choice, Alex. You have to make yours."

"I've made my choice, Alex," Leonard mimicked in a simpering voice. "Fuck you, Pierce—fuck your family, and fuck your God."

Leonard fired two shots into Alson's chest. My friend fell against the table, holding himself there for a moment before dragging the cloth down after him with a clatter of dropping guns and toppled Communion vessels. I believe he was alive until he fell. I believe he lived long enough to see Alex Leonard insert the gun into his own mouth and fire.

In happier days, before the tragic events that have shaken every one of us, Alson and I used to play a fanciful game called Heaven and Hell. The way it worked was that each of us got a turn at describing his version of hell or heaven, sometimes both, depending on the mood of the moment. Once we were at a convention in Philadelphia, and Alson started up a new round of the game by leaning over and whispering to me, "Hell is an eternal convention." I turned to him and whispered back, "Of clergy!"

On another occasion, after my computer had just lost a sermon I'd been working on for the better part of a week, I called up Alson and told him to tell Cynthia, who was quite a computer whiz, that in my version of heaven there were no computers. Either that, or infallible ones. And that's how it went, more whimsy than theology, but it kept us amused, and I suppose it kept us from taking ourselves too seriously.

We stopped playing after Alson's tragedy. There seemed little point then in asking him to describe his version of hell.

But among some old correspondence I managed to find a letter of his in which he describes heaven, and I'd like to close with that. I'm not including it to suggest where I believe he is or is not right now, but to remind us where he once was. And when we remember our friend, it's important to remember that his life contained joy as well as sorrow. We should thank God for his joy.

The letter is dated May 22, 1993.

I think, Andrew, that I may have at last found my perfect version of heaven. It is a beach in Maine, with boulders studding the sand, and tall cliffs covered with pine trees rising on either side of it. Cindy and I are sitting on a blanket watching the waves go in and out under an azure sky. Though the sun is shining, the air is raw, and we have not worn our suits. A few intrepid sun worshipers lie exposed to the wind, but the handful of others on this beach are wrapped in blankets and kerchiefs, or dressed in hooded sweatshirts. We keep our distance from these strangers and we exchange no words with them, but we do exchange smiles whenever someone passes, and I feel a sublime affinity with everyone here.

Cindy and I are warm-blooded enough to have braved the day in our shorts and bare feet. We see our flesh in the dappled sunlight. What is there in the whole creation more beautiful than human flesh? Cindy lifts her golden knee from the blanket, and I can hear all the hosts of heaven sigh in the receding surf. On both

of our knees and shins we see bruises, scratch-
es, bug bites, and even scars that we did not
know we had, and cannot remember how we
got—and I feel a certain glory in thinking I
am able to forget such injuries, and I feel
grateful for the scars and bruises because
they remind me that I *can* forget.

I know, as I clasp my wife's hand, that
there are better beaches elsewhere—warmer,
sandier, washed by tropical seas. "In my
Father's house are many mansions." And I know
that throngs of people have found their way
to those beaches. For all I know, the Lord
Jesus himself is oiling his body on one of
them, preparing to darken his skin and drink
a washtub full of wine. Didn't he say he would
not drink of the fruit of the vine until he
drank it again with us new in the Kingdom of
God? Well, I do not see him on my beach, but
I know he knows me, and I can feel his love and
favor in the grace of the sun whenever it
comes from behind a high puffy cloud. I also
know, just as surely, that the woman and the
boy who are with me deserve to be on one of
those warmer beaches, but they have chosen this one for the sake of having me close
by. And who knows where else we might find
ourselves in the stretches of eternity?

For now, we are here. My wife's arms and
legs are pressed warm against mine, and in the
miraculous simultaneity of heaven, in the
echoes of the seagulls crying out above us, the
love we made last night and shall make for every
night hereafter is as present to us as the

331

rolling sea and the kindly sun. She kisses my cheek and whispers into my ear; the kisses and the whispers and the crashing waves all speak to me of love.

Out at the foamy edge of the water, in bare feet on the dark, smooth sand, dancing like a diminutive clown, stooping to inspect every object that God ever put on a seashore and pronouncing each one a priceless treasure, is our little boy.

"Look at him," Cindy whispers.

He runs toward us, grinning, then turns abruptly and runs toward the fathomless sea, then comes to us once again, back and forth, and back and forth forever, like the love of the Holy Ghost.